THE
HIDING
ROOM

JONATHAN WILSON

THE
HIDING
ROOM

VIKING

VIKING
Published by the Penguin Group
Penguin Books USA Inc., 375 Hudson Street, New York, New York 10014, U.S.A.
Penguin Books Ltd, 27 Wrights Lane, London W8 5TZ, England
Penguin Books Australia Ltd, Ringwood, Victoria, Australia
Penguin Books Canada Ltd, 10 Alcorn Avenue,
Toronto, Ontario, Canada M4V 3B2
Penguin Books (N.Z.) Ltd, 182-190 Wairau Road,
Auckland 10, New Zealand

Penguin Books Ltd, Registered Offices:
Harmondsworth, Middlesex, England

First published in 1995 by Viking Penguin,
a division of Penguin Books USA Inc.

1   3   5   7   9   10   8   6   4   2

PUBLISHER'S NOTE
This is a work of fiction. Names, characters, places,
and incidents either are the product of the author's
imagination or are used fictitiously.

Library of Congress Cataloging in Publication Data
Wilson, Jonathan, 1950.
The Hiding Room / Jonathan Wilson
p.   cm.
ISBN 0–670–85603–7
I. Title.
PR6073.I4679S4   1995
823'.914—dc20   94–41253

This book is printed on acid-free paper. ∞

Printed in the United States of America
Set in Janson
Designed by Katy Riegel

To the memory of my father,
Lewis Wilson

Forget the flowering almonds.
It's not worth it:
in this business
what cannot come back should not be remembered

NAZIM HIKMET

heavier than war the scents of youth

KEITH DOUGLAS

THE
HIDING
ROOM

PART ONE

JERUSALEM

1 9 9 1

In the first days of April I quickly concluded all the preparations for my mother's burial. She had never been a sentimentalist, and I was taken by surprise when the lawyer read the will. She requested (she would never stipulate) that I take her body to Jerusalem.

The initial arrangements had to be made very fast, but El Al, the Israeli airline, was extremely cooperative. My mother wanted to be laid to rest on the Mount of Olives, but unfortunately the hillside had a waiting list, and as speed was of the essence, I had to make other, less dramatic, arrangements. I found a cemetery not too far from where I am now staying, a somewhat neglected place in Sanhedria, the graves all grown over with crabgrass, but almond and cherry trees were in blossom, and as I stood by the prospective plot, a feeling of peace (although it may have been tiredness) came over me, and I said to the young man standing next to me (who might just as well have been selling cars), "This will do."

All the authorities, the bureaucracies of death in both England and Israel, have been very helpful and efficient. My mother's request was not unusual. In Israel, apparently, the burial of foreign Jews is booming and has become a macabre branch of the tourist industry. There were two other corpses unloaded from my plane: one from Manchester and one from London. In the airport lounge at Ben-Gurion, while we were waiting for the deceased to pass through customs, the son-in-law from one of the grieving families told me about an irate Israeli couple prevented from taking their seats at Heathrow because they were accompanied by the family cat. Normally, there wouldn't have been a problem (the cat had a ticket), but Jewish law forbids the proximity of animals to the dead.

After they lowered my mother into the ground, uncoffined, draped in a prayer shawl, a shovel was handed to me. I dug it into the ground and dropped the earth onto her body. It fell in dark clods, and I thought, for a moment, that she might flinch when the dirt hit. A hoopoe bird flashed across the grave in quick beats of black and white; the sky, which had been streaked with orange throughout the funeral, seemed suddenly to drain of color and became a gray slate hung over the hole in the ground.

It was after the funeral, which was attended by myself, a rabbi, and a handful of paid mourners, that I decided to stay on. My mother has brought me here for a reason, and it is up to me to discover it. I have no obligations at home: My marriage, a disaster for many years, fell apart for good six months ago. My wife, my ex-wife, Anna, has moved to Florida with her new friend, an airline executive she met while walking the dog on Hampstead Heath. As for my job, my employers at the BBC, disgruntled by my failure to adapt to the new editing computers that they purchased at enormous cost, and disappointed with my recent performance cutting a six-part medical documentary—divorce is no longer an excuse for anything—were alarmingly happy to grant me an extended leave of absence.

And so I have lingered into early summer, with the wrong clothes in my suitcase, a laptop computer, and a bottle of cheap whiskey that I bought in the duty-free but have not yet opened.

After my mother's death, I returned from the hospital and sat for a while in her small Finchley apartment (not the home in which I grew up). In the terrible calculations that we make despite ourselves in these situations, I scanned the rooms, deciding what I would sell or give away and what I wanted to preserve. I discovered that I had very little attachment to the few objects of material value that she owned—silver candy dishes, a set of Delft dinnerware, a pair of brass candlesticks—but to my surprise, I found myself stuffing a nylon bag with the entire contents of her mahogany dressing table's four drawers: head scarves, pins, torn stockings, letters, old diaries, photographs, and jewelry. When I left for the airport I brought this bag with me. I don't know what was going through my head. It seems that I could not let her travel empty-handed.

I have been here now for six weeks. It is my first trip to the Middle East. From the window of my room I look out over the red-tiled roofs of a neighborhood called Nahla'ot, where narrow streets descend in steep steps and curves. There are courtyards full of garbage, where stray cats forage, and others where thin-stemmed wild roses clamber beyond tall grass. I am on the top floor of a three-story dwelling, the highest on the block. If I stand on the balcony I can see all the way around the western perimeter of the city. It is a smooth line of low brick buildings, pink by day, tinged deep blue at dusk. Here and there, a high-rise penetrates the skyline. The tallest of them, the Hilton Hotel, has displayed on its roof, in huge, garish white bulbs, the age of the State of Israel: 43; the nation is seven years younger than me.

It is the middle of May; a dry, hot wind blows through my open window as if someone were holding a giant hair dryer a few inches away from my face. But in with the wind comes the scent of roses and, at night, honeysuckle.

Last night, a Friday, I took a walk through the city. After twenty minutes or so of directionless strolling, I found myself outside the walls and barbed wire of a police compound. Saxophone music poured out from a sidewalk café nearby. Apparently, the area has become a small haven for secularists who wish to celebrate the Sabbath in a less than traditional manner. I entered the café, sat at a small table, ordered a glass of white wine, and ate from a bowl of green olives that was immediately placed before me. An enormous, bearded man blew the sax, while a long-haired drummer kept time with the brushes. The room was crowded with a rough miscellany of individuals, young and middle-aged, black and white. As the evening wore on, they spilled out into the street and danced trancelike under the high stars. Some carried small children on their shoulders; others moved their bodies close, gliding together, and turning down the pavement until they were out of sight.

Shortly before I was about to leave, a woman sat down at my table, offered me a cigarette, which I declined, and struck up a conversation. She asked me what I was doing in Israel. I told her that I had come to bury my mother. She launched into a long story of her own: She was an immigrant from the old Soviet Union, hard-pressed by poverty and anti-Semitism. She had come to Israel to make a new life, but so far there was only more of the same. She had left her old mother behind in Russia, and before she could send for her, the old lady had died. Perhaps I would like to go back to her room with her and we could drown our sorrows together over a bottle of vodka.

I assumed she was a prostitute and her story an empathetically seductive gesture. Nevertheless, I was reluctant to give up on her companionship. I suppose, too, that at the back of my mind, the promise of sex, no matter how tawdry, was appealing. I had not met anyone new since my wife left. I didn't miss her all that much (I *know* she didn't miss me—I have a trenchant postcard from

Boca Raton), but it's hard to sleep alone after twenty years of marriage.

We went back to her place and entered through a warped and rusty metal door set in a long stone wall. From the outside it looked like the kind of barrier that might conceal a wild dog. I am over six feet tall and had to bend almost double under the lintel. The door led into a flagstone courtyard overhung with a trellis; a vine clambered across it and blocked out half the sky; a few tiny grape buds had begun to swell. A step up, and we were in her room: the same broad flagstones, a large bed, a ceiling that bled plaster, and walls oddly hung with pink bobbled curtain sashes and posters of American movie stars. She offered me a drink and then a stick of marijuana. I took the joint, held it to my lips, and sucked in the smoke. She allowed me one drag, then carefully stubbed the remainder in an ashtray. She got up and walked efficiently over to the chair next to the bed and began to remove her clothes.

"Well," she said, looking over her shoulder at me. "Shall we do it?"

I was, as they say in the books, "vaguely stirred" when she reached across her freckled back and unhooked her bra, but the arousal was insufficient. I made an effort and attempted a half-hearted, awkward embrace, but when she broke away to step out of her skirt, I gestured for her to stop and told her that I would have to be going. She asked me for money. I had wasted her time, and time was money. I left a fifty-shekel note on the table and walked out.

I strolled for a while, settling finally on a bench in a small courtyard near a playground. I could see through the open windows of the small house opposite me, into the kitchen and parlor. A small child sat cross-legged in the white light from the television; his mother cleared the dinner table, while the man of the house, potbellied, in shorts and a T-shirt, moved aimlessly between the two rooms. As I rose to move away, the woman in the kitchen looked up from her work and caught my eye. Her long brown hair was pulled back from her head, and unlike her husband and child, she was pale, almost wan. She smiled at me, and I saw my mother's young face hung like a moon in the kitchen window of our tiny suburban London house. I remembered standing outside in the garden, slamming a football against the wall, pretending indifference but glancing up every so often to make sure that my mother was still there.

I felt a sudden surge of warmth, toward both my dead mother and the woman in the window, which pulled me out of the melancholy mood that my clumsy tryst with the prostitute had induced. I waved in the direction of the kitchen, as if the young Israeli woman and I had known each other for years, and walked on.

It was after this that I thought for the first time that I could feel my mother's presence in the city. Whatever I knew, I knew, of course, in only the obscurest way. My mother had never been forthcoming about the past. She occasionally mentioned the time that she had spent in the Middle East as an interlude on her long journey from Hitler's Europe to an untroubled life in England. She talked about the friends she had made along the way, people who had helped her, mainly in Jerusalem. But for the most part she was reluctant to go into the subject. I suppose she was trying to protect me, or herself, or both of us.

She kept a postcard of the pyramids on our mantelpiece at home. In the foreground were three mangy camels, their necks bent to the ground. It never occurred to me to turn the card over until I was about ten. There was no address, but a message scrawled in brown ink: "Desert blossom as the rose? You must be joking!" I asked her if she had ever been in Egypt as well as in Palestine, and she replied, "Briefly." When I pressed her she described Cairo as if she were telling me a story from the *Arabian Nights*: the Sphinx in the moonlight, that kind of thing. After I grew up she became taciturn on the subject. Like everything else

to do with the "missing year" in her life—that is, the time between her escape from Austria and her arrival in England—Cairo
was coated in a film of forgetfulness.

Of my father she spoke very little. He appeared in different
versions: as a fly-by-night, a young man, "it was the war." The
contours of his being were indistinct, vague and indiscernible, almost mythical, so that she might just as well have described him
as a disembodied voice, or a shower of gold. There were no photographs, because they had not been "sweethearts" and never
posed against a romantic backdrop. He was tall, she said, which
accounted for my own spindliness, and had green eyes. As to his
nationality, it was as indeterminate as everything else about him:
at times she intimated that he was a Palestinian Jew, a member of
an elite unit in the Haganah, while at others he was a boy from
Vienna with whom she had escaped from Austria; and sometimes
she hinted darkly that he was someone else entirely. In all his
metamorphoses his character remained ambiguous, a necessary
figure but ultimately spurious, loving but cruel, temporary but vi-
tal, as if she herself were not yet quite sure what she thought of
this man whom she had loved for only a short time before he (or
was it she) disappeared. He still haunted her dreams so that she
would sometimes cry out his name at night (or so I thought), and
it would come to me, muffled, through the wall that separated
our bedrooms, as variations on sounds that simply attached
themselves to the word "Father."

As a child I put almost no pressure on her to give me the full
story—which she would not have done anyway—preferring the
status quo, the world of shadows and allusions. In his discarnate
state my father could not be dead, which meant that some somnolent evening, my mother at work, the sitter slumbering in the
chair next to the fire, me upstairs staring out the window toward
the station, I would see a figure emerging from the steam left by
a departing train, and as in the corniest postwar movies, which
were chock-full of miraculous and unexpected returns, I would

run out to meet the lanky stranger, who would know me immediately, lift me up, and twirl me under the spinning stars until I
was dizzy.

Perhaps it is for him really that I am here, to turn a magnifying
glass on the print of his presence in her life, the print that is the
spiral of my own existence. Did he walk down this street to meet
her? Where, and in what room, and at what time of day, did it all
begin?

CAIRO
1 9 4 1

1

Whenever he came into the office the refugee was there, in the waiting room. The first week, he told his secretary to say that he was busy. He sat behind his oversize walnut desk with its absurd secret drawers, its elaborate combination lock, and he decoded and encoded messages, filed reports and made phone calls. When he went out for lunch she was there, sitting with the others, the informers and the petty spies. She always looked straight at him when he walked past. She had deep-brown eyes, made darker by her thick black eyebrows; there was a small white cicatrix across the bridge of her nose. If she hadn't been so skinny, she might have been pretty.

When she stared at him he didn't detect any anger. She looked as if she was used to waiting. Well, she could wait a little longer. That's what Phillips had said: "Make her wait. She's only going to tell you the same cock-and-bull story as the other one. Harfield threw him out on his ear, the little scrounger. He had Shylock; now you've got Jessica."

He would go and sit in Kamil's garden café with some of the other lower echelon officers who didn't drive across to the club for lunch. He listened in silence as they complained about the wogs and being gypped in the Muski every time they tried to buy something there. Their brick-red faces ran with sweat and they tugged in discomfort at the collars of their uniforms. They were all "browned off."

After lunch, when the ceiling fan in his office seemed to revolve even more slowly and ineffectively, and the room started to feel like an oven, she was still there. It was even hotter for her. There was no fan in the waiting room; no point in encouraging *them*, and with luck they would lose a few at siesta time. "Work English hours": Phillips again. "It throws 'em off." When he looked up from his desk he could make her out through the frosted glass of his door. He saw her face like a palimpsest behind the back-to-front letters of his own name, 2LT A. RAWLINS. Her features were fractured by the distortions of the glass. Sometimes one of the others would rise and say something to the secretary; whoever it was would leave the room for a few moments and return with a cup of water. She never shifted from her place. In the end he would have to see her. And then it would all begin. He knew when he looked at her that she was going to be the end of sleep.

2

"Name? Christian name last, please."
  "Christian name?"
  Rawlins blushed ever so slightly.
  "Forename. First name."
  "Esta."
  "Esta . . . ?" He waved the pen over the form.
  "Esta Weiss."

"Date of birth?"

"February 5, 1919."

He looked up, surprised. The year was the same as his own. He had her pegged a few years younger, maybe seventeen.

"Place of birth?"

Her head sank, and she spoke into the ground.

"I'm sorry. I didn't . . ."

"Piotrkow Trybunalska . . . Poland."

"And you lived there until . . .?"

"Until I was seven. Then we moved to Vienna."

"Where you attended school?"

"And the first year of university."

"Current address?"

"Why do you need to know that?"

"It's something we ask. What if we need to get in touch with you?"

"You won't need to. I will come here. You can listen to me here."

He stood up. "Look, I don't know if I can listen to you at all. When I ask you a question, you answer it. All right?"

She waited, the way a patient mother waits for her son's tantrum to blow over. He walked smartly over to the door and opened it.

"Harriet, tell Lieutenant Harfield I'll be five minutes."

Harriet smiled at him, the way she always did, as if there were something secret between them.

Once he'd returned to the desk, the refugee began to talk, and as soon as she did, he wanted her to stop. Harfield and Phillips had both warned him. They had told him what to expect. Her story was preposterous: not the part about returning to Poland to visit relatives—that was all credible enough—but everything else smacked of lies and exaggeration. But why would she lie? Why would the other one, Harfield's client?

Occasionally, he interrupted her.

"First you said everyone in your grandmother's apartment building? Now you are telling me everyone in the immediate neighborhood? Is that what you are telling me?"

She began to talk about the digging, the walk and then the digging, the children with shovels. Had he heard her properly? She spoke in a low, flat monotone, her voice conveying no emotion. A pale lemon light filtered through the blinds; he saw that there were flecks of gray in her thick black hair. "It's your job," Phillips had said, "to listen and to figure out exactly who she is, who she works for, and what she's after. I think you know the word from on high. They're up to something with these stories. We've had 'em out of all kinds of places, wherever these people wash up, and believe me, where they wash up is no accident. It's all about Palestine, old chap. The worse things are over there (he gestured back to Europe with his thumb), the more pressure there is to let 'em in over here."

Rawlins heard the shovels scrape in the mud, saw the ditch in the forest. Was there a way not to listen? To concentrate on the spinning fan, or the knots in the wood floor, or the cries of the street hawkers rising through the open windows. He had been in Egypt only a few weeks and he knew no Arabic, but he could distinguish the call of the water vendors. If he were outside now, he would approach one of the men with outsize copper teapots on their backs and trays of glasses balanced on their hands. He would kneel and have cool water poured over his head.

Harriet knocked on the door, opened it, and stuck her head round.

"You have a meeting with Captain Phillips. Did you forget?"

She glanced toward the refugee, taking her in with a quick up-and-down sweep of her eyes. Harriet noted with distaste the young woman's heavy brown skirt, creased blouse, and tangled hair; then she looked back expectantly at Rawlins.

"Well," he said, letting out an involuntary sigh, "that seems to be that for now."

Harriet closed the door. Rawlins started to tidy his desk and noticed with embarrassment that he had left Palgrave's *Golden Treasury* of English poetry visible, the binding facing toward her. *"Keep silence now, for singing-time is over."* He hastily put the book in a drawer.

The refugee rose slowly, as if rousing herself from a dream, and passed through the door that he held open for her.

"Do you live close by?" he asked, but she continued walking through the outer office and into the corridor. He found himself staring at her legs.

3

Rawlins didn't sleep well that night. He couldn't get what she had told him out of his mind. The images came in stops and starts, arrested moments: a German soldier kneeling to shoot a child, a young woman's body rolling slowly into a pit. In the brief term of his enlistment he had heard all kinds of things from men returning from the front, but this was different. The obscene deaths that soldiers had described to him, cruel and violent as they were, did not register in the same way. It was the elements of shame and humiliation in her narrative, the overwhelming sense of the victims' impotence, conveyed in a voice that never trembled, that worked now on his imagination.

When he finally slept, an old, forgotten nightmare from childhood returned to haunt him: A thick mist rolled over him from out of his bedroom wall. He was hopelessly alone in the fog, desperate and calling for his mother. Rawlins must have emitted a few muffled cries before he woke, because he heard Harfield murmur, "Steady on, old boy," from his bunk on the other side of the room.

The following morning she was there again, sitting in the waiting room, her hands clasped in her lap, her face lifted and directed toward his office door. He tried to make himself busy, banging in and out of other people's offices, stepping briskly around the rooms, shouting orders at the secretaries.

"We are in a rush this morning, aren't we?" Harriet said, giving him her winning smile.

Two weeks earlier, half the office had put in for a day's leave and taken a drive up to Alexandria. After swimming, Harriet placed her towel next to his on the beach. She teased him about his pale skin (she had been in Egypt for six months, and her face and body were smooth and brown). Rawlins felt awkward and embarrassed. He didn't quite know why; he had had girlfriends, he had one now in England, and he was used to flirting. Perhaps it was something about their circumstances: the proximity of the war; there was a heaviness in him that playful chat couldn't lighten. All afternoon she tried to engage him in conversation. He responded politely, but he felt withdrawn, indifferent to her friendliness. The sun slid down and touched the surface of the water, turning it liquid gold, as if some ancient god had dissolved the weapons of war and suspended the solution in the sea.

In the front seats of the jeep on the way back to Cairo, Harfield had yelled across to him over the shuddering of the engine and gestured his thumb back at Harriet, following in the car behind. "She's yours if you want her!" But Rawlins didn't want her.

Nevertheless, he returned her smile this morning, reminded her not to forget the carbons to KGP, and asked her if there were any outstanding jobs, the kind of dreary paperwork he usually put off, that he might catch up on. He was in the mood for clearing his desk.

In this way he occupied himself for the morning and on into the afternoon. He had already told Harriet to announce that he would not be seeing people today and that those waiting might as well go home, but as was usually the case, the directive was ignored and no one left the room.

At around three, Harfield called him on the phone:

"I'm leaving now, old boy, and if you want a ride to the briefing, you'd better come with me now."

Rawlins rose, put on his hat, and prepared to leave the office. Looking down through his window into the street, he saw the refugee come out through the main door. He watched her stop at the curbside. The slope of her shoulders suggested vulnerability, but this was contradicted by the deft, businesslike manner in which she brushed the hair back from her face. She turned and glanced up at the building. Rawlins stared as she straightened her skirt and opened the top button of her blouse. He wished now that he had let her in. There were things he wanted to ask her: how she had escaped, for example; she hadn't spoken about that. Quickly, without thinking, he stepped into the other room and asked Harriet to tell Harfield not to worry, he would catch up with him later. Then he sped out of the office. As he clattered downstairs, he told himself that it wasn't going to be an important briefing anyway. Unlike the others, he had already had two months of mechanical training before being transferred. There was nothing Intelligence needed to know about MK-III Crusader tanks that he didn't already know.

Out on the street she moved very fast, darting in and out of the crowds, dodging the trams and the horse-drawn carts with their huge chariot wheels. In the heat and the terrible humidity, it was a trial to keep up with her. Above him was a sooty gray sun; it looked as if someone had pulled a dirty eraser across the sky and rubbed hard at the stubborn orange spot at its center. From time to time, birds rose and wheeled in dark revolving clusters, in imitation of a spring migration. He followed her south for more than an hour. She moved down streets parallel to the narrow arm of the Nile on his right. Occasionally, the river would come into view, a flash of deep green rippling under dusty air. Once, she seemed tempted to jump on a tram, but the press of bodies clinging to the surface of the vehicle appeared to put her off; once, she lingered for a moment by a fruit and vegetable stand. He watched her slip two small pears into the pocket of her skirt. Had she proffered money? He didn't think so, but perhaps he was mistaken.

They entered a part of the city with which he was completely unfamiliar. The streets were narrow and loaded with garbage. In one corner an old man sat on the ground next to a pile of water-melons; he was smoking a *shishah* and wearing heavy sunglasses. Suddenly Rawlins felt conspicuous in his uniform. As if to disguise himself, he removed his beret and rolled down his knee socks. He was pretty sure that she hadn't noticed him. He had kept his distance.

He turned one more corner and found himself next to a foul-smelling dump; two black-and-white pigs were rooting in the garbage. Where was the refugee? From out of nowhere, a small group of ragged children gathered around him. The exposed parts of their bodies were covered with dirt, and their eyes were clouded by trachoma, but at the sight of him, they grinned from ear to ear. They beckoned, gestured, chattered, and tried to take him by the hand. When he failed to respond, two children in stained, grimy galabias pushed him from behind. They were pointing at a low hut at the edge of the dump. Suddenly decisive, Rawlins shrugged off the children and headed smartly toward the hut. Could she be in there? Had they seen him following her? He bent down and peered in. A young woman, half her teeth missing, lay on the ground, smiling up at him. Her dress was pulled up over her thighs. She nodded her head enthusiastically for him to enter. Rawlins stared at the black triangle of her pubic hair. The woman slid her hands up and down on her thighs, gyrating a little. Rawlins turned his back to her. She began to scream at him. He wanted to run, but instead, slapping the children aside as if he were swatting flies, he walked away at the speed of a fast march.

He thought he had lost her now. Where was he? Asking for directions would only be asking for trouble. Some time ago, he now realized, the familiar minarets that he had used for almost two months as landmarks to guide himself around Cairo had vanished. In their place was a cluster of church spires.

He emerged onto a small square and found himself next to a tall flight of steps leading up to the broad doors of an ancient church. He sat down for a moment, wiped the sweat from his face, and then he saw her. Halfway down a narrow lane leading off from the square, she was scaling a short ladder at the side of a building. He watched her disappear through a hole in the wall, then reach out and pull the ladder up and in after her. He rose and walked over to the building. The entrance, indented where a set of doors had been removed, was blocked with thick planks that had been nailed across. The windows, too, were boarded up. Above the portal were two barely visible Stars of David. Now that he had found where she lived, he felt awkward and a little perplexed. Had he followed her because she had intrigued him and he wanted to know more, or because she seemed so defenseless and in need of protection? Or was there some other reason, which he didn't want to acknowledge? She was intelligent, that was clear, and everyone else he had met in Cairo was so, well, predictable and dull. And when she sat in his office, even though she had been telling him those awful, chilling tales, he had wanted to touch her, to run his finger down the seam of her stockings. He felt ashamed.

By the time he made his way back to GHQ, almost everyone in his department had left. A couple of indignant, preoccupied secretaries remained, no doubt typing overdue documents. They paid him no attention. He went into his office, closed the door, sat down, and began to review his notes from the interview: "set a fire in the house, then ordered to run into the street, shot as they ran"; "taken to the cemetery and shot"; "father and son forced to beat each other at gunpoint until they refused to go on and were shot." And then the brief notes on the walk into the forest; here he had almost stopped writing. But how had she got clear? It hadn't been explained.

There was a tap on his door. Phillips's large blond head appeared. "Thought I saw you come in, old man. How's it going with Jessica?"

Rawlins shifted a pile of papers over his notepad.

"Oh, much as you predicted."

"Lots of jolly little tales of atrocity."

"Something like that."

"They really should try to do a better job of getting their stories straight. Shylock told Harfield he was from Poland, but spoke with a Romanian accent. Harfield's got an ear for languages, you see. Double first."

"Does she know him?"

"Who?"

"The other one?"

"Beats me, old chap. Never seen 'em together. Like the Fool and Cordelia, never see 'em onstage at the same time." Phillips laughed and gestured to the waiting room. "But I'd hazard they have their meetings. What about a drink? You look about done. Coming over to Shepheard's?"

"Not right now. I've—"

"Wait a minute. Weren't you supposed to be getting briefed?"

"Something came up."

Did Phillips give him an odd look, or was he imagining it? They didn't really like him, Harfield and Phillips. He knew that. It wasn't that he had gone to the wrong school or otherwise defiled their beautifully standardized origins. It was worse; it was because he had gone to the right school but emerged with the wrong ideas. He wasn't a good "social type," he couldn't banter, and if you didn't banter, it meant you were on unhealthy terms with reality.

"Well, your loss, old boy. See you tomorrow."

After Phillips had gone, he sat a long time at his desk. He tried to write a letter home but could get no further than "Dear Mother and Father." Eventually he left the building and, in the gathering dusk, started to retrace his steps back in the direction of the hole in the wall.

Rawlins felt pulled forward through the Cairo streets, as if the refugee were tugging on an invisible thread that he held in his hand. He passed a row of barbershops, the hairdressers lounging outside, then a man squatting, almost walled in by a stack of coal, and another, who seemed to be offering for sale only a single, shriveled lemon. By the end of the street, he was running, his heart pounding and his breath coming in short, sharp bursts.

4

Her body was like white marble, and he could see the blue veins running through her arms and legs. She lay naked on her side, with the thin cover thrown off. When he scrambled through the hole (two crates from the street had been enough for him to heave himself up) she shivered but didn't immediately wake up. He called to her: "Miss Weiss, Miss Weiss," and then it started, but afterward he wasn't at all sure how everything had begun. Suddenly he was astride her, and she was tearing at his shirt and pushing down his shorts. He began to enter her, but she reached down and pulled him out. She bit his neck and pressed her hands hard against his buttocks, pushing him up so his penis was between her breasts. He wanted her to take him in her mouth, but she turned her head to the side. She pulled his right hand down and pressed it between her thighs. He worked his fingers for a while, but then she whispered, "No. You. You," and grabbed him. The come spurted out of him and onto her breasts.

He lay in silence in the stuffy room. A musky odor rose from their bodies. There was no mattress; they had clung together in dust, bonded by sweat. Rawlins's knees and elbows were bruised. By the light that came in through the wall, he made out her suitcase, open on the floor. On a stool next to it was a hurricane lamp and a box of matches. A book, he thought, perhaps an address book from the thick leather cover, lay facedown on the floor. She was turned back on her side. He ran his fingers along the thin ridges of her shoulder blades. "You should go," she said. There was nothing recriminatory in the voice, and nothing affectionate.

When he jumped down to the ground he landed badly and twisted his ankle. He hobbled along for a while, then, when he reached a main street, hailed a passing taxi. He sank into the back seat and closed his eyes. He would have to ask for a transfer first thing in the morning. He couldn't see her again. He told the driver to take him to Shepheard's Hotel.

5

He stood on the terrace outside the Long Bar, nursing a beer. His ankle was burning and swollen. He looked out to where the moon cast a silver light on the palm trees of the Azbakiyah gardens. A few yards away, a group of the Long Range Desert Group men, one of whom he recognized from a briefing (they never wore uniform), were huddled together, smoking and chatting. Inside, raucous and strident, with Phillips and Harfield among them, was the bunch known to everybody as the Short Range Shepheard's Group. How did the song go? It was one of the first things he had learned after his arrival in Cairo. "We fought the war in Shepheard's / And the Continental Bar. / We reserved our punch for the Turf Club lunch / And they gave us the Africa Star."

"Mind if I join you?"

He gave a start. The figure approached out of shadow on the corner of the terrace.

"It's a beautiful night, isn't it? You wouldn't think there was a war on."

He was tall and thin, with a shock of graying curly hair. Rawlins looked for the unit and rank insignia on the speaker's uniform but failed to make them out in the dark.

"Mendoza. Captain Gerald Mendoza."

Rawlins stiffened a little at the mention of rank.

"I saw you by yourself, and I thought . . . I hope I'm not intruding. It's rather noisy in there, so I came out, and, well"—he gestured toward the other end of the terrace—"those chaps can be a little cliquish. You are . . . ?"

"Archie Rawlins."

Mendoza extended his hand. Rawlins shook it but quickly withdrew his own hand; was the smell of her body still on him?

"Based in town?" Mendoza continued, in a friendly, cajoling voice. He wasn't going to give up.

"Garden City."

"Been out long?"

"Since April."

"Action?"

"No. I'm a pen pusher."

Rawlins leaned forward onto the wrought-iron balustrade. In the street below, a man in an ash-blue galabia and a lavender headband was pushing a hand-held cart loaded with empty baskets. He stopped under a streetlamp near the entrance to the hotel. A shining, noiseless automobile cruised by, holding, no doubt, some exiled dignitary. The city was full of them.

Rawlins thought he'd better make an effort. The other fellow was getting embarrassed.

"And you?" he asked.

"I'm the chaplain."

"Oh, I'm sorry. . . . I didn't recognize. I haven't attended. I really should have. I did promise the parents. I mean. For myself as well. I would have wanted . . ."

Mendoza laughed.

"No," he said, "it's all right. I'm the Jewish chaplain."

Rawlins wanted to run away, to clatter down the stairs into the street and conceal himself under the fellah's handcart. But Mendoza was continuing to talk, trying to engage him, and he found himself answering questions about his home, his education, his family. Finally, he blurted out, "I'm sorry. Got an early-bird meeting with the top nobs at GHQ; got to get some sleep."

He turned away, but Mendoza reached out and caught him by the elbow.

"Would you mind if I ask how old you are?"

"I'm twenty-two."

"And you said you were an Oxford man."

"Oxford, yes; Magdalen."

"Do you know, I believe there are other chaps, other officers . . ."

"From my college? From Oxford? Yes, yes, I suppose there are."

"I do believe I've bumped into a couple. Chap named Caudwell, and another fellow . . ."

Rawlins was irritated by this small talk and looked around in a quiet panic.

"Not too lonely, then? Because it can be, you know. I see people all the time, but even so, there are times . . ."

"Yes, I can imagine. Look: I'm terribly sorry, but I really must be going."

"Of course."

Mendoza had kept his hand on Rawlins's arm, but now he removed it. He reached into his tunic pocket for a pencil and pad, scribbled quickly on a small piece of paper, folded it, then handed it to Rawlins.

"If you ever want to get in touch. It's all so chaotic, isn't it? This is where you can reach me."

"But I'm not . . ."

Mendoza gave a wan smile. "My job doesn't limit my conversations to HM's Jewish servicemen."

"No. Of course not. I'm sorry. I didn't mean to imply . . ."

Rawlins wanted to turn away, but Mendoza held him with a look. There were crow's-feet around the outer corners of Mendoza's eyes, thin white lines exacerbated by his tanned skin.

"Listen: I'd like to talk. Some other time."

"Yes. Don't let me keep you."

Rawlins walked away and into the bar. Phillips spotted him and yelled his name over the din. Rawlins went over to join him. He had told Mendoza he was returning to barracks. What if he saw him? So what? He didn't owe him anything.

"That's better, old chap." Phillips had his arm around him and was bellowing in his ear. "You can't sit all night with one drink. It isn't good for you."

From his protected situation among the carousing officers, he glanced from time to time over Phillips's broad shoulders. Eventually he saw Mendoza, alone and looking straight ahead, angling toward the exit.

6

In the morning, he sat in his office and waited for her to appear. If she did come he would hand in the letter. He had already written it out, and now it lay in front of him on the desk: "want to be closer to the action . . . feel I can be more useful nearer the front . . . experience with tanks . . . and therefore am requesting an immediate transfer . . ."

She didn't come all that day, or the next day. On the third day, after returning from lunch, he put the letter back in the top drawer of his desk. Within half an hour of his having done so, she appeared in the waiting room. He immediately rose from his seat, opened his door, and told Harriet to send her in. There was a general stir in the room. Voices were raised in complaint. "Excuse me, sir, but we have been waiting all day." A small, heavyset, bald man with a thick mustache shouted, "Important information. I have important information," as if he were hawking pots and pans on a street corner. Harriet threw Rawlins an angry look. It made her job harder when the queue was disrupted. What was more, she didn't like the way the girl stepped toward him: such a proprietary manner, as if she had rights.

Rawlins ushered Esta into the room. He thought he caught the odor of saffron around her, the scent that permeated the streets when the hour for cooking rice arrived in the poor quarters of the city.

"Did you think you wouldn't see me again?"

"I . . ."

"I'm not a whore."

"I didn't . . ."

"Why did you come in the first place? Why did you follow me?"

"Could you keep your voice down, please?"

"I am speaking quietly."

"Look: What do you want me to do?" He felt his ankle twinging. He had strapped it too tight.

She reached down and opened a battered brown leather handbag that she had set beside her chair. As she bent her body, her long hair fell forward, and he had a flash of his face lost in the mess of her curls, the loud response to his orgasm muffled as she tugged his head down.

"I want you to report what I told you"—and here she fumbled with the square of paper that she had produced—"to General Dryborough."

"Where did you get that name?"

"What does that matter? He is the person, isn't he? He is the chief of your Intelligence."

He saw that despite her bravado, she was trembling, shivering. He almost wanted to reach out and lay a calming hand upon her shoulder. But what if Harriet should come in, or be looking through the glass?

"And what makes you think that what you told me is something the general doesn't already know?"

"He may know, but he doesn't believe. No one believes."

"And why should he believe me?"

"Because *you* believe *me*."

Rawlins wondered if he did believe her. He knew enough about Harfield and Phillips not to trust either of them. But could he let that mistrust go all the way up to the very top?

"That place you live in . . . ?"

"Yes."

"How did you find it?"

"By mistake. I was looking for the synagogue in Shari Adly Pasha—"

"So you're in contact with other Jews?"

"I didn't say that."

Rawlins wanted to ask her about the "other one," the thin boy in the ill-fitting suit who had been summarily dismissed from Harfield's office. The phone rang on his desk. He let it ring four times before moving to pick it up. Whoever it was had already rung off.

"I asked someone," she continued, "for directions to the synagogue. I thought I might get help there, shelter, make *contact*. But the old man I had asked sent me the wrong way, toward Fustat. There was a synagogue there, but not the one I was looking for. This one was abandoned. Still, I found the hole in the wall."

Rawlins got up and walked toward the door of his office. He turned the handle, making sure the door was firmly closed, then he returned and stood in front of her.

"Do you . . . do you have food?"

She stared at him. He reached into the back pocket of his trousers for his wallet, took out two notes, and handed them to her. She took the money, zipped it into an inside pocket of her handbag, then snapped the clasp shut. The phone rang again. She stood up. Rawlins stretched out a hand toward her face, and touched his finger to the scar on her nose.

"You will speak to General Dryborough?"

He walked away from her, picked up the phone, and said "Yes" into the receiver.

He went to her three nights that week. He told Harfield he had a friend, a girl who knew his family, in from England. It wasn't uncommon. Egypt was officially neutral, and Cairo, with its odd wartime abundance—French wine, cigarettes, strawberries and cream, meat on the restaurant tables—had attracted its share of adventurous society girls. They came out to join in the fun, dance in the open air at Groppi's with wreaths of jasmine hung round their necks, connect up with old lovers, snare an officer. They found work as "secretaries" in hastily created staff jobs away from the front. The real army girls, like Harriet, resented these intruders. It was all one big aristocratic charade. Rawlins sometimes thought the war was like the accounts of the Crimean War that he'd read in school. Families coming out with their picnics to watch the battle, sitting pretty on distant hillsides. The women in long, elegant dresses.

If Harfield had known where he went, there would have been trouble. Rawlins changed into civvies, took the number 1 tram down Canal Street, dropped off in Old Cairo, and circled the Al

Mu'allaka church until the square was more or less empty. He whistled to her, and she lowered the ladder. There was always a moment before she appeared. He would stare up in anticipation; the tops of the trees by the synagogue wall looked like giant sponges absorbing the stars.

She took him always as the first time. She wouldn't let him come inside her. She barely looked him in the face. She rubbed hard against him, pulled at him, scratched him, bit into his shoulder with her small, slightly discolored teeth. He sucked at the nipples on her thin breasts, then pushed them together and into his mouth. She murmured and moaned very softly, but the noises she made were out of key with their lovemaking. Why was she doing it? To make him speak to Dryborough? At some point every night she would ask him when he was going to go forward. He would answer that Dryborough was away from Cairo but returning soon, and that he would speak to him as soon as he could. But there was more to it than blackmail, and in any case, hadn't he come to her? He felt that his body was like food for her, meat for a starving person. She wanted to lick it, savor it, tear chunks out of it, and taste the grease around her mouth. But at the same time she didn't want his body in her, didn't want to be penetrated, or nourished, or to grow strong.

With the money that he gave her she bought tea, fruit, and pita bread. On the third night, he shouted at her because she had bought a bunch of anemones. The flowers stood in a small can of water that she had previously used for brewing tea, their fat stems already bending, wide purple and red heads tilting to the floor.

At daybreak, when he crawled to the hole in the wall, he saw, every morning, a small rose-colored hawk circling high in the sky. It was his sign to leave. When he got back to barracks, and to the room that he shared with Harfield, he crept under the rough blankets on his bed for five minutes' rest. Harfield would pretend to be asleep, but at breakfast in the mess, when they were sitting with the other officers from their division, he would say, "Well, you must be having quite a time with the family friend." Rawlins would lower his head and attend to the food.

That night he went to her and she wasn't there. No one responded when he whistled. It took him a while to find two crates sturdy enough to hold him while he clambered up. She wasn't there. The thin gray blankets that he had stolen from the barracks were spread on the floor. The folded clothes that she used as a pillow were in place. The flowers, paper thin now, with the color almost drained out of them, drooped to the floor. She had taken her handbag with her, and the address book that he had seen lying by the bed on that first night. He had wondered several times if he should try to get a look at it, see who she knew.

He waited an hour or so, sitting with his back against the warm stone wall. He felt bored, a little angry. What a mistake he had made. He rose, walked to the far corner, and urinated into the enamel bucket that was her toilet. A line from Palgrave's came into his head and stuck there: "So faire a church as this, had Venus none." The heat of the night fed in ripples around the room, bounced off the black walls—or were they white, or pink, or brown; he never noticed, had never visited by day, and when the hurricane lamp threw light and shadows, he took in not the room but his and Esta's bodies entwined in monstrous shapes on the walls.

In this airless room he thought, suddenly, of Lensbury, the place he had been taken by Shell-Mex, his prospective employers, shortly before the outbreak of war. In the gloom and heat of this Cairo storage room, he conjured the green cricket field, half mown, patchwork style, against the grain, the quick thunks and grunts that came from the tennis courts, the people in white bathing caps who shouted happily in the swimming pool, and then the tea dance where he had met Claire, who had been with the company for a year. And what had she said to him that he had thought so utterly banal and yet charming and appealing at the same time? "It always seems as if the sun is shining here." She was working as assistant to the administrative head of finance, or some such post. Rawlins liked her. They had gone out dancing a few times, to a concert at the Albert Hall, and once to tea at Lyons. Since he had been in Egypt, she was the only person outside of his family who wrote to him. What would she make of all this if he were to tell her about it?

He thought he heard movement outside, someone scuffing along the road. Was there a call? Did someone call Esta's name? He went to the hole and peered out. A thin figure hugged a shadow by the entrance to the church on the opposite side of the road. It wasn't her. A sliver of moon sliced through thick cloud, and Rawlins caught a glimpse of a young man in a suit moving out of the shadow and away from him.

He retreated into the room. The heat seemed to rise in jolts; his shirt and undershirt were soaked through with sweat. When he couldn't stand it any longer, he got up to go. He fumbled around in his pocket for something to write on, produced a scrap of paper, but then thought better of it. Best not to leave a written note. Instead he folded the blankets, army style, as he had been taught to do in base camp; that would be message enough.

He let himself through the hole, jumping down and trying to land as gingerly as he could; he couldn't prevent hot pain searing through his ankle.

He thought he'd go to Shepheard's, or maybe everybody was at the Continental tonight. But what would he do there? He couldn't talk about *her*—the others would make a few predictable and ugly remarks about Jews, or maybe a joke or two, and that would be it. He had to find someone to share her with: that, he realized to his own surprise, was what he wanted to do. He found himself staring at the piece of paper that he had apparently retrieved from his pocket moments earlier. He hailed a taxi and gave the driver the name of the street nearest to the barracks that housed the Jewish chaplain.

When he entered the room, Mendoza was sitting at a desk, making notes in the back of a small book. A pool of light thrown by a desk lamp illuminated his face and lent his gray curls an iconic glow. At first Mendoza didn't recognize Rawlins, but when he did he smiled quickly and urged him to sit down.

"I came—"

"Yes, I see that." Mendoza laughed.

"There's something I'd like to discuss with you . . . well, tell you. It's personal."

Mendoza closed the book on his desk.

"Please . . . go on."

"It's about a woman. I've been seeing a woman."

Mendoza passed a hand over his brow and spoke softly.

"I don't. *We* don't. That is, I don't take confession, you know."

Rawlins started, as if a small electric shock had been run through his chair.

"I'm sorry." Mendoza spread his hands on his desk. "I didn't mean . . . That was in poor taste. I'm sure I misunderstood."

Rawlins was silent for a moment, shifted in his seat. He could see that Mendoza thought that he had lost him, and again, as he had felt on the balcony at Shepheard's, Rawlins felt the need to disembarrass the man.

"Were you busy? I'm sorry I interrupted."

"Don't worry about it. It's a book I've been revising. Stationery Office in London was kind enough to print up a few."

"May I?"

Mendoza pushed the thin volume across the desk. It was small enough to hold in the palm of a hand, a cheap printing job. The title was in heavy black lettering on a khaki cover, *Prayers for Trench and Base*, by G. S. Mendoza. Rawlins turned the page and read: "Issued by H.M. Stationery Office with authority of the Chief Rabbi. 5701-1941." 5701? Jews, it seemed, lived in different time. He turned one more page and found, to his surprise, a dedication "To the memory of my great friends Simon H.

Leonard, killed in action, 11 May 1915. Colin A. Meyer, killed in action, 26 Feb. 1917. Frank W. Rossman, died of wounds, 14 March 1917. Samuel G. Wasserstein, killed in action, 7 June 1917." He read on into the prefatory note: "This little book of prayers, written and adapted by Captain G. S. Mendoza, should prove a welcome aid to private devotion in the trenches and at the base, and a valued companion to the official 'Prayer Book for Jewish Sailors and Soldiers.' May these simple prayers—mostly written during Captain Mendoza's active service—be a solace and a strength to the individual soldier, even as they are a touching memorial to the brave men with whose names they are linked. J. R. Gevertz, Chief Rabbi. Rosh Chodesh Elul, 5701."

Rawlins felt Mendoza's eyes upon him and sensed that he was reading too intently, had become too immersed in the little book.

"You can keep it if you wish. Would you like to? I have *many* copies." Mendoza laughed, "Not all our Jewish servicemen, you see, are interested in prayer."

Rawlins replaced the book on the desk. Mendoza left it in place.

"This woman?"

"I thought you didn't . . ."

"Well, as a friend. No harm in my listening, is there? You have something on your mind?"

Rawlins looked around the room. The walls were bare, no pin-ups, of course. The desk, however, was cluttered with memos, books, newspapers, and framed photographs, of which Rawlins could see only the backs. One of the newspapers was called the *Jewish Chronicle*; by the tattered look of the paper, it must have been a month or two old. It was folded in two, but Rawlins could read the upside-down headline: "Indiscriminate Round-ups Continue."

"She's a Jew."

"Local?"

"Yes. No."

"Well, which is it?"

"How much do you know?"

"About what?"

"About what's going on. About what's happening . . . to the Jews."

Mendoza's face darkened. He pushed a pile of books to the side of the desk, adjusted some papers.

"I know no more or less than you. I look, I read, I hear. Are you suggesting that I have some special information?"

"I only thought . . . perhaps. . . ."

"What did you think?"

Rawlins could not prevent himself from glancing at the *Jewish Chronicle*. Mendoza caught the drift of his eyes and laughed again, but this time it came out as a cracked half-snort.

"Old news. From London. They round Jews up there too, you know."

"Round them up?"

"Surely you must be aware of that. I thought you chaps over in Intelligence knew everything. Well, never mind. Internment. I suppose it's inevitable. Can't take risks, have to be rigorous. It's absurd, of course. A while back, they rounded up the entire German-born staff of the BBC—twenty announcers and translators! Fifth-column panic. Can you imagine? But tell me more about the girl."

Rawlins was beginning to regret that he had ever come. This rabbi was relentless.

"There are Jews being massacred." Rawlins spoke in a murmur, as if perhaps he could take back what he was saying if he said it quietly enough.

"Yes."

The two men were silent. Mendoza closed his eyes momentarily, and Rawlins felt as if two blue searchlights had been switched off.

"Then it's true."

"Isn't that what *you* are telling *me?* And what, if anything, does this have to do with your girl? Who is she? What's her name?"

"Esta. Her name's Esta. That's a Jewish name, isn't it? She came into my office. We talked, that's all. I've been visiting her. Look, if you'd like to meet her I'll take you. But not tonight. And this is between us. Is that clear?"

"Why on earth should I want to meet her? Are the two of us the only Jews in town? Or is there something else that you have to tell me? Is she from Cairo, from London, from Berlin? What exactly is the issue here? Are we talking about the fate of the Jews or a pregnancy?"

"Oh, for God's sake!"

Rawlins heard the wild rise in his voice. He had gone much too far. What was he thinking of? Take this rabbi to her? He must be out of his mind. He tried to get up quickly, but his ankle gave way beneath him and he stumbled out of the chair, against the desk. Mendoza helped him to his feet. Rawlins heard him mumbling, "Watch what you're doing, now. No need to get all worked up," then Mendoza pressed something into his hand. The book, the damn prayer book. Rawlins could almost have laughed if the whole thing hadn't been so pathetic. He heard Mendoza saying, "Now tell me what's going on." Rawlins shrugged him off.

"Leave me alone!"

Before Mendoza could reply, Rawlins hobbled through the door. Out in the street, he took great gulps of air and tried with all his might to calm the febrile activity of his brain.

7

Rawlins made his way out of the city through the melee of dust-covered army matériel that clogged the streets. On his route, he weaved in and out between tanks, lorries, scout cars, and jeeps. Sometimes the drivers would lean out the windows, yell a question at him, then ask for cigarettes. Nobody seemed to know where they were headed. He stopped once and bought stale coffee from an Assyrian vendor with an immense brass carafe strapped to his back. The pavement cafés were crowded with card and domino players. Leaning against a wall to sip his drink, he heard the city's music turn harsh, backfire and bagpipe overlaying the local ring of bicycle bells, the slow clop-clop of horse-drawn carriages.

By the time he had crossed the bridge, he could already see the horses on the polo field. He watched their soundless, swift galloping in some measure of astonishment. He knew, of course, that such life always continued undiminished somewhere, but the brilliant gleam of the horses' flanks, and the resplendent green of the ground they traveled over, disarmed him. It was all too bright, as if money and class, obscured and softened by cloudy England, were now dazzlingly exposed. He had heard of an officer, heir to a tobacco fortune, who had brought his own hunters out to Egypt with him to serve as chargers. One of the horses had fallen sick at a railway station in France at the beginning of the journey. The waiting room was requisitioned and a corporal seconded to remain with the animal until it was cured. Eventually the duke of Gloucester had collected the horse and ordered a railway car for its safe transport. And Rawlins was part of all this; a small part, because he had never hunted or fished or shot, and his father wasn't a country gentleman but a self-made businessman, and his boarding school, Stowe, was better known for producing intellectuals than cavalrymen, but a part nevertheless.

He worked his way through the straggly crowd on the sidelines and arrived at the pavilion. Most members of the teams had already mounted and were out waiting for the next chukker to begin. A short figure was standing alone, caressing his horse's muzzle and whispering in its ear. Rawlins recognized Dryborough. The general had come to the mess and addressed the new officers on Rawlins's first day in Cairo. Dryborough had made one of those

"No need to discuss the need for our final and full victory, no matter how long it takes or what its agony" speeches. At the time, Rawlins had been moved, his spirits lifted after the long sea voyage, but the first night spent in barracks had quickly grounded him. Harfield was up all night, groaning and retching: he complained of "Gyppy tummy," even though he had been on land for less than twenty-four hours and had eaten nothing but his NAAFI rations.

Dryborough had his foot in the stirrup and was about to swing himself up.

"Excuse me, sir. Could I talk with you?"

"Rather busy."

Dryborough eased up into the saddle and adjusted the reins.

"It's important, sir."

"Look here, who are you?"

"Rawlins, sir. Second Lieutenant Archibald Rawlins, GHQ Intelligence, sir."

"Come on, Teddy" someone shouted from the middle of the field. "We haven't got all day."

Dryborough waved to indicate he was on his way, then turned to Rawlins. "Go through the proper channels."

Rawlins stared at Dryborough, hoping to communicate by the flat expression on his face that the channels, in this instance, were unreliable. Dryborough remained impassive.

"I can't, sir."

"*Ted*dy." The drawl from center field was more insistent.

Dryborough was about to spur his horse, then seemed to catch himself. He turned back and spoke with a small, exasperated sigh.

"Do you know where I am?"

"No, sir."

"Well, have Ogden over there give you directions. You'll come this evening. Seven o'clock sharp."

Dryborough dug his heels into his horse's sides and cantered off, looping his mallet in slow, easy circles.

Rawlins had the afternoon to kill, and in any case, he thought he had better show up at the office. He'd been absent too much recently. Often, the reason was entirely innocent, an extended trip to the Muski, or a message that needed to be delivered by hand. But on one occasion he had gone by day to check if she had returned. She hadn't. When he got back, Harriet had given him a dirty look, and Phillips, passing him in the corridor, had murmured, "Missed you, old boy. Got some 'road watch' in, needs deciphering *tout de suite*."

Between two and three, he interviewed a butcher, who told him a long story about a local man supposedly selling vast quantities of meat to a beautiful Romanian woman who was undoubtedly a spy in the service of the Italian secret police. It took Rawlins a while to unravel the motive behind the report. The "local man" was a rival butcher, who had opened a new shop just two doors from the informer's own. "We'll put a watch on it," Rawlins assured his visitor. The story may have held some truth, but it was of no consequence. Rawlins had been notified early on that all the local espionage women were known to British Intelligence. Most of them maintained some sort of diplomatic status, some string to a neutral embassy. Some even lived at Shepheard's or the Continental. They dressed smartly, danced well, inhabited cocktail lounges and clubs like the Extase; they were not treated seriously.

Soon after Rawlins had got rid of Mr. Afify, Phillips came into the office.

"Did I see you headed in the direction of the club this morning?"

Rawlins shuffled some papers on his desk. "That's right," he replied.

"I was on my way back, got a lift from a chap in a two-ton. Damnedest thing happened. Arab ran out from behind a lorry, right across us, driver caught him with his mudguard and broke his right foot more or less clean off under one wheel. Arab vomited blood all over everyone. Got him off to hospital, then we had to make out an accident report to some local gendarme. Suddenly I see you strolling happy as can be down to Gezira. Didn't know you liked to mix with the smart set."

"Don't you?"

"But that's different, old chap. Born to it!" Phillips laughed and slapped Rawlins across the back. The distinctions, however slight, and in however jocular a manner, always had to be noted.

"By the way," Phillips continued, moving to stand directly under the ceiling fan in the middle of the room. "How's the family friend? Any chance of catching a glimpse?"

"She's left."

"Has she? Where to?"

Rawlins worked hard not to hesitate but could not avoid a small stutter as he spoke.

"P-Palestine. She has a sister there, came out as a nurse."

"Well, bad luck for you. Back to your left hand, is it? Or do you take trips down to the Berka. I saw something down there the other night—"

The phone rang, mercifully, and Rawlins was able to wave Phillips out of the room without offending him. "Yes," said Rawlins into the receiver. "I'll have them done as soon as I can."

For the rest of the afternoon he decoded descriptions and numbers of supply trucks spotted by the LRDG in the far reaches of the western desert.

It was still light when he left headquarters, but barely. A brown effluence from the setting sun seemed trapped between land and sky, and he walked through it as if through mist. There was more than an hour to go before he was due at Dryborough's, plenty of time to change his mind. "Just a misunderstanding, sir. All cleared up now. No need to bother you."

If he had gone straight back to the barracks, he would not have seen her. Perhaps he would never have seen her again. But he had decided to walk aimlessly. She was sitting at a round table outside

a small café off Shari Adly Pasha, not far from the main synagogue, the one she claimed to have got lost trying to find.

She was not alone. A thin young man with a sallow complex-
ion, looking hot and uncomfortable in an inappropriate wool
suit, was with her. They were both sipping from tall glasses of tea.
Rawlins approached the table. He was red in the face and shaking. He looked directly at her, turning his body sideways to shut
out her companion.

"I've been looking for you."

"Why don't you sit down?"

Her composure took him by surprise, unsettled him, and he
could only repeat himself.

"I've been looking everywhere for you."

"And now you've found me. You might as well sit down."

Rawlins snatched at a chair from the next table and dragged it
over. He remained standing, however, pressing his hands hard on
the chair back as if the metal might absorb his shaking.

"This is Falik Hafner." She gestured toward the young man,
who extended his hand. Rawlins did not reciprocate. Instead he
tipped his head back, as if to avoid a cloud of sour breath. Hafner
withdrew his hand and tugged at the grimy white collar of his
shirt. His gray, malarial face, his dirty, broken fingernails, the
threadbare suit, all repelled Rawlins.

"I did it," he said, looking only at Esta. "Now perhaps you'll
leave me alone."

"Leave *you* alone?"

"I saw him. That's what you wanted me to do, wasn't it?"

"And what did he say?"

Rawlins looked at the young man, who was eagerly staring him
in the face, waiting for an answer. Rawlins felt his eagerness and
hated it. Impulsively, he let go of the chair and grabbed Esta by
the elbow. He pulled her roughly away from the table. Hafner
stirred, but quickly settled back into his seat.

"Not here," Rawlins whispered at her, with barely controlled ferocity. "Harfield threw him out. Do you realize . . . ? You told me you didn't mix with Jews."

"I didn't ask you to meet me here, and I didn't tell you anything of the kind."

The scent of her body up close and the feel of her bony elbow cupped in his hand sufficed to give her back to him as a lover. He resented this intrusion on his anger, but when he spoke again he softened his tone. He felt, instantly, that he had lost control: a voice was speaking through him, imitating his own.

"I'll come tonight after I've spoken to Dryborough."

"I thought you'd already . . ."

"I have. I have. It's just . . . there's more. And look: Is this why? Is this the only reason?"

She looked at him. Rawlins noticed that her lips were sunburned and swollen. Where had she been?

"Would it matter?" she asked. "Would it make any difference? You certainly seem to think I'm capable of using you."

Abruptly, he turned away. He had heard English voices, someone laughing, then whistling "I'm in Love with the Girl I Left Behind Me," a song that, up until this moment, Rawlins had thought he liked. He wheeled around, but whoever had been there was already lost in the crowded street. Rawlins had to step aside in order to avoid a man carrying a tray of colored icing sugar on his head. He took in the porter's elevated hands, stained crimson by the cochineal dye.

He saw Esta return to her table, and realizing with a start that he was late for his appointment with Dryborough, he hurried off. It had been his authority, not his anxiety, that he had wished to assert, and now he felt that she had outwitted him. Why did he continue to act on her behalf? As he moved toward the broader streets and wealthier residences of Garden City, a new moon, thin as an arched eyebrow, appeared in the sky above him. He would pass on the information to Dryborough and then be finished.

8

A servant led him out into the garden. A soft breeze agitated the palms and rustled the branches of an old banyan tree. At the foot of the terrace he could hear the hidden waters of the Nile, gently lapping. The city's heat magically diminished here, and Rawlins, for the first time that day, found that he had stopped wiping his brow. Above him, two searchlights desultorily searched an empty sky.

It was twenty minutes or so before Dryborough emerged into the garden. He was still in uniform and walked smartly out, as if he had only recently returned to his house and had not yet begun to unwind. Rawlins watched him approach. He was short, with dark, wavy hair tinged with gray. His nose was broad and fleshy; a pair of horn-rimmed glasses sat squatly on the bridge. It flashed across Rawlins's mind that Dryborough looked Jewish. But perhaps this was only because Dryborough was always described as shrewd, "the cleverest man in the army."

"Rawlins, wasn't it?" Dryborough acknowledged Rawlins's salute and motioned for him to sit down. His irritation from the afternoon seemed to have dissipated. He called to the *safragi*. "Drinks, please, Hassan. This young man is thirsty."

They sat in wicker chairs at an old stone table overhung with palm branches.

"And you have something you wish to tell me that cannot be told to anyone else. Is that right?"

"Yes, sir."

"Before you begin, may I ask you something?"

Dryborough did not wait for Rawlins's nod of affirmation.

"What is the mainspring of war?"

Rawlins, taken aback, opened his mouth to reply, but nothing came out.

"Would you tell me 'revolution in ideas and government'? If

you did, you'd be wrong. After the last war there was a strong hope. I heard it everywhere expressed. I didn't share it. It went something like this: We've had the experience of the trenches and we've learned from it. What we know now will save man from future self-destruction. Well, take a look around. We have at present several hundred million people caught in a condition as barbaric as the Thirty Years' War. What's gone wrong? Forget nations, consider man as a whole. How did our civilization get in such a fix?"

Rawlins didn't answer. Momentarily, he raised his eyes away from Dryborough's face and followed the thin moon as it slipped through a wispy patch of clouds overhead.

"It looks as if something has been pressing on modern man, doesn't it?" Dryborough continued. "But I'll let you in on a secret, and I'll wager it's bigger than the one you're about to tell me." Dryborough leaned forward in his chair and lowered his voice to a whisper. "Modern man is not modern at all." He sat back and gave a short laugh.

Rawlins wondered if Dryborough was drunk, but there was no trace of alcohol on his breath, no evidence at all to support the intuition. A servant stepped onto the terrace, holding a plate of fruit. Dryborough waited until he had set the plate and paring knife down.

"Modern man is just, momentarily, ahead of himself. You and I can witness a lopsided spectacle here, the result of thirty years' bad government tied to thirty years of technological improvement. Our science chaps, our inventors, our engineers: they've supplied a new world in the mechanistic network. But they've made a mistake. They forgot something. They haven't been supplying new men, or new statesmen. No corresponding development, you see, in the mind or spirit. A hundred years ago, we were still dying like flies every time the weather turned bad. Don't do that anymore. All to the good, you say. Is it? I say, better when the tools matched the environment. We haven't only got health, you see; we've got wings, webbed feet, iron claws. Think all this is a little batty, don't you?"

"No, sir."

"Oh, yes you do."

"I think I understand you, sir. You're saying war is an instinct and there's nothing to be done. Couple that instinct with technology, and you've got a formula for apocalypse. But can't the destructive instinct be modified, controlled by others that are more powerful?"

Dryborough smiled. "My, my. They do put the intelligent young men in Intelligence, don't they? And I do believe that here in this delightful Egyptian garden you are talking about love."

Rawlins blanched. The word "love" brought him back to his mission. Dryborough had begun again. "Would you give a small child a hammer to play with near his baby brother?" but Rawlins interrupted him.

"Sir?"

"Yes, yes, Rawlins, your business."

"I'm sorry, sir . . ."

"Quite all right. I do tend to go on, known for it. . . . Well, what is it?"

"I've had a report."

"What kind of report?"

"Eyewitness."

Rawlins felt for the notebook in a pocket of his tunic. As he pulled it out, the thin pamphlet of prayers that Mendoza had thrust upon him fell to the ground and dropped in front of Dryborough's chair. Dryborough bent down to retrieve the little book. Rawlins reddened. Dryborough glanced briefly at the cover before returning it to him. Rawlins began quickly to flip through his notebook.

"Shouldn't walk around with that."

"I'm sorry, sir." Did Dryborough meant the prayer book? No, he was gesturing at the notes in Rawlins's hands.

"Best to leave it in the safe. Well, let's hear it."

At some point while Rawlins was reading, Dryborough had thrown his head back in his chair and closed his eyes. Now that he had finished, Dryborough remained immobile, and Rawlins wondered if he had fallen asleep. Figures moved across the windows of the house, shadow puppets on squares of orange light. Dryborough roused himself.

"We've had these before, you know."

"Yes, sir."

"And your superiors . . .?"

"Not interested, sir."

"Quite right, quite right. But you thought . . ."

"I believed the witness, sir. It seemed to me that she was telling the truth. I understand, sir, about the dangers of Jewish propaganda. I know we don't want a rush on Palestine. But this, well, it seemed so . . . out of the ordinary."

Dryborough asked for the notebook, and Rawlins handed it over. He didn't open it but slapped it against his knee.

"Let me give you a general rule. Jews are inclined by nature to exaggerate. Does that sound harsh? It's what makes them such fine entertainers—I'm sure you love the Marx Brothers as much as I. Don't misunderstand. They have been done unto. But they have a tendency to magnify their persecutions. You're too young to remember, but after the last war all kinds of stories circulated: pogroms in Poland, that sort of thing. I was in the war office at the time. We investigated them all. The charges were fully examined; truth is, little substance. There are always rumors—"

"But this is more than a rumor—"

Dryborough held up his hand.

"I would be the last to dispute that atrocities are taking place. The German war machine is large and very ugly. And your informer has been among the unfortunate who have got in its way. But let us exercise some cautious reserve. Every war will have its atrocity. Can't let it govern policy. Hate to say it, but it's a brush fire. The way to stop the brush fire is to douse the monster flames. Got to smash the Nazis, here as well as there. As you say, no merit at all in stirring things up in Palestine. So I would say, treat your informant kindly; looks like she's seen some things a young girl shouldn't. Don't lose sight of the job, though; might even see if you can get something out of her a little more useful. Good you passed this stuff on to me, but best for now, *keep it under your hat.*"

Dryborough handed the notebook back to Rawlins.

"Your job's the larder, isn't it?"

"Yes, sir."

"Well, I'd stick to the larder. It means a lot, you know. If your enemy's not eating, he's not fighting."

Dryborough rose from his chair.

"Glad you came by."

When Rawlins departed, Dryborough went into his study, closed the door, and picked up the phone.

9

Rawlins started back to Esta, feeling like a fraud and a failure but hating her for getting him into this. What should he tell her? Hadn't Dryborough more or less ordered him to be kind to her? Did that mean stringing her along? Lying?

Outside the Restaurant Balalaika, on Opera Square, he bumped into Harfield and Shaw from Signals. They dragged Rawlins in and sat him between them in the front row. A team of Egyptian muscle dancers took the floor. The sign outside had promised NON-STOP COMEDY, SENSATIONAL DANCING, NEW MU-SIC. There were six girls: a towering gold-toothed brunette in the center and five shorter, bulkier colleagues in a circle around her. As they danced, they carried on a running conversation with one another (the non-stop comedy?), emitting little yips at unexpected moments, as if they had been surprised in the monotony of their movements.

"It's a terpsichorean miracle," said Harfield.

Shaw leaned forward in his seat, trying to dip his head to the level of the dancers' undulating bellies. A waiter brought a bottle of *zebeeb* and three glasses. Rawlins watched the colorless drink turn white as Harfield added water from a jug. Rawlins drank two quick glasses, told Harfield he was going to the toilet, and strode out of the club, into the street.

Halfway back to her, he stumbled into a camel train. The gawky animals, tied nose to tail by long, thin ropes, were brought in each evening from the desert. An Arab rider sat on every second or third camel and controlled the animals' progress. Rawlins heard the tinkling bell of the lead camel but was not quick enough to get out of the way. Before he knew it, he was tangled in the ropes and a bunch of men began shouting at him, urging him out, and trying to rein in their camels. He struggled like a creature lassoed, emerging with rope burns on his forearms and across his chest. As he moved off down the street, he heard laughter ring out behind him.

When he climbed into the room, she was kneeling with her back toward him, writing in her book by the light of the hurricane lamp. He went and gripped her round the waist from behind and rolled her onto the bed. He felt sick inside, but the knowledge that he was deceiving her seemed only to increase his desire. She undid the buckle on his belt, snapped the buttons of his fly, and reached her hand inside.

"No," he said. "I want to make love to you."

She lay back, compliant for once, not grabbing or snatching at him. She was giving him a gift, and it was terrible because he had not done anything to deserve it. But why should he have? Hadn't she said it wasn't blackmail? What was it, then? Loneliness? Desperation? Not love. Then he was inside her, and her hands were caressing his back, and he was calling her name, banging her body on the hard floor, raking his fingers through her damp hair; perspiration streamed on his chest, and he rubbed his body close into hers so her breasts could take the sweat.

When he had come, she held him inside her for a few moments. It was the first time that he felt she wanted tenderness from him. But she soon pushed him off. The room held their bodies' odor, circulated it, mingled it with the sour smell of urine from the open bucket. She began slowly to gather up her clothes.

"I want to hear everything," she said.

10

They were waiting for him in his office. Phillips was there and an older man whom he'd never met. Phillips stared at Rawlins, a look of contempt in his eyes. The older man, who occupied the seat behind Rawlins's desk, asked him to sit down and indicated the visitor's chair. Phillips stood in the corner.

"Would you mind telling us what the hell you've been up to?" Phillips spat the words out. He could barely contain himself.

The older man ignored the outburst and began in firm but modulated terms.

"I'm sorry. I haven't introduced myself. I'm Arthur Graham. I'll be conducting this little investigation."

The buckles on Graham's cross-belt had been well burnished by his batman, as had the buttons on his tunic and the insignia on his hat. His fastidiousness reached all the way down to the pair of shiny shoes that poked out at the foot of the desk: Rawlins noticed that the bows on Graham's laces fell in identical lengths. Everything about him seemed scrubbed and shining: his face, his manicured nails, his silver eyebrows and well-groomed mustache.

Graham turned over Rawlins's copy of Palgrave's *Golden Treasury*.

"Like poetry, do you?"

"Yes, sir."

"Who have you been reading?"

"Swinburne, sir."

"Milton's a great favorite of mine."

"Yes, sir."

" 'What though the field be lost? All is not lost.' Eh?"

"Yes, sir."

Graham laid the little book square in front of him on the table.

"Did you know she sees another man?"

He could feel Phillips's eyes on him. He had to hold himself in check, even though his heart was beating fast and he could sense his cheeks reddening. But even more than his fear and embarrassment, he had to contain the hot spurt of jealousy that Graham's words had loosed in him. He took a breath. A refulgent yellow light rippled through the windows; it seemed intensified by the heat and reflected off the glass onto the faces of his interrogators. Phillips walked over and lowered the venetian blind.

"I don't know what you mean, sir."

"Well, you leave, and he comes. At least that's how it's been for the last couple of weeks. Has it been going on longer than that, do you think?"

"I think he's her friend, sir."

"Her friend? Harfield thinks something quite different. Harfield thinks he's her accomplice."

"In what, sir?"

"Ah. Now, that's the question, isn't it, Rawlins? And that's where we thought you might be able to help."

"They're refugees, sir. I believe he's also from Poland."

Graham took his pipe and a tobacco tin from a pocket of his tunic and began to fill the bowl.

"Did you know Sir John Waterlow?"

"No, sir."

"Splendid chap. Minister to Greece. Had to turn back a refugee ship bound for Palestine last year. Didn't want to. Had his
hand forced by London. Good results for us, though. The Egyp-
tians were very pleased. They're very anxious about Palestine,
you know, and we're very anxious about . . . well, Suez for a start.
The oil, you see, Rawlins. Well, you know this, of course: the oil
for all our tanks, lorries, field guns, it all comes through Suez. At
the other end, up in Haifa, there's the pipeline, of course.
Wouldn't like to see some angry Arabs blow that up, would we?
Not in the middle of a war. Not telling you anything you don't
know, am I? Elementary stuff. Except for this, you see. Sir John
Waterlow came over to see us. Must have been just before you
came out. Isn't that right, Phillips?"

"Last March, sir."

"Someone shot him. Dead."

Graham paused, much as Rawlins remembered his old form
master doing when he waited for a sinner to confess. Then Graham continued.

"We really can't allow that kind of thing to go unpunished,
you know."

Rawlins wanted to say, "It could have been anyone. Everyone
hates us here." But instead he remained silent. Graham puffed on
his pipe, coughed a little, and looked expectantly at Rawlins.

"I'm sure Miss Weiss had nothing to do with it, sir."

"What makes you so sure?"

"I know her. I mean, it's not possible."

He heard how lame and pathetic he sounded. He was an intelligence officer talking like a schoolboy. Graham waited and stared
blankly at Rawlins until he seemed assured that the young man
had secured a sense of his own foolishness.

"And her friend, or lover, or whatever he is. Would such a
thing, an assassination, be 'possible' for him?"

"I couldn't say, sir."

Rawlins saw how Graham was trying to provoke him, and saw, too, how he could stumble and fall so very easily. It would be simple to tell them what they wanted to hear—about her address book, or the unease that he felt in her company—anything to leave this excruciating interview behind him.

"It would seem, wouldn't it, that the kind of organization that pursued a murderous and terrorist policy toward us might very well search out someone like yourself—someone, shall we say, a little bit green: a setup, a possible conduit of information. Wouldn't you think so?"

Before Rawlins could collect his thoughts to reply, Graham had started on another tack.

"Do you know Mendoza, the rabbi?"

Rawlins blushed deeply.

"Fine chap, apparently. Decorated in the last set-to. One of those enthusiasts who went in early, at sixteen, I believe. *Do* you know him?"

"I've met him. . . ."

"Yes. And you've spoken with him."

"Yes, sir. Briefly."

"What's your impression?"

"I'm not sure, sir."

"Not a susceptible type, you wouldn't say?"

"What do you mean?"

"Simply that, really. Nothing hidden. Interested in your assessment of his character, I suppose."

"He likes to talk. . . ."

"He likes pretty boys." Phillips stood smugly, with his arms folded. Rawlins couldn't tell if Graham approved of his interruption.

"Well, you shouldn't have any problem with that."

Phillips leaped forward across the desk. "Why, you little—" Graham held him back with an outstretched arm. "Go and fuck your little Jewess. Or don't you want her now you know someone else has been in the hole too? Some friend of the family. What's it like, Rawlins? Is she teaching you Hebrew?"

Rawlins knew that Graham was watching him, weighing his responses, deciding what to do with him.

"You really are in quite a bit of trouble, old chap." Graham spoke in a low voice. His pipe had gone out, and he felt around in his pocket for matches to relight it.

"Captain Phillips, would you mind leaving us for a while."

Phillips looked angrily at Graham and glared at Rawlins. He walked smartly to the door, stepped out, and closed it behind him.

"Gets a little overexcited, does he?"

"You might say that, sir."

"Still, loyalty's not a bad thing, you know."

"I'm not disloyal, sir."

"Perhaps not. You didn't tell General Dryborough quite everything, though, did you? I mean, that she is your lover."

"Lots of the men have women here, sir."

"Not quite the same. There are the English girls; then there's the Berka—that is, if you don't mind catching something. There are even the Egyptian women; very beautiful, some of them, very European looking—and, I'm glad to say, old chap, 'officially neutral,' so they're not quite out of bounds in the same way as your Miss Weiss. Especially given what we know. . . ."

"What you know?"

"Well, all right, what we think we know. What Harfield is pretty damn sure he knows."

"Has he conducted an investigation, sir?"

"Look here, Rawlins. We're going to give you a chance. I don't think you're a bad chap. I think you let your willy lead you astray, and there's hardly a man alive to whom that hasn't happened. But there's more than that, isn't there? Do you know what the most corrupting element that we have to contend with is, Rawlins? It's not power, or money, or sex. It's pity. You pity her, don't you?"

Rawlins's voice caught in his throat. He didn't know what he felt about her. Sometimes it was desire, sometimes almost hatred.

"You didn't see her yesterday, did you?"

"No, sir."

"Or the day before?"

"I left at dawn."

"Do you know where she goes when you don't see her?"

"No, sir."

"Nor do we."

Through the gaps in the blind, Rawlins glimpsed the dense foliage of the mango tree that he had spent hours staring into from his desk. The room itself had taken on an ocher tinge; the softer light on the furniture and the aroma of the smoke from Graham's pipe took him back for a moment to his front room at home. He caught a glimpse of his father, ear glued to the radio, heard his mother's voice calling from upstairs. But then they were gone. Graham had begun to talk to him again.

"You see, we'd very much like to know where they go. Harfield isn't too competent, I'm afraid. She's been giving him the slip, and now her *friend* has disappeared completely. But you . . ."

"I see, sir."

"Shall we say forty-eight hours? You know in the end we'll have to pick them up."

"They . . . she hasn't done anything. Didn't General Dryborough tell you, sir? She's been through hell. . . ."

"I think all this can be resolved, Rawlins. I can't promise, of course. But I do think things may just work out."

Graham got up to leave. When he reached the door of Rawlins's office, he turned. Rawlins had risen from his chair and was standing with his back to the window.

"One more thing. I'd stay away from the rabbi, if I were you. We do have our own chaps on board, you know."

11

Mendoza was sitting at his desk in his pajamas. His gray curls were pressed flat on the side he had been sleeping on. When Rawlins knocked he had woken, shifted in his chair, and turned the desk light down and away. Now a waste bin stuffed with paper was illuminated, but the rest of the room was in semidarkness.

"They told me to stay away from you."

Mendoza sighed. He buttoned his pajama jacket at the midriff, where it had fallen open.

"I need your help."

"Is it the girl?"

"Yes."

Rawlins was still panting a little, trying to catch his breath. The room was hot; he could smell the sweat coming off his body. He had run the last quarter of a mile, crouching in doorways every now and then, like a fugitive. He had thought that if he came immediately, that night, they might not follow. Hadn't he been given forty-eight hours? In some stupid part of his being, he still trusted them.

"Is she in trouble, or are you?"

"It's both of us."

"Who's onto you?"

"People from my department."

"Senior officers?"

"Yes. And higher."

"What do you want me to do?"

"I want you to get her out."

Mendoza raised himself up in his chair.

"Out of Cairo? Out of Egypt? Out of the war?"

"Anywhere. Just out!" Rawlins took deep breaths, sucking in the spoiled air, and wiped his brow with the back of his hand.

"What makes you think I have the capacity to spirit someone away?"

"Surely you must have contacts. In Palestine!"

Rawlins regretted it as soon as he had blurted out the words. Mendoza flushed deep red, but whether with embarrassment or anger Rawlins couldn't tell.

"What are you trying to imply? Do you think I am a Zionist agent?" Mendoza gave a short laugh. "I see that you know very little about English Jews. Perhaps I am the first Jew you've ever met? You're not from London, are you? If you were, you might have heard of my family. We have been there since the seventeenth century. My relatives are quite well known merchant bankers." Mendoza caught himself short. "But perhaps we had better not talk about banking. It's not quite the same—is it?—as if *your* relatives were merchant bankers."

"I'm sorry; I didn't mean to suggest that you were . . ."

"Disloyal?"

"That wasn't what I was thinking."

There was silence. Rawlins shifted in his seat; he felt sweat trickling down his arms and chest. His mouth was dry. He asked Mendoza for water and gulped at the canteen that the chaplain handed him.

Mendoza seemed to relent a little.

"And what about you?"

"I'll take care of myself."

"Is she alone?"

"Yes." Rawlins didn't falter in his response; to do so would be fatal. Mendoza would know that he was lying.

"You'll have to explain—"

"I can explain."

Rawlins told the story without once mentioning Falik Hafner. His mind felt like a block of wood and the name Hafner like a drill going in, making hole after hole. When he described Esta's experiences in Poland, Mendoza turned his face away and closed his eyes.

Rawlins finished speaking and looked quickly in panic around

the room, as if his recent interrogators might suddenly materialize out of the walls.

"You say she has been implicated in a murder."

"Yes."

"And what reason do you have to believe that Harfield—is that
his name?—has got it wrong?"

"He hates Jews."

"That's as may be. There are probably plenty of Jews who are
not too fond of him."

"It's a frame-up, a game. I see how they work."

Mendoza squeezed the neck of the lamp and directed light
back onto his desk. He started to fumble through some papers,
then sat back as if he had decided that whatever he was looking
for would be of no help.

For a minute, the two men were silent. Then Mendoza spoke.

"I really think it's too much. And what could I do anyway?
Perhaps I could speak to your superior officer, find out exactly
what's going on. On the other hand, if they've already told you to
stay away from me . . . Really, I don't see how I can help you."

"But you must, you must!" Rawlins leaned over the desk, gripping the edge, then moving his hands in small circles to wipe off
the sweat.

"You're asking me to do the impossible."

"Didn't you understand what I told you? You know what she's
been through."

"Look here. I have more than twenty years of service. Do you
have any idea how difficult something like this is for a man in my
position?"

Rawlins softened his voice. "I don't mean to compromise
you," he murmured.

"Then what do you mean to do?"

"She's a Jew. Doesn't that mean anything to you?"

There was a noise in the corridor. Rawlins flinched. Two men
talking in loud voices clattered past the door. One said, "One

more drink and I would 'ave 'ad her." The other replied,
"One more drink and you wouldn't 'ave been able to get it up."

Mendoza rose slowly from his chair and stumbled over a pile
of books on the floor. He came around the desk and stood next to
Rawlins. Rawlins could see the mat of hair emerging at the V of
his pajama top, like stuffing from a mattress.

Suddenly Mendoza raised his hand and began to tug and pinch
at the flesh on Rawlins's face. Rawlins slapped him away.

"What are you doing?"

Mendoza grabbed Rawlins by the arm. A steel shaving mirror
was propped on a pipe that ran along the perimeter of the room.
Mendoza dragged Rawlins over to it and shoved his face an inch
away from the glass. Rawlins saw a pair of bloodshot eyes ringed
with dark circles, the bridge of his nose, the pores in his skin
breathing sweat. Now, for the first time, he smelled the liquor on
the rabbi's hot breath. Rawlins's ankle began to throb, and he felt
a sharp pain in his arm where Mendoza was twisting it.

"I could lose everything, everything," Mendoza muttered in
his ear. "And they'd love that, wouldn't they? 'Knew all along he
couldn't be trusted. Not really one of us, you know. Like to look
after their own first.' "

He let Rawlins go, took two steps, and slumped back exhausted into his chair. The heat rose in waves, as if someone were
pumping blasts of hot air up through the floor. Rawlins stood
with his face buried in the palms of his hands.

"Do you love her?" Mendoza asked.

Rawlins dropped his hands and looked at him.

"I don't know."

12

He had to go to her now. They would be waiting and watching
somewhere outside the synagogue, but that didn't matter. He was

on their mission. At least that's what they thought. He wasn't so sure. He didn't know what he was going to do, only that he had to see her.

He picked up a horse-drawn taxi outside Shepheard's. A *safragi* in a gold-embroidered crimson jacket and white pantaloons tried to help him into his seat, but he shrugged him off. He shouted the address to the driver. For this one night on his way to her, Rawlins could be as noisy and conspicuous as he wanted. He took note of the usual crowd up on the balcony, drinks in hand. Was Phillips among them? Had he spread the word? "Rawlins has a little Jew." Probably not. Graham must have kept him quiet. They wanted their arrests.

If they were following him, he didn't see them. The horse clopped slowly past the brightly lit clubs that dotted the center of town. They turned a corner, and Rawlins saw a group of latecomers rushing toward the entrance of one of the open-air movie theaters. High above him on the screen, the enormous forms of Robert Montgomery and Madeleine Carroll were locked in a passionate embrace. The taxi moved on and out into the semideserted streets that marked his passage to her. Two lost Tommies, drunk and red-faced, swayed and tottered down a side street. A girl, her face garishly made up, called out to them from a second-story window. Rawlins felt almost princely in his carriage, oddly light-headed. He laid his head back and gazed up at the stars and the sharp, hot splinter of moon. From the seat back he caught the aroma of Turkish cigarettes mingled with perfume.

He stopped the cab right beneath the hole in the wall and whistled. When she looked out he waved his cap, and she laughed.

He climbed onto the crates and scrambled in. The room was full of the thin, sticky light that came from the hurricane lamp, as if someone had smeared pale yellow on the walls. For the first time, he didn't want to make love to her immediately. He needed to deal with the problem at hand, in one way or another, and *then* one last time, and it *would* be the last time.

She was pleased to see him. Ever since he had told her how he had confronted Dryborough, and how Dryborough had promised to report her story at the highest levels in London, she had softened toward him. "He's going to pressure the Foreign Office and the Colonial Office," Rawlins had said, "and believe me, he has clout." Now when they made love she said his name. "Archie." She whispered it, and he liked the way it sounded. Her accent was absurd but lovely, "European," not Jewish.

Her lips, when his brushed against hers, were harsh and chapped. He remembered how sunburned she had been at the café. He had to ask her. He had to find out; not for them, for himself.

She pulled him toward her. This change had come too, things happening at her instigation.

"Where have you been?" he said.

"I was away."

"Where do you go when you're 'away'?"

She kissed his face and began tugging his shirt out of his trousers.

"Esta, where do you go?"

"To the desert."

"Why?"

She leaned back from him, holding on to his belt with one hand.

"You still don't trust me, do you?"

She let go of the belt and stepped back.

"What would you do if I left Cairo? Would you be very sad? Would you be 'heartbroken'?" She laughed when she used the phrase, as if it was the first time that it had crossed her lips and the possibilities of the words having real meaning had only now struck her.

"Are you planning on leaving?"

"Yes."

"When? How? Where are you going?"

"I see that you would not be all that 'heartbroken.' "

"No . . . I . . . It's just . . ."

"I am going to Palestine."

Rawlins felt his face redden. "Why Palestine?"

"Because I have someone there, and besides—"

"Who do you have? A lover?"

"No; a relative."

"A relative? Who?"

Esta lowered her eyes. He felt for a brief moment as if he were interrogating her again.

"My father."

"What do you mean?"

"He lives in Tel Aviv. He left Vienna eight years ago. He was supposed to send for us. He wrote and said he didn't have the money."

"I assumed. . . ."

"I know what you assumed."

What other information had she withheld?

"So you see," she was continuing, "I must go to Palestine."

"But you can't. I mean, it's not possible. Not for you."

She came back to him and took his head in her hands.

"My poor Archie," she said. "Do you think I can stay in this room for the rest of my life?"

"You'll be blocked at the border."

"There are ways."

"When are you leaving?"

"When it can be arranged. It may take weeks. We are a small group. We meet to arrange things. We have to be very careful. Eventually someone will take us across."

"Can't you go faster than that? What if there's an emergency?"

"An emergency? What do you mean? Are you in a hurry to see me go, Archie?"

"No. But perhaps I can help. I want to help. Tell me what to do. And I'll come. I'll come to you in Palestine. I can request a posting."

She looked away from him.

"Do you have someone else? Is it him? Falik? Are you his lover?"

Esta laughed. "Didn't you notice?" she asked. "I'm your lover. Do you think I am insatiable? Poor Falik. Falik is a ghost. More than I am. His body hasn't come back to him yet, not at all, not one bit. He is still in the land of the dead."

Rawlins thought of Falik's face, his jaundiced cheeks and sunken eyes. She had begun to pull at his belt again.

They made love. He tried to take her whole body into his memory by touching her everywhere, as if his fingertips might remember, like a blind man's, even if the rest of him forgot her. Because even as he was thrusting into her he knew that everything he had told her was a lie. He was a coward and she thought he was brave; and he planned to forget her. There was a whole life ahead of him in England, Sunday lunchtimes in the village pub, and Claire, and the long stream of days of clear thought in cool weather; there were friends, his family, that job with Shell-Mex, reunions with other chaps who'd been in the war, and they would talk about things just like this: the women they'd had beneath them, the breasts and cunts of exotic, strange women; foreign sirens who'd nearly pulled them out to sea and drowned them. First you read about them in the poems, then you got the practical education; maybe that's what going abroad was all about.

A thin blue vein stood out in Esta's breast; it ran from her nipple almost to the flat of her chest. Rawlins ran his finger along it, and she shivered. He turned her over and ran his tongue down her spine, over her tailbone, and into the crack beneath it. He was marking her now, marking her with his saliva; he had a claim. Afterward, when she was lying in his arms, she whispered:

"Do I mean something to you?"

"Everything," he replied.

"And if, after I go, I write and tell you where I am, you'll come to Palestine?"

"Palestine," he repeated.

13

"So you came around."

Rawlins didn't respond. He was alone with Phillips in Phillips's office.

"You're *damn* lucky." Phillips smacked his swagger stick on the table. "Well, where are they?"

Again, Rawlins was silent.

"Look here, Rawlins: If you don't plan on speaking, let me know now, and I'll make the necessary phone call to Graham, and we can have you under lock and key by morning."

"They meet in the desert. There's a little hut out near the Saqqara pyramid. It was being used by some archaeologists working the necropolis. Now it's abandoned."

"When's the next meeting?"

"Tomorrow night."

"Are you sure about that?"

"Yes."

"Why do they go there?"

"They're planning to cross the border into Palestine."

Phillips wrote everything down.

"Is that all they're planning?"

"Yes."

"As far as you know."

Rawlins was silent.

"Well, you can leave the rest to us. Colonel Graham says you're to take a few days off. Clear your head."

"Where am I supposed to go?"

"Damned if I know. Go wherever the hell you like. You came damn close, Rawlins."

"What are you going to do with them?"

"I'd take those days off if I were you."

14

He was going to Tel Aviv. He knew it was perverse to travel to Palestine, but when Harriet heard that he was taking a furlough, she offered him a ticket to the Palestine Philharmonic Orchestra. Phillips was in the room, hanging back, listening to every word, and Rawlins had to accept. Harriet might, she said, join him at the concert if her own leave came through. He saw Phillips smirk before he stepped away.

He set out down Adly Pasha, hoping to pick up a ride. In the street, a slow convoy was on the last leg of its journey back to barracks from the front. Rawlins could see what he already knew from his paperwork, that out in the desert things weren't going well. There were bashed-in trucks bearing the skeletons of torn tanks and airplane fuselages, ripped-up wings; jeeps and field kitchens; semidestroyed trailers and scout cars; pulverized motorcycles riding in piles on the backs of trucks.

Every car was crusted with a heavy hard dust; the windshields looked as if they had been coated with enamel. The joke circulating in town was that Rommel had sent a telegram to Shepheard's, reserving the hotel for his Nazi officers.

It was astonishing to Rawlins how the city continued to go about its business. Here was a parade of the beaten and weary, at its head the field ambulances with their cargo of battered bodies and torn minds, but in Cairo, on the threshold of battle, destruction, and death, there was music every afternoon under the palm trees in the garden at Shepheard's and a floor show each night in the roof cabaret of the Continental. The officers and club members were still playing cricket. This morning, he had heard Harfield describing to a group of men how the Imperial Harlequins had beaten the Wilcocks Sporting Club by an innings and forty-two runs. "*Huge* crowd. Simply enormous. Took me an hour to get out of the stadium."

Rawlins secured a lift in a two-ton as far as Jerusalem. The ride was long and bumpy. At first he simply stared out at the billowy white sand and the road unwinding in a dark ribbon before him. When it grew dark, he asked the driver to stop so that he could go into the back and stretch out.

He slept badly most of the way, waking in cold sweats, sick with guilt, her name on his lips, the taste of her in his mouth. Outside, the stars were hidden and the air was chill. He was glad when it began to get light. Through the back flap of the truck he watched dawn unfurl over the hills on either side of the road, in bolts of pink and yellow.

When the domes and spires of the Old City came in sight, the driver pulled off the road.

"Breakfast?" he yelled back at Rawlins.

They stood against the back of the truck and cradled mugs of tea that the driver had brewed up. He was a sergeant in a camouflage corps ("Nobody wants it, nobody does it"). A short, thickset squaddie with a head of blazing red hair. His name was Ross.

"Been here before, sir?"

"First trip."

"Well, watch out."

"For anything in particular?"

"The place is stiff with refugees. They'll steal every piece of equipment you've got."

Rawlins shivered. "Surely not."

"They'll take everything they can lay their hands on, sir." Ross made a mock grab at his own balls. "I'm not joking, sir. Some of these young women will do anything. They love a British passport. Most of 'em didn't want to come here anyway. Soon as Hitler's gone they'll scoot right back, mark my words. If you ask me, we're doing 'em a favor when we turn 'em back. They wind up in Cyprus or Italy or somewhere. Gotta be better than here. This is a bloody sweatbox. Mosquitoes. Filth."

Suddenly Rawlins felt the impulse to brag to Ross. He wanted to say he'd fucked one of them himself and she hadn't managed to put a dent in *his* equipment. He wanted to tell this ginger-haired squaddie that *he*, Rawlins, had taken *her* for everything she had. It was as if now that he had betrayed Esta he had to hate her in order to make her disappear. He wanted to tell Ross about her body, how he hated it—her thin breasts, the black-and-blue marks on her arms where he had banged her against the stone floor, the stupid scar on her nose—hated the desperate clutch of her fucking, her neediness. She had tried to take from him, but he hadn't given her anything.

They drove into the city in silence. Ross dropped Rawlins at the train station. For a few moments before buying his ticket, he stood under a dusty eucalyptus tree and breathed in the warm air. A mixed scent of petroleum, coal dust, and almonds hung over the station. Two Jewish women, thin, dark-haired, walked swiftly and purposefully down the street toward him. He stepped aside to let them pass. They looked at him without smiling.

It wasn't until the train began its snake wind round the foot of the Judean hills that he began to feel embarrassed. The journey had been so simple. A few hours' discomfort, and he was in Palestine. Whereas with a wave of his hand, or so it now seemed, he had banished Esta forever from the promised land. More than this he didn't want to think. He told himself that she couldn't have got in anyway. Whatever he had done or said, they would have caught her eventually and turned her back. All he had done was to speed up the inevitable. He tried to put Harfield's "report" about the Waterlow murder out of his mind. That was just play; they were toying with him, scaring him. At worst they would take Hafner. At worst she would spend a few days in jail.

There was a wedding party in his carriage, an excitable group fussing around the groom on his last journey as a single man. Rawlins had watched them arrive on the platform: a portly father, his face beet red; a mother in a wide-brimmed straw hat with a fake bunch of cherries on the headband; two small sisters in blue-print cotton dresses; and the groom, probably about his own age, besuited but tieless, his broad-collared cream shirt open at the neck. Unlike his father, the groom was pale and on the skinny side.

As soon as they had settled down, Rawlins felt the groom's eyes upon him. He thought, at first, that it was his disheveled appearance that was drawing attention. He had tried to smarten himself up before getting out of the lorry, but he had been unable to shave, and Ross, whose hair was spiked and hard, had no need of a comb and hadn't been able to lend him one.

The long stare continued until Rawlins began to feel oppressed. They were all staring at him. He realized that it wasn't the state of his uniform but the uniform itself that had silenced them and brought their joy to a halt. Ungrateful bastards, he thought.

The train chugged slowly west beyond terraced hills covered with olive trees. Rawlins could see the red and tan roofs of small settlements, and then, as the train rounded a corner, the coastal plain came into view. The members of the wedding party began to talk among themselves again. There was something about the groom that disturbed Rawlins. He knew what it was: the groom reminded him of Hafner. Hafner, who had been unable to look him in the eye and had sat so passively that time in the café when he grabbed Esta's arm. But look at him here, this Hafner, comfortable and confident. The groom's father rose and pushed open a window. A rush of soft fresh air penetrated the carriage.

It's me, Rawlins thought. I'm the Jew here. His lips moved silently and involuntarily around the phrase.

15

Rawlins found a room in a square, off-white boardinghouse with a balcony overlooking a narrow street. The outside was badly in need of a fresh coat of paint, and there were no window boxes or potted plants decorating the place the way he had seen at some of the establishments closer to the shore. But Rawlins had deliberately chosen a place away from the seaside hotels. He didn't want to share accommodation with other soldiers on leave, if he could help it. The proprietress, a short, dark-haired woman in a floral-patterned housedress, led him up the stairs and gave him a key. The room was low and constricted. Rawlins shoved his kit bag under the bed, while the woman stood watching him.

"Do you want to eat here?" She spoke English with a heavy European accent.

"No."

The woman shrugged and moved toward the door.

"No more than one person in the room, please."

Rawlins paid her no attention. He had shifted to the room's only window and was looking across the street toward a small grocery, partially obscured by a mulberry tree. In front of the shop, two small children, a boy and a girl, barefoot and bare-chested, played in sand that swirled in ripples over the pavement; another, bigger boy endeavored to climb the tree. An awning of rags hung over the vegetables and fruits. Further down the road, a soda vendor approached, stopping his cart to pour drinks for thirsty customers.

When Rawlins heard the proprietress close the door behind her, he moved out onto the balcony. The smaller children outside immediately stopped what they were doing and waved up to him.

The older boy shouted something in Hebrew, and the little ones laughed. Rawlins felt foolish and retreated inside his room.

He lay on the narrow bed. The sun pressed in through the wooden slats of the shutters and striped dark bars across his body. He heard the sound of clinking glasses and rolling wheels, then the high-pitched squeals of the children running across the street. He turned his face into the pillow and slept.

When he awoke, it was almost noon. The air in the room was heavy and still, as if before a summer rain that would never come. Rawlins felt the weight of it pressing him down to the bed. He was covered with sweat. He stripped off his uniform and underclothes and washed himself at the sink. The water came out rust-colored; he brushed his teeth anyway, swilling and spitting the warm liquid but not feeling the least bit refreshed. He tried to wrap around him the rough white towel that had been provided, but it was not quite long enough to encircle his waist, and he let it drop to the floor. Sitting naked in front of the mirror of a small dressing table that the owner had squeezed in between the sink and a wall, Rawlins watched indifferently as a fat cockroach scuttled out from under the bed and over the tiled floor. When a second appeared, he picked up his boot and brought it crushing down on the insect's soft shell, leaving a small patch of brown blood at the foot of the sink.

He flicked through a pack of postcards, purchased on his walk through town, and searched for the right picture to send, first to his parents and then to Claire. He could barely remember Claire, her face, her hair, her voice, the times they had spent together, but he needed to bring her back, to have her phantom foremost in his imagination. He wrote to her: "Here on a three-day pass. It's hot, hot, hot. You not being here is a howling great gap in my life." Then he tore the card into pieces.

Toward one, he went out. The shops were closed, the streets more or less deserted. The sun blazed, and he felt heat rise off the broad flagstones through the soles of his boots. He walked toward the sea.

At the shore it was a different story. Excited groups of youngsters bobbed in green waves; young women lay stretched out on towels; further back from the water, a line of striped deck chairs with odd little canvas roofs housed the older members of the beach population. Rawlins leaned over the rails of the promenade, let the breeze blow into his face, and watched a cluster of gulls wheel and dip in the wake of a fishing boat. He spotted a group of English soldiers playing soccer in the dark apron of sand at the edge of the sea. By the look of their pale bodies, they were new arrivals. Their voices floated up to him like the strains of familiar songs. "You kicked it, you get it." "Jump in the bloody sea, that's how." Two of them were trying to start a conversation with a girl on the beach. Back in Cairo it had been obligatory to repeat the mantra "You can't beat British girls," but Rawlins saw now that you could. Nevertheless, he wasn't aroused. For him, the bright beach and the women in low-cut bathing suits had nothing to do with sex.

He walked north, away from town, hugging the shoreline. Eventually he found a semideserted spot and stopped. As he laid out his towel, two men on bicycles pedaled slowly past, paying him no heed. Rawlins lay down on his back; two planes, Bostons, familiar to Rawlins from the desert, flew in low over the water, no doubt heading for the air base at Lydda. He closed his eyes. He was playing on the beach at Broadstairs. His father dug in the sand with a child's red shovel, making a car for him; he pressed shells into the dashboard and gave Archie a cricket stump to use as a gear lever. The steering wheel was a piece of blanched driftwood, dressed in seaweed.

Rawlins got up to swim. The sea was calm and warm, but its salt stung him, penetrating the deep scratches on his back where Esta had dug her nails. Afterward he lay in the sand with his face pressed down on the small towel. The sun burned into the salty scratches.

He lay on the beach, half asleep, until the sun began to drop. Rousing himself, he headed back to the boardinghouse. His shoulders began to burn; when the sun went down, the pain would increase. That didn't matter.

He had her father's address, 6 Ezekiel Street, scribbled on a piece of paper in his pocket. On his last night in Cairo, after they made love, Esta had fallen asleep and he flipped through her leather book, memorizing the address. He wrote it down as soon as he had left her, along with the name of the place in the desert, the one that she had told him and that he had given to Phillips.

When he got back to the boardinghouse he washed himself at the sink, pouring cups of the warm rust water over his shoulders and down his back. He sat on the bed and took out his Palgrave's. He tried to read some poetry, but the words had no meaning. Nothing had anything to do with where he was, what he had come to.

He went downstairs and asked the proprietress for directions to Ezekiel Street. She called to the cook, who shouted a response from the kitchen. Then he emerged, wiping his hands on his food-stained apron.

"Ezekiel? Why do you want to go there? There are nicer parts of town."

"I'm looking for someone."

"May I ask who?"

"If you could just give me directions."

Outside, the blue vault of the sky was rapidly darkening; purple shadows formed on the walls of the restaurants and small hotels in the neighborhood. This was a busy time on the street, children outside playing, families gathered on their balconies, talking or listening to the radio, mothers drawing in the laundry that hung on pulleys across the narrow streets. The smell of cooking mingled with sea air and a wilder, more exotic scent, which Rawlins couldn't identify. Orange blossom?

He walked through streets that broadened into tree-lined boulevards, then narrowed again as he neared his goal. He stopped one or two people to confirm directions, and each time he was greeted with questions rather than answers. After forty minutes or so, he took a turn down an alleyway and found himself on Ezekiel Street.

At one end were a few dark garages and mechanics' workshops. Beyond them, backing onto a dank, narrow waterway, stood a single three-story apartment house. Rawlins sat on a low wall outside and waited.

Shortly, a man approached. He walked slowly down the street, swaying slightly from the weight of the shopping bags he held, one in each hand. He wore a short-sleeved shirt, long khaki shorts, a pair of leather brogues, and dark socks. On his head was a battered broad-brimmed straw hat. Rawlins couldn't get a clear look at the face, but he noticed a pair of long silver sideburns and a hard growth of gray stubble on the cheeks and chin.

The man stopped in front of Rawlins and put down his bags. Rawlins saw that the leather soles of the man's shoes had curled away at the toes.

"Can I help you?"

He spoke in the same busybody tone as the boardinghouse landlord.

"I'm not sure."

"Well, if you're not sure, you're not sure. Are you looking for someone?"

Rawlins averted his eyes. "No, I don't think so. No."

"Then what are you doing? Taking a rest?"

Down the street, someone kick-started a motorbike, and the pop, pop, pop of backfire echoed between the buildings. Rawlins noticed dark patches of sweat under the man's arms. The air was thick, as if it had been coated with a slick of grease.

"You don't seem to know very much."

The man's voice was heavily accented, but Rawlins couldn't place it (no "double first," he thought bitterly). It could be Esta's father. He could find out just by asking. But his tongue felt anchored in his mouth.

He watched the older man walk into the apartment building, and then he followed him, tracking him up to the third floor and noting the number of the door that he entered. He quietly descended the stairs and checked the residents' names on the mailboxes in the hallway. They were all written in Hebrew.

16

Rawlins walked aimlessly at first, tracking the path of the narrow river that ran behind the old man's building. The dark theater of the sky enclosed a dome of stars. As he walked, shafts of moonlight slanted between the walls of warehouses and cramped apartment buildings. He intended, eventually, to make his way back to the boardinghouse, but on an impulse, he felt suddenly for the pocket of his tunic; it held the symphony ticket that Harriet had given him. He stood under a streetlamp and scrutinized it. If he found his way quickly enough, he could make the concert.

It was only after he had taken his seat that he became aware of the slovenliness of his appearance. He had a two-day growth of beard—he hadn't shaved since leaving Cairo—his uniform was creased and grimy, his hair was uncombed. There were a few British officers in the audience, and Rawlins caught them casting glances in his direction. The seat next to his, the one for Harriet, was empty. At first he was pleased that she hadn't shown up; in fact, until he sat down he had forgotten the possibility of her coming to Tel Aviv.

He was glad when the concert began; he slumped back in his chair, hoping that the music would stop his mind from whirling, calm him. A cellist took center stage and drew from his instrument the sober opening notes of an adagio. Rawlins thought it might be a Haydn piece, but he hadn't bothered to purchase a program. The audience seemed alert and appreciative, glad to indulge a kind of collective deep melancholy, but for Rawlins, the music that he had hoped would soothe him only named a terrible loneliness. He had set out to do good, and he had fucked up everything.

Harriet arrived during the intermission, weaving her way through the crowded aisle, smiling her cheerful smile and waving at him from a distance. She was wearing a long black skirt and a white blouse. Aside from the day at the beach in Alexandria, it was the first time that Rawlins had seen her out of uniform.

"I'm so happy you're here," she said, squeezing past him and into her seat. "I wasn't sure you'd come."

Rawlins looked hard at her.

"Any activity in the office?"

"Well, you really don't go in for small talk, do you? I thought we were here to get away from the office."

"Has anybody been brought in?"

"What on earth are you talking about? I left the day after you. Who were you expecting?"

"Never mind."

Harriet settled back. She seemed momentarily dispirited, but before the intermission was over she had returned to her old self, chatting in a vivacious manner about the comedy of her train ride from Cairo. When the second half of the concert began, she slipped her hand into Rawlins's. He didn't resist.

17

The room was full of mosquitoes, which buzzed in his ear and caused him to slap and smack at his face. Beside him in the bed,

Harriet was crying softly. She lay on her side, facing away from him, her arms held across her breasts. Rawlins watched the mosquitoes land on the fleshy part of her arm and sit there until they were finished. Red marks proliferated on her neck and shoulders.

"What's the matter?" He tried to inject a note of genuine concern into his voice, but he knew the effort was a dismal failure.

Her crying diminished, and she replied in a broken voice: "You were rough."

"I thought you wanted—"

"You were rough, and now you're like a dead man. It's horrible."

It was she who had suggested they take a walk after the concert. She who had stopped him under the tamarisks and pines to raise her face to his, begging a kiss.

Rawlins stared straight ahead, then looked back at her. One breast had broken free of its protective barrier; a mosquito immediately alighted close to her nipple and began to suck. Harriet shifted her arms, turned her face away from the wall, and lay on her back. She pulled the sheet up over her body as far as it would stretch.

"Did you sleep with her? That refugee?"

"What makes you think that?"

"You have scratches all over your back."

Harriet's voice was muffled, hoarse with resentment.

"I went to the Berka. That's what everybody does."

"She must have been a very passionate whore."

"You don't have to worry. I didn't catch anything."

"You have a soft spot for her, don't you?"

"I have nothing for her."

"It's because you have a Jewish mentality yourself."

"What's that supposed to mean?" Rawlins snapped.

"Injustice. You think everyone's against you. I've seen the way you act at the office. You wouldn't allow Harry and Robert to be your friends, no matter how hard they tried."

"You have no idea."

"Oh, God," she sighed. "I wish I'd never come here."

He hoped that she would fall asleep. It wasn't her fault that he was disgusted with himself, but he knew that if she stayed awake he would pretend that was the case.

They lay without speaking for a few moments, until Harriet broke the silence.

"It could be all right between us, but you won't let it be."

She rolled over and laid her head on his chest. Rawlins lay stiffly, with his arms limp at his sides.

"Do you miss England?" she asked.

"We're supposed to, aren't we."

"Well, do you?"

Harriet half raised her head, and her loose fair hair brushed against his neck and under his chin.

"I thought I did. But what I missed was only an idea about my future: a feeling of certainty. I want something else now, but I'm not going to be able to get it."

"What else?"

"I can't put it into words. It's a feeling. I want to go past the limits, to break them. You can't do that in England."

"Isn't that what the Germans are doing, breaking all the rules?"

"I'm talking about a certain kind of passion that you can't find at home."

"That's silly. Of course you can, whatever it is. We're human beings, you know, like everyone else. I hate all that Mediterranean nonsense. Those men in the office, ogling every time a beautiful dark-skinned woman comes in. It's so unfair."

She moved her hand between his legs and began to rub his balls and stroke his penis. He felt his erection returning.

"See, you can have passion."

Harriet had misunderstood him entirely. It wasn't about sex, or not only about sex. With Esta he hadn't known who he was, and that had scared him, and so he had given her up rather than give himself up. What he had done was beyond forgiveness.

Harriet moved her mouth over his chest and circled her face down and over his stomach. He grabbed at her hair and tugged. He wanted her to continue and take him in her mouth, but at the same time a terrible rage was building inside him, which he felt powerless to control. He pulled harder on her hair.

"Stop! You're hurting me."

Harriet tried to pull away. Why wasn't she grabbing him, fighting back, biting, drawing blood? Suddenly he snatched the sheet away from her and began beating at her naked body with his fists. Harriet screamed, "Stop it! Stop!" She raised her hands and held them protectively over her face. Rawlins continued to punch at her, raising blue marks on her thighs and arms. It was as if his soul could be cleansed only by his reaching a state of utter shamelessness. Someone was hammering on the door, yelling at them, and then it burst open and the burly cook pulled him off Harriet, while the proprietress screamed, "I told you no more than one in the room! This is a decent place."

Harriet scrambled into her clothes. A look of terror had spread across her face when he started to hit, but now her cheeks were bright red with embarrassment. She straightened her skirt and began vigorously to smooth her hair with her hand.

The proprietress stared contemptuously at Harriet as she stood buttoning her blouse; then, turning away from her, the woman addressed Rawlins.

"You pay me now and you go. I don't want you here."

Harriet grabbed her bag and ran toward the door, slamming it behind her as she left. Her footsteps echoed as she clattered down the stone stairs.

Rawlins stood naked, still clasped in the cook's bear hug. His shoulders began to shake. The cook released his grip, and Rawlins dropped to his knees, convulsed in tears.

18

"You again."

Rawlins was stretched out on the wall on Ezekiel Street. The sun had been up for perhaps an hour; the street was bathed in a pale-green light. Toward dawn he had fallen asleep, waking now to see the man in the straw hat standing over him.

"What are you? A drunk? You come here every night?"

Rawlins roused himself. Grit from the wall had pitted and grazed his cheek; his hair was tangled and his mouth dry.

"What is it? You're a deserter or something? You look like you haven't washed for a week."

"I'm on leave."

"You want a coffee. I don't have money for a coffee, but I'll buy you one anyway."

Rawlins stood and brushed himself off. He followed the man down the street and into a three-table café on the corner. Without any order being given, a woman appeared from behind the counter with two cups in her hands. She put them down in front of them, spilling coffee into the saucers as she did so. Men in overalls filled the other tables.

"Once they start work, it's noise all day. Would you like to live with that? Unfortunately I don't have a choice. I'm a poor man."

Rawlins looked his companion over. He was in his late fifties, perhaps his early sixties. His eyes were dark, like hers, but beyond that there was no resemblance. Rawlins noticed the way the man's stomach spread over the belt of his shorts; he may have been poor, but he wasn't underfed.

"So?"

"I got thrown out of my boardinghouse."

The man laughed. Rawlins listened for Esta's voice in his, but heard nothing.

"You've been having a little too much fun. That's a dangerous thing. Were they religious? You chose a religious proprietor. That was your mistake. Or maybe not. Maybe you did something else."

"Zev!"

Rawlins turned. A man had come in and was greeting his companion. So it wasn't him. Rawlins felt a mix of relief and disappointment. Her father's name was Wolf; he had seen it in the address book: Wolf Weiss, Ezekiel 6.

"I have to be going."

"You haven't finished your coffee."

Rawlins remained in his seat. He was too tired to move, and something else kept him, a glance, the way his companion had looked at the friend who had come in, something familiar in Zev's expression.

"Mr. Wiener. Come sit, sit with us. We have here a young man on leave from the British army. It's his first trip to Palestine. *Is it* your first trip?"

Rawlins nodded.

"As I say. He's a little out of sorts. Perhaps some conversation can cheer him up."

The new arrival pulled up a chair. He was better dressed than Zev; his shirt was pressed, and his shoes had been shined.

"Do you play chess?" he asked Rawlins.

"Not for a long time." Perhaps not in this world, Rawlins thought: a coal fire burning in his parents' parlor, the chessboard set up on the middle table from the walnut nest, his father pressing a knight under the tip of his heavy finger, saying, "Two forward and one to the side, *or* two to the side and one forward, *or* the same thing going backwards."

The man spoke again in a teasing voice. "Well, Herr Doktor Professor Weiss, and what is your plan for today? A few hours in the Tel Aviv library, perhaps." He laughed.

Rawlins didn't hear the jokey reply. His head was spinning. Weiss. It had to be him. Not Wolf, but Zev, but it had to be him. And now that he'd found him, what was he going to do, or say?

The two men were still bantering. A group of workers got up from the adjacent table and bumped heavily, a little too heavily, past him in the cramped space: one man dug his elbow into Rawlins's side, another flicked the back of his head.

"Don't mind them," Weiss said. "They're young."

"They don't know how to be grateful," his friend added. "Let the Nazis come to Palestine, then ask them how they feel about the British army."

A ragged dog appeared in the doorway and barked. One of the workers, on his way out, aimed a kick, and the dog limped away, disappearing behind an overstuffed garbage can buzzing with flies.

Weiss's high spirits continued. He was nothing like her. Everything was a matter for laughter or a caustic comment. Rawlins began to feel angry. He, Weiss, was the betrayer. What kind of father left his family in a hostile country? And here he was, alive and well, draining his coffee cup and asking for a refill.

"Listen," Weiss was saying, and he began to tell a joke. "A man finds a lamp and rubs it. Out pops a genie. 'You can have any wish you want.' The man thinks a little. Finally, he says, 'World peace.' 'World peace?' The genie looks at him. 'Excuse me, sir, but that's a tough one. There's never been such a thing. Anything else, ask me anything else.' The man thinks for a bit." Here Weiss lowered his voice to a whisper. " 'How about getting my wife to give me a you-know.' " Weiss pointed quickly from his mouth to his groin. " 'No problem,' says he genie. 'Oh, just one thing. Is your wife Jewish?' 'Surely,' replies the man. 'Now,' says the genie, 'when you talk about "world peace. . . ." ' "

The two older men laughed; their bodies shook. Weiss nodded his head at Rawlins, saw that he wasn't smiling, and gestured with his hand, as if to wave away his own joke. He adopted a serious demeanor and said:

"How about if you come with me? There's something you can

help me with. We've had coffee, now we need breakfast. Come back to my apartment."

They walked down the street. The metal shutters on the workshops slid up, and garage grease monkeys began to hammer and drill. The first customers pulled up and got out of their cars, shouting and cursing. A welder poured bright-yellow sparks into the air; boys who looked too young to be at work wheeled tires almost bigger than themselves and ran with tools to mechanics lying supine under jacked-up trucks. Rawlins felt that he walked through a heightened reality, one in which color had been mysteriously enhanced and sound magnified. It was partly because he hadn't slept, but also because the events of the last three days had thrown his whole being off kilter. He should have stumbled down the road instead of walking, because that was what he felt like: a man staggering, a man whose body refused to obey the directions coming from his brain. But the opposite was also true. Hadn't his body told him to rescue Esta, sent him scurrying to the rabbi? And when the words that he spoke to Phillips came out of his mouth, his body had resisted: his tongue curled, his throat swallowed the sounds, he had heard himself talking in slow motion. The voice wasn't his. But it was!

Weiss labored up the stairs to his apartment, breathing heavily and stopping once on a landing to suck in air and explain to Rawlins, "My heart doesn't work so good." He opened the door into a small room.

In one corner was a sink and next to it four burners. The blinds were drawn on the windows, and the room was in semidarkness. A smell of boiled vegetables, which reminded Rawlins of his old school dining room, permeated the atmosphere. A birdcage was set on a stand behind one of the kitchen chairs; its two small, brightly colored inhabitants rested silently on their narrow perch.

"Take a seat." Weiss nudged a stool toward the small kitchen table. He lifted the blinds and pushed windows open. Light spread through the room, like ripples off a green pond.

"In Vienna I lived like a proper person. But here . . ." He gestured hopelessly, spreading his arms.

Rawlins sat and watched Weiss as he diced a tomato, cucumber, and green pepper, then mixed the vegetables together in a bowl. He doused the concoction in oil, vinegar, salt, and pepper, spread half onto a plate for Rawlins, and kept the half in the bowl for himself.

If Rawlins was going to say something, now was the time to begin. He had an opening. What was he waiting for? He glanced around the room. An uninspired watercolor of marigolds in a vase hung on one wall, but there were no photographs. Off the main room there was an alcove, which must have served as Weiss's bedroom, but Rawlins could not see into it.

"This is where I need your help." Weiss fumbled through a pack of envelopes slid in next to his radio. Rawlins noticed the names of the places on the dial; London was one of them.

"I'm writing to the high commissioner. There's all kinds of refugees get blocked at the port, at Haifa. Nobody knows who's on the boats. They send them off to strange places. Someone told me Africa. Maybe you know more about this than I do."

"It's possible."

"I've written a letter asking to know about the names. I've got family over there, in Europe: my wife, my daughter. Who knows, maybe they got out on one of these boats."

Rawlins took the letter in his hands. The handwriting was firm and clear, but words were misspelled and the syntax was confused. Esta's name and that of her mother were written in bold capital letters. He could have said then: "I know where your daughter is," but something—he decided it was something in Weiss's attitude—held him back. Was it that Weiss didn't seem to care enough? He wasn't crying; he didn't have his head buried in his hands. Ten minutes earlier, he had made a crass joke.

"How long ago did you leave your family?"

"Eight years. First I went to a cousin in America. Two years of the Depression, then I came here."

The birds fluttered briefly in their cage, letting forth a quick flurry of melodic notes.

"How was I to know that there was no money here either? For a while I worked on a kibbutz near Petah Tiqwa. But it wasn't for me. Don't get me wrong, I'm not afraid of hard work. But I couldn't stand communal living. No privacy."

Weiss's eyes searched around his apartment, as if to confirm that now he had what he wanted, but the dead look that he maintained indicated to Rawlins that the confirmation he sought continued to elude him.

"I did all I could," Weiss continued. "I took whatever work was available, but I barely made enough to feed myself, let alone a family."

"What did you do in Vienna?"

Rawlins felt himself falling into his familiar interrogatory mode, as if Esta's father were one of his Egyptian informers.

"What did I do? I bought and sold. Scrap metal mainly. I was a wheeler-dealer. Does that make you an evil person?"

"It's possible I could find something out for you."

Weiss looked at him suspiciously. Rawlins realized that his appearance suggested he could hardly help himself.

"Let me take the letter."

"What could *you* find out?"

"If your wife and daughter have passed through Haifa. I know some people up there."

Weiss snatched the letter back. "Write down the names; that's all you need, the names."

"I'll make inquiries. I'll come back tomorrow."

He wanted to leave now. To be out in the street before he had to say, "It's me who is your daughter's jailer, not the Nazis, not the port authorities in Haifa." He rose from the stool and began to walk toward the door.

"Wait a minute. You haven't even told me your name."

Rawlins stuttered a moment.

"I'm Phillips. I'm Harry Phillips."

19

Rawlins spent the rest of the day searching the cheap hotels around Hayarkon Street for another accommodation. He settled finally for a room in a stark concrete building with yellowing walls; judging from the presence of British-uniformed soldiers, frequent door slamming, and an overcrowded lobby, it was probably a bordello. He didn't care anymore about remaining anonymous. He might as well be where he belonged, among the whores and pimps and their clients: all those who bought and sold flesh.

He wondered if Harriet had gone back to Cairo and spread the rumor of his brutality. Perhaps she would be afraid to implicate herself. But what did it really matter? Everyone already thought so badly of him, how could his reputation deteriorate? What if she was still in Tel Aviv? He hoped he wouldn't run into her, latched onto the arm of some stupid officer who would feel obliged to fight him.

Rawlins stood in the bathroom at the end of his second-floor corridor and ran one hand over the stubble on his face. He looked quizzically into the small cracked mirror. He had to think rationally now, to work out a plan. He had framed lie upon lie, and now he had compounded everything by raising false hopes for Esta's father.

He spent the night tossing half asleep on the room's camp bed. He could hear the sea churning and, over it, a sporadic accompaniment of slaps, laughter, bangs on the walls and ceiling, and, at one point, a harsh scream that brought him out of sleep to the window, where, peering through a thumb-wide hole in the mosquito netting, he saw a woman on the ground, whether Arab or Jew he couldn't tell; blood ran from a gash in her arm. A few yards on, the man who had slashed her turned a corner and walked indifferently away.

The morning restored him, almost against his will. He washed, shaved and stepped out into the sunlight on the street like a vacationer setting off for a day at the beach. Two women stood arguing on the hotel steps; one pointed to the washing line outside her room. Rawlins guessed she was accusing the other of stealing her clothes. The sky was bright blue, and the buildings on the street, all stucco and plaster, in an odd symmetry, half built or dilapidated, had taken on a fresh, appealing quality, as if the foam pounding on the shore had stretched its creamy fingers and washed them clean.

Rawlins knew that he should go straight to find Weiss, but he didn't. Instead he headed toward the old port of Jaffa. The previous night he had seen its minarets and domed roofs silhouetted in the distance where the bay curved west, and now a distractive inquisitiveness drew him along the sand dunes. He wanted to disburden himself, to lose his way again in the alleyways and markets of an Arab town, as if by repeating, or imitating, the movements of the last few weeks he might recover his equilibrium.

But the streets of Jaffa hung in a slow torpor: there was none of the bustle and commotion that characterized his journeys through Cairo. Such enterprise as was visible did not seem to go much further than a man slumped on the ground next to a donkey cart piled high with watermelons. Perhaps Rawlins had arrived too early.

He climbed some winding stone steps behind a mosque and emerged onto a whitewashed flat roof overlooking the bay. A battle cruiser was in dock, its thick-barreled guns pointed toward the shore; not far away, longshoremen drove back and forth unloading crates from a merchant ship.

What if the Nazis should come, as Weiss's friend had proposed? He realized that he had almost forgotten about the war. That struggle had been utterly subsumed in his own. He had stopped thinking about Hitler, Rommel, advancing armies, friends who were at the front, family at home surviving the blitz. Even his own fate as a soldier, posted to a city that could be occupied, failed to engage him. There was only the terrible fact of his betrayal of Esta, the impossibility of putting things right, and the inevitability of making things worse when, as now, he tried to make them better.

He walked to the edge of the roof. Beneath him, the town had begun to wake up. In courtyards open to the sky, women washed clothes and sat peeling vegetables. Immediately below, in a narrow lane, a rug merchant unrolled on the street a vermilion square decorated with dark arabesques. Rawlins could throw himself down, disappear into the dark vault that would open for him as he descended.

Someone was yelling his name from the street below.

"Rawlins! It is Rawlins, isn't it?"

He looked down. At first he failed to recognize the speaker, but then the face came back to him. It was a chap called Livock, who had been with him on the boat over from England.

"What on earth are you doing up there? Come on down and have a drink."

Rawlins descended the stairway. He thought that he would dash off and lose himself in the surrounding alleyways, but there was no escape. Livock was waiting for him at the bottom.

Together they entered a narrow bar tucked in between the rug dealer's and a spice merchant's. Livock ordered a bottle of arak. The proprietor, a tall, powerful man with a round, sleepy, boyish face, came over with the drink and two glasses. Livock quarter-filled Rawlins's tumbler and his own. Rawlins downed the drink without waiting for Livock to add water.

"My, my. You are enjoying your leave, aren't you?"

Rawlins took the bottle and refilled his glass.

"Who are you with?" Livock asked.

"I'm still in Cairo. GHQ. I can't give you the details, I'm afraid."

"Oh-oh. Secrets; that's very nice. Not much chance of getting your boots blown off. Wish I had your luck."

"Where are you?"

"Sherwood Ranger. Bow-and-arrow stuff, but for big boys. Tanks."

Rawlins remembered how drawn he had been to Livock on the boat. Livock was "a hearty," but Rawlins hadn't minded that. He had struck him as a good man, not bright but a genuine chap: "brave in the body," was that the phrase? On the journey, they had teamed up, talked about everything: family, childhood, girls, university—Livock had played rugger at Cambridge. But now Rawlins looked at him as if he were from another planet, and perhaps he was: the planet England.

In the dark-brown light of the bar, a place that might have exploded at the walls if more than ten people had entered, Livock tried to take up the conversation where he and Rawlins had left off all those months ago. But Rawlins didn't participate; he could only listen. While Livock talked, Rawlins drank: the liquor in the arak bottle diminished until there were only finger-thick dregs left in the bottom.

Livock had been in battle. He began with stories of daring and bravado, but his narrative soon took a darker turn: he described to Rawlins how he had watched wild dogs exhume a face from a body dumped in a shallow desert grave, then recounted how he had stood and watched helplessly as his best friend burned to death in a tank.

As he continued to describe horror upon horror, Rawlins realized that Livock had remained curiously untouched by his experiences; he was still the lighthearted, good-spirited fellow he had been when they played chess on the liner.

While Livock had been in the desert, Rawlins had been in that room, with Esta. He had smelled, not rotting limbs, but the heavy scent between her thighs, the piss bucket, some heady aroma from the flowers he had yelled at her about, the forest of her hair when he buried his face in it, a smell of apples on her breath, her sweat, his come. And because he had been in that room, he was not the young Englishman who had set out for Africa anymore. How to understand it? Perhaps he never had been who he thought he was. He was waiting, on all those long, quiet afternoons in school and at university, for his other self to emerge: the self that would rip and tear at a woman's body, that would lie and betray. It was hidden, like a dormant virus in his body, waiting for a shift in his metabolism to release it.

When the bottle was finished, Rawlins rose sluggishly and swayed loosely on the balls of his feet.

"Are you all right, old chap?"

"Got to go. Someone I have to see."

"Back in Tel Aviv? I'll walk along with you."

He was going to refuse, but before he could speak, Livock shoved a supportive arm under Rawlins's folding body and dragged him out into the air.

"A little bit of sea air's what you need."

Livock walked Rawlins along, taking the full weight of his body as it draped across him. The dunes loomed up before Rawlins like vast yellow mountains, and twice he slumped into the sand, swallowing mouthfuls and spitting gravelly saliva from his mouth. Livock dragged him down to the edge of the sea; surf ran over their boots, and a high salt spray blew in their faces. Livock forced Rawlins around so that the wind was at his back, and Rawlins knelt to vomit. After he was done, Livock fed him water from his canteen.

"I suppose you want me to thank you."

Livock stiffened but said, "No need for that, old chap."

Rawlins wiped at his mouth with the sleeve of his shirt. "I'm sorry. I shouldn't have said that."

Livock looked down the beach and muttered, "Strong stuff, that arak."

The wind whipped up, and a larger than usual wave, having gathered strength from way back, crashed down on the shore, soaking them both up to the waist.

There was no point in their trying to dry themselves off. They simply walked on. The sun was high and hot. Rawlins's trousers felt clammy against his legs, and his mouth was parched, but he didn't want to ask Livock for more water. After all, this was only a walk along the beachfront, not a fortnight in the western desert. He should be able to stand it.

"Quick march, old boy, left right—have you forgotten everything?"

Livock tried for a while to keep up a cheerful banter, but eventually Rawlins's silence wore him down. At the outskirts of Tel Aviv the two men parted. Livock gave Rawlins's hand a firm shake.

"You all right, old boy?"

"Yes, I'm fine now. Thank you."

"Sure nothing's the matter? Anything I can do, you know, for an old shipmate."

Rawlins shook his head. He had the impulse to ask Livock one of the banal questions that were disallowed in the army's officer corps, and he suddenly turned on him.

"Why are we stuck here?"

The sun beat down. Rawlins felt himself on the edge of fainting, but he couldn't, not in front of Livock, not after what had already happened. His mind was spinning. He continued to mumble at Livock, but he wasn't even sure what he was saying.

"I'm sorry, I don't follow your drift, don't quite get the question."

Rawlins leaned near and spoke in a hoarse whisper. He remembered now what he had been trying to say.

"I said, 'Is it because of the Jews?' "

"Oh, I don't think you can blame them." Livock, taken aback, seemed shocked. He withdrew a few steps, an expression of repugnance on his face.

"Look: I don't know what's been happening to you back in Cairo or anywhere else. But you'd better get ahold of yourself. See a doctor. Maybe you caught a dose. But for heaven's sake do something."

He turned smartly on his heels and walked away.

Rawlins remained still for a moment, then backed up into the shade. He stood leaning against a nearby wall, which was covered by posters advertising various musical and theatrical events. His head throbbed, his face burned, and his heart beat against his rib cage. He noticed two streetwalkers about to approach him, and heard the click-clack of their high heels on the pavement. With a great effort, he pushed himself away from the wall and continued on his way.

By the time Rawlins got to Ezekiel Street, the sun had just passed its zenith. The garages were closing and their workers heading home for lunch and a siesta. The rusty metal shutters on the workshops looked hot to the touch. Rainbow pools of oil dotted the dusty road. The ground seemed to steam, as if a swamp were seething beneath it.

Rawlins went first to Weiss's apartment, but when he knocked on the door the only result was a yell from Weiss's neighbor, who was probably trying to sleep.

He found Weiss sitting in the same spot at the corner café. His straw hat was placed on the table before him, and as Rawlins approached, Weiss picked it up and began to fan himself with it.

"Ah," he said when he saw Rawlins. "Captain Phillips. I've been expecting you. Come, come and sit down."

The correct choice of rank—correct for Phillips, that is—unnerved Rawlins. He had forgotten that he had used a false name.

"So? Do you have news for me? What have you discovered?"

Rawlins sat down and waited until the waitress had brought his coffee. He stirred in a spoonful of sugar and concentrated on the tiny whirlpool in the cup.

"I have news about your daughter."

"What is it?"

He could tell him now. Why not? The man was suffering. He didn't know if Esta was dead or alive. But as in Weiss's apartment, Rawlins held back. He wanted to punish Weiss; he didn't know if it was because of his own betrayal or Weiss's. He remembered the look on Esta's face when she had described her father's failure to send for her and her mother. But what gave him the right to play the avenging angel? Perhaps he wanted to hurt Weiss, in the same way that he had wanted to hurt Harriet: because prolonging Weiss's pain prolonged his own. And if he did tell the truth, what could he say? "Your daughter is a murder suspect, and although I believe her to be innocent, I turned her in"? There was no next step from that.

"Well, come on—what's holding your tongue?"

"Your daughter came into Haifa but was sent away again. I'm afraid I don't know the destination. As you know, the boats go to a variety of places. But she is alive, and if she's in British care, I imagine she's well."

Rawlins, still unable to look Weiss in the face, heard himself speak and recoiled from his absurd embellishment of his lies.

"And my wife?"

"I'm sorry. I couldn't locate her whereabouts through my

friend. It was only luck that we happened upon your daughter's name."

Weiss buried his face in his hands. He remained in the same position for several minutes. The hot black coffee burned Rawlins's tongue. He asked the waitress for a glass of water, gulped it down, and requested a refill. Finally, Weiss spoke, but when he did so it seemed more to himself than to Rawlins.

"Well, if Esta is safe, then probably they wouldn't be separated. There's a reason to hope." He looked up at Rawlins. "So where have they gone?"

"I told you, I don't know. Boats evading the blockade have been redirected to Mauritius. Some return to Cyprus. No doubt you will hear soon."

Weiss reached out and grabbed Rawlins's arm.

"Are you telling me the truth?"

Rawlins flinched. Weiss's body was fleshy, but his grip was hard and bony, like hers. Rawlins pulled his arm back.

"I've done the best I can. I'm not a captain, I'm a lieutenant. I'm not involved with Jewish refugees. I happened to have a friend, that was all."

Rawlins knew now what he was going to do. He had to return to Cairo and somehow secure her release. He would testify on her behalf, go to the highest authorities, back to Dryborough if he had to. Dryborough wasn't a fool. He would know that whatever charges they brought against her were trumped up. Esta hadn't shot any British official. All she wanted to do was come here, to this mosquito-infested cauldron.

He looked at Weiss without pity. It wasn't for him that Rawlins wanted to rescue Esta. It was in order to walk straight again and look people like Livock in the eye.

"You'll hear from your daughter, you can count on that."

"How can you be so sure?"

"She's being held for her own good."

Weiss spat. "Her own good is to be here, with me and with her mother."

Rawlins found himself on the edge of replying, "Perhaps you should have thought of that before," but he held back.

"Trust me. You'll hear."

20

As soon as he was dropped off, Rawlins went straight to Mendoza's room. The door was open, but someone else was behind the desk.

"Where's Captain Mendoza?"

The young man looked up. Rawlins noticed that the desk had been tidied and the newspapers beside it placed in neat piles on the floor.

"I don't know, sir."

"When's he expected back?"

"Don't know, sir. A lot of people have been looking for him today."

"Looking for him? Why?"

"Couldn't tell you, sir."

Rawlins was exhausted. He slumped against the wall of the office.

"Who are you?"

"I'm Adler, sir. I'm his batman."

"And you have no idea where he went?"

"He must have driven somewhere, sir. His car is not in its usual spot."

Adler sounded exasperated, as if he had been through all this before.

"How long has he been away?"

"Three days, sir. He could be at the front. He sometimes has special duties there. He may be stuck. It's happened before."

"And who are the people who've been looking for him?"

Adler stared, taking in Rawlins's red eyes and three-day stubble.

"I'm sorry, sir, I'm not at liberty—"

"Look here, Adler: I'm from GHQ Intelligence, and when I ask you something you damn well better answer it."

Rawlins heard his own voice and felt a pang of remorse; he had shouted at Esta in just this way.

"Then I'm surprised you don't know, sir. It was your people. They've been over here a couple of times."

Rawlins tried to pull his thoughts together. What was going on?

"Listen: As soon as Captain Mendoza gets back, you let me know. All right?"

"That's what I'm supposed to do anyway, sir. Call Captain Phillips."

"Well, tell Mendoza to call me first. Do you understand?"

Rawlins wrote his phone number on a piece of paper and handed it to Adler.

"Who shall I say it's from, sir?"

"Rawlins. Lieutenant Rawlins."

"That's you, sir?"

"Of course it's me."

Adler got up from his chair and moved around the desk.

"I'm sorry, sir: could I see some ID?"

"What on earth for? What do you want?"

Rawlins turned and looked toward the door. What was going on here? He pulled his dog tag from around his neck and showed it to Adler.

"I have something for you, sir."

Adler reached inside his trousers and extricated a small buff envelope from the band of his underpants. He handed it to Rawlins.

Rawlins took the envelope and ripped it open. There was a small square piece of paper inside. Rawlins read it.

"Let me use this phone."

After he had dialed, Rawlins crunched the paper into a ball.

"This is Rawlins."

He listened intently, then said, "Yes, I'll come right away."

He left the room and hurried down the street outside the barracks. The Egyptian sun was a red fireball; it seemed closer to earth than it had in Palestine. A dust-filled desert wind blew up and temporarily deadened the sounds of traffic that surrounded him. He walked as fast as he could without attracting undue attention. Heat hung in the air like fog. Near the International Hotel he found an empty gharry. He got in and whispered an address to the driver, but the vehicle moved so slowly through the dense traffic that he quickly got out and began to walk again. He paused to catch his breath under a palm tree rooted in a bed of white sand. Opposite him, a taxi pulled up near a crowded tramcar stop. Rawlins moved toward it but stopped in panic when he saw Phillips and two other officers emerge from the back seat. Had they seen him?

Rawlins began to run, dashing in and out of traffic. He thought he heard a voice yelling after him, but he didn't turn. Soon he was lost in the cacophonous blare of the Cairo street.

PART
TWO

PART
TWO

JERUSALEM

1 9 9 1

Three weeks: I have spent almost all my time acquainting myself with the city. I walk the rabbits' warren of narrow streets and alleyways that surround my apartment. Heaps of rank-smelling vegetable garbage from the nearby market surround intricate wrought-iron gateways, and thick-scented roses clamber over blue doors stamped with the deeper blue hand that wards off the evil eye.

I have scouted the semirural landscape in the vicinity of my mother's grave. For a week, I made a daily pilgrimage there, partly because I had nothing else to do and partly because I hoped that in the peaceful setting of the cemetery the secrets of the past would unfold and reveal to me a picture of my father. I stood over the marked patch of earth that holds my mother's decomposing body and tried to remember a chance remark, a face in a hidden photograph, an overheard telephone conversation, or perhaps even a meeting from childhood. But nothing stirred in my memory, and I abandoned these morbid journeys.

In a secondhand-book shop on King George Street (I remember the English names more easily), I found a prewar *Walker's
Guide to Jerusalem*, and ignoring, as far as possible, the sites and
places of interest constructed since the establishment of the state,
I attempt to follow some of the routes around town that I imagine my mother and her lover might have taken more than fifty
years ago.

In augmenting intervals, as I take the walks, the city begins to
work its numinous magic on me. I am over my jet lag, but I still
feel heady, almost dizzy, as if the whirling contours of olive terraces near my mother's grave are spinning in the crucible of
my head.

When I go out, even in the heat of the day, I rarely take the
bus, preferring to walk whenever I can. There are flowers everywhere, almost too many; the municipality has gone overboard in
laying out its plots and gardens. At every corner, small groups of
Palestinian workers are bent over the soil, ankle deep in marigolds, pansies, or snapdragons; they adjust sprinklers and re-
arrange lengths of hosepipe. I notice that the walkers in the city
give them a wide berth. There has been a spate of recent knife at-
tacks on civilians by members of Hamas, and the inhabitants of
the city are skittish and nervous.

Beneath the walls of the Old City, a few fat-tailed sheep still
meander, but a broad road, half under construction, has cut a
swath in the path of their grazing. The traffic is heavy, as drivers
head out toward the new shopping mall or the clean suburbs that
ring the throat of the city like a heavy limestone necklace.

By day, it is hard for me to conjure the places that the lovers
walked. The old guidebook shows a barren, pockmarked city of
blistering unshaded pathways, a dirty brownstone police station,
"Taggard Fortresses": the architectural litter of the British man-
date. But at night, when the air is charged with honeysuckle and
jasmine, and I wander, as I have taken to doing, through the religious quarter of Mea She'arim, I feel their presence. Here noth-

ing has changed. The Hasidim amble to prayer, kerchiefed women pull in their washing, the proprietor of a hatshop hurriedly closes his shutters. I peer through a window and see the remains of a meal on a kitchen table: chicken bones, chipped plates, and cheap cutlery; there are wine stains on the white cloth, illuminated by candles half burned down.

I imagine my parents arm in arm, walking these same cramped streets and broad courtyards, turning their faces toward each other with the air of detached amusement appropriate to a couple of young sophisticates: they have seen it all in the first years of the war, and the ultra-Orthodox Judaism of their ancestral contemporaries is entertainingly alien.

But the fantasy always crashes around *him*. The Jew, Christian, or, for all I know, Muslim, the multiaccented figure, spinner of worlds and small boys. I return to my room and try to read, or I lie in bed and think of reacquainting myself with the Russian prostitute.

My mother's possessions are on a table next to my bed, set out like the lettered exhibits in a courtroom: a bundle of correspondence tied with brown string; a box of buttons, a folded plastic hat that she carried in her handbag in case it rained on her way back from the hairdresser's, a brooch in the shape of a fan held by a Spanish dancer, a small khaki hardcover book that I took to be a diary and, of course, turned to first, only to discover that it was a prayer book for Jewish servicemen; hairpins, a darning needle, a gold-leaf-framed photograph of myself aged twelve.

Before sleep, I turn these objects in my hands like rosaries or worry beads. The moon crowds my bedroom window and fixes a brilliant silver light on the objects.

There are more than a hundred letters, and most of them appear to be from me. I read through five or six and was embarrassed by my false, jolly, upbeat tone. Everything was fine at university, wonderful in my first job with an advertising agency, ecstatic in the first year of my marriage. Could that have been so?

In 1971, Anna and I were living in a semidetached in Ealing, a half hour's commute from work. My wife, God bless her, was already conducting her first affair, with the hippie jeweler who sold us our dope. Perhaps we needed to cement our relationship with children; it never happened. I realized that my letters to my mother, written in a large, childish, forward-leaning scrawl, were all fiction, directed at her loneliness and contrived out of guilt.

On two or three envelopes I failed to recognize the handwriting and removed their contents with great excitement: here, surely, would be the dramatic answers to my search, the revelatory paragraph in a letter from a long-lost friend that would, with Dickensian appropriateness, reveal the name of my father and perhaps one or two useful starter facts about his background. But nothing of the kind appeared; instead I read unhappy accounts of evolving poor health and other family tribulations, as reported by my mother's few friends writing from their homes, or the homes their children had placed them in, in South Africa and Canada; one had remained in Vienna.

When I was very young, my mother, like most parents, would read to me or tell me stories. Her English was perfect, although her accent was strong. She was always proud of her proficiency in her second language and claimed that despite the drawback of coming from a distinctly unacademic family, she had always been at the top of her class, both in school and at university.

There was a story game that she used to play with me, and I had forgotten it until I came to Jerusalem. Esta would ask me to name three objects, and I would select, let's say, a comb, a ring, and a toy soldier. She would begin to tell a story, gradually relating the fates of the three objects until the liquid shifts of her narrative miraculously solidified.

Is there a way for me to connect the articles on the bedside table: to link the rain hat to the buttons, the prayer book to the brooch?

This morning, possessed by the strange mixture of boredom and excitement that her death has engendered in me, I searched, once again, through the letters. Among the more recent missives of sympathetic loneliness from friends, I found one that I had previously overlooked: it had been posted in England, but the address at the top of the letter named a street in Jerusalem. In a large, unruly script, the correspondent described in detail a recent operation for cataracts, which had not been altogether successful. The sentences recorded, in slow, poignant terms, withdrawal from the world of sight and receding colors: "As I write, I look up and out of the window with my left eye, and it's considerably darker and fuzzier than with the right." The letter went on: "I have just had a terrible night . . . ," and here I paused, unwilling to face yet another limning of the appalling future that is in store for us all. And indeed, someone close had suffered a heart attack, not fatal, as it turned out, but enough to put the victim on the critical list. The signature at the bottom was the indecipherable flourish of a single letter, a *C* or *G* or perhaps an *O*.

I had never heard my mother refer by name to any friends in Jerusalem, and with the sheets of paper in my hands, I broke into a cold sweat. The address was perfectly clear, and I decided to pay an immediate visit.

My taxi drove to an address in Talpiot and stopped outside an ugly stucco house, the first of its type that I had seen in Jerusalem. Its walls were discolored and the casement windows grimy and opaque—I thought, inevitably, of the cataracts.

At first I received no answer to my knocking and ringing, and I was about to leave when I heard a shuffling behind the door. It was pulled open, and I was greeted by a tall, angular figure with a shock of white hair. He leaned on a cane and peered at me through thick glasses, the left lens of which was patched with white surgical tape.

"I'm Esta Weiss's son," I said, my heart beating very fast.

He bent toward me as if it was an effort to discern the contours of my body from the wave of light that I had caused to wash into his house. And then he replied in a polite English cadence that took me by surprise:

"Perhaps you would like to come in."

JERUSALEM

1 9 4 1

1

Rawlins approached a garage at the bottom of a narrow alley behind the synagogue on Adly Pasha. As he did so, its wooden door
pushed open; a hand reached out and beckoned him through the
narrow gap.

Mendoza's car, a battered station wagon with the word CHAP-
LAIN painted in rough purple letters across the doors and hood,
was parked inside, the engine running.

"Get in, and for God's sake keep your head down."

Mendoza opened the garage doors, then climbed into the driver's seat. He drove as fast as he could through streets cluttered
with wagons, donkeys, trucks, cars, bicycles, and a host of individuals on foot. On one corner, Rawlins, peering up for a second,
saw a group of what, by the look of their dress, must have been
foreign residents. They were carrying bundles toward a line of
waiting cars. One tall, angular woman held a spaniel on a leash
with one hand and in the other clutched a velvet-covered jew-
el box.

"Where are they going?"

Mendoza freed his hand from the gearshift and forced Rawlins's head back down.

"East to Palestine, south to Luxor. We're in luck: there's a flap on. The Germans have reoccupied Cyrenaica; the whole of Egypt's in a fluster. Should make things easier. Not a lot of bodies available."

"They're looking for you."

"Do you think I don't know that?"

"Do they know what you've done?"

"I doubt it. Not yet. They're speculating. They have to be a bit careful, you know. I may be a Jew, but I'm not a nobody."

They drove for half an hour or more in silence. Whenever an army vehicle pulled up next to them, Mendoza veered away down a side street, his bald tires screeching on the dusty road. When they reached the outskirts of Cairo, Mendoza permitted Rawlins to sit up.

"Is she safe?"

"Yes."

"Is this where she's hidden?"

Rawlins looked among the ramshackle houses at the roadside, their windows shuttered against the sun. A coppery light spread over the rooftops and down onto the street.

"I want you to take me straight to her."

"You're already with her. She's here."

Mendoza gestured with his thumb toward the back of the station wagon.

Rawlins turned quickly. There was a shape, he now saw, barely distinguishable under a pile of blankets strewn with prayer books, old newspapers, two spare tires, a jerrican, a bedroll wrapped in a Tropal coat, and a baggy haversack. The shape was enclosed by a smell of camphor and gasoline. It didn't move.

"Esta." Rawlins reached back and stretched out his arm.

"Leave her!" Mendoza shoved his hand away. "If she's sleeping, let her sleep."

"But for God's sake."

"Shut up."

Mendoza pressed hard on the accelerator, and the car sped forward. Rawlins laid his head back. As they drove, Mendoza occasionally reached to his side, pulled up a bottle of brandy from between the seats, and took a swig.

"You changed your mind."

Mendoza pretended that he hadn't heard.

"Why?"

"I went to see her, that was all. I didn't have anything in mind. Although I'm not without feeling, you know, for you as well as for her."

"For me?"

Mendoza looked across at Rawlins. "Is that such a surprise to you?"

Rawlins blushed.

"I'm sure they must have told you about me. I'm not the best-kept secret in the army."

"I'm sorry."

"Sorry? Why? You're not to blame for the randomness and stupidity of my infatuations."

Mendoza took a deep draft from the brandy bottle.

"You spoke to her, then. You must have understood. She's absolutely innocent. You saw that too."

"It seems that way."

"Only 'seems'?"

Mendoza was silent.

The car approached Suez at dusk, then turned north; the water was a turquoise strip lying between darkening flats of sand. A deep-red glow surrounded the ships in dock. In the distance Rawlins saw a large warship move fitfully through the desert, smoke puffing from its funnels. It looked like a piece of scenery jerked along by an invisible stagehand.

Light ebbed on the edges of the desert. Mendoza waited until it was dark before pulling off the road. A yelping dog zigzagged in nervous haste across their path. Mendoza turned off the headlights.

"Get out." His mood seemed suddenly to change, and he spoke with a barely restrained savagery, as if he could hardly bear his own daring.

"What now?"

Mendoza reached into the back seat of the car, grabbed a uniform and threw it at Rawlins.

"Well, what are you waiting for? Come on."

"Come on, what?"

"Get it on."

In the rear of the station wagon, Esta stirred.

Rawlins began to remove his clothes. He knelt down to loosen his puttees and began to unlace his boots.

The two men stood opposite one another. The moon, hidden behind wispy clouds, cast a ghostly net over their bodies.

"You're a good man, Mendoza."

"Hurry up."

"I say you're a good man."

"Don't patronize me."

"But you are."

"Am I?"

Esta emerged from the car and took two faltering steps toward them. Rawlins rushed over and embraced her awkwardly, as if he were propping her up. He was embarrassed to feel himself almost naked, pressed up against her body.

Esta's clothes and hair reeked of gasoline: her forehead was smeared with grime. Rawlins touched his fingers to her cheeks: her skin was rough and chapped where it had rubbed against the blankets in the back of the car. She shivered in his arms, but her body was on fire.

"She's burning," he shouted to Mendoza.

Esta shivered again and took a step away from him.

"I'm fine. It's only from the blankets," she said.

But she could hardly stand. Mendoza walked quickly over and helped Rawlins lift her into the front seat of the car. He placed a hand on her forehead, then pressed his canteen into Esta's hands. She hardly had the strength to lift it to her mouth, and water dribbled down her chin and onto her neck.

Rawlins began to pull on the shirt and trousers that Mendoza had given him. He tightened the leather belt and breathed deeply. Mendoza had left the engine running, but now, still tending to Esta, he cut it. The abrupt silence took Rawlins by surprise. It was as if his own momentum had suddenly halted: the rush of movement that had taken him from Tel Aviv back to Cairo and now to here. He looked up at the dark sky: the constellations had wheeled into view, and, momentarily, Rawlins was back in England and ten years old, sitting on the back porch outside his parents' house in Sherbrooke, picking out the Plow and Orion's Belt. There was no war, and all his thoughts were concentrated on the smells of cooking coming from the kitchen. It was spring, the trees in the Rawlins's back garden had burst into blossom; the night air was scented, plum-laden. He hadn't betrayed anybody.

He walked back toward the car. Esta sat slumped to one side, pushing off the blanket that Mendoza was trying to pull over her. Mendoza gave up and instead reached between the seats and extricated the bottle of brandy. He unscrewed the cap and pressed it to Esta's lips. She swigged, choked, and spat.

"Try to swallow some down," Mendoza said. "It will do you good."

"I don't need it. I'm all right."

Mendoza hesitated a moment. The bottle was in his hands. He was about to slide it into a pocket of his tunic, but with a quick movement that seemed both to incorporate and to disguise an effort of will, he rammed the flask back under the driver's seat. Esta glanced at him, and their eyes met.

Rawlins noted the exchange and, although instantly ashamed of himself, felt a moment of exclusion. It was horrible, the bubbles of evil that surfaced unbidden in his brain: Jews, clubby, look after their own, not our types, stick together, no loyalty, wouldn't trust a single one of them. Who was speaking? He turned to Mendoza.

"But what about you?"

"I'll get back tonight."

"What are you going to tell them? I mean, the station wagon, everything?"

"Well, I'm not going to tell them the truth; you don't have to worry about that."

"I wouldn't want . . . I mean, you didn't have to . . ."

"Listen, you asked me to do this, but neither you and your pretty face, nor her, are the only reasons I got involved. For all I know, she may have shot Waterlow. I doubt it, but I've been wrong before. I've been compromising too long. My whole damn career. I'll take the risk. If they want a Jew to play with, let them take me. Whatever she's done, this woman's suffered enough. And as for Waterlow, I wish I could say I was sorry. Do you have any idea how many people died when that ship he sent back went down? Hundreds of Jews."

Rawlins was shocked to hear him speak like this. Mendoza was drunk, that was the only explanation. He had to believe her innocent, otherwise this whole escape was a sham. On the other hand, in the depths of his heart, Rawlins himself remained uncertain.

Mendoza gripped Rawlins's arm and walked with him around to the back of the car. In a sharp slant of moonlight, Rawlins took in the stubble on Mendoza's face, his bloodshot eyes.

"She has people in Palestine. She knows where she's going, even if you don't."

"Will she be all right?"

"How the hell should I know? For God's sake get going, and when you do, get a move on."

Rawlins got in and started the car. For a moment, the wheels spun, threatening to sink into the sand, but then they achieved a purchase and Rawlins pulled the car back up onto the tarmac. Mendoza's figure quickly receded, became a thin sapling, a stick, a shaft of light.

2

Mendoza stood alone and stared as the taillights of the station wagon dwindled to white dots and merged with the stars on the edge of the horizon. He would wait to flag down a truck or a jeep to take him back to Cairo. It wasn't all that unusual for him to leave headquarters for days at a time. Jewish servicemen were spread all over the place, and he knew as well as they did how chaotic things were out in the desert. Still, they were looking for him now, and well aware of his connection to Rawlins.

Mendoza dumped Rawlins's uniform under a bush, then sat down against the back of a palm tree and stretched out his long legs. He felt in his pocket for the flask of brandy, as if somehow a miracle might have occurred and he hadn't after all left it in the station wagon. He was forced to drink instead from his water canteen. He put it to his dry lips, swallowed, then laughed to himself. Perhaps, if he prayed, God would change the water into brandy. He began out loud: "O God, and God of my fathers, thou art one, and thy name is one, and thou art from everlasting to everlasting . . ." His voice trailed off, but then he began again, imitating the radio announcers from the forces network: "And now, selections from *Prayers for Trench and Base*, with Rabbi Gerald Mendoza." Mendoza intoned in a portentous monotone: "Thou hast called me as a child of Israel, and I humbly beseech thee to help me fulfill my holy mission." He laughed to himself, then continued in a somber voice: "When heavy burdens oppress me, or when I am disheartened in my tasks and the gloom of failure settles upon me . . ." That was it, he thought, "the gloom of failure." He had started out in search of piety, but his character had let him down. He couldn't think of a single person who had been really helped or transformed by his rabbinical attention. Lots of empty thank-yous, and the terrible times when he had let his appetites get the better of him, for drink, for other men. Years ago, the head of Jews' College had advised him not to take on a community; he wasn't "cut out" for dealing with families. He had disappeared into the army, a job no one wanted. His colleagues had a right to scorn him. And yet he continued to feel that the battles of the spirit were worth fighting, even if he had lost every one. But not this time. He would face them down. Let them bring him in, let them come with their clever, polite interrogation, their sharp, nimble minds. He would tell them about every joke or slight, every offhand remark or ugly gesture, every "jewed me out of this" or wringing of the hands.

Out in the far distance, two pale circles of yellow light appeared and began to enlarge, like some dark creature of the desert opening its eyes. Mendoza remained stretched out. That wasn't right, he thought, not the petty stuff. It was Europe that he had to talk about. They knew, oh, they knew and knew. He had sat around once with a group of senior officers listening to Radio Roma: "The Axis isn't making war on the Egyptian people. It means merely to liberate Egypt from the domination of the British. Don't worry! No harm will come to you. But see that the Jews don't get away." Laughter and bravura responses had stopped at the mention of Jews, to be replaced by an awkward silence, until someone said, "Well, I suppose we're going to have to lock you up in a cupboard, Rabbi," and everybody, including him, had laughed again.

But it wasn't a joke. If the Nazis came, they'd all be done for, all the Jews. The British would open the damn cupboard, hand him right over. Him, the Weiss woman, anyone else they could lay their hands on. No one was fighting for the Jews.

Mendoza looked up into the blazing desert night. "I will multiply thy seed as the stars of heaven." That was God's promise. But God wasn't keeping it. That's why he had to help her, save the seed. Mendoza closed his eyes.

The headlamps from the approaching truck illuminated his sleeping figure in a pool of light. He woke from dreaming with a start. The driver leaned out the window.

"What have we got 'ere, a desert napper?"

"I need a lift."

"What are you?"

"Chaplaincy."

"You're joking. How'd you get out 'ere?"

Mendoza got up slowly and began to walk around to the back of the truck. He climbed up and squeezed himself in between two large cans of food supplies.

"Some people," the driver said, and revved the engine.

3

Rawlins gripped the wheel tight and peered through the dust-and-insect-smeared windshield.

They drove with the windows three-quarters shut. Even so, the dust of the desert swirled into the car, raising a thin, lung-stinging mist. Esta lay in her seat with her head thrown back, first tugging at, then throwing off, the blanket. Rawlins saw now that she was dressed in a nurse's uniform. Not bad for the traveling companion of a rabbi.

She began to speak, a slurred, delirious flow interrupted by raspy coughs. Rawlins inclined his head to hear her above the sound of the engine. She spoke in German and Polish, but whispered repeatedly and urgently in English, as if addressing a child, "Have to keep still. Keep still."

Occasionally, single trucks or small convoys of vehicles passed them, headed in the other direction. After a while, Esta settled into an uneasy sleep. Rawlins maneuvered the station wagon around an escarpment, took the corner too fast, and nearly went off the road. Esta was flung from one side of her seat to the other but did not wake. Rawlins stopped the car to settle himself. Though exhausted, he was oddly lightened, now that the irrevocable decision to flee had been taken. He looked across at Esta. Her face, pale as ash, emerged from the top of the blanket, and at the bottom one bare leg poked out, skinny and bruised, from its coarse cocoon. He bent toward her and kissed her forehead and eyes; he tasted the sweat on her skin and inhaled the fever-induced salt scent of her body. The kisses were the first real gestures of affection he had ever made toward her that were not a prelude to making love. Esta murmured, opened her eyes, stared wildly for a second, then twisted her head and fell back awkwardly in the seat.

The engine ticked over. He couldn't stop for long. Only a moment, that was all. Rawlins leaned forward and rested his head in his hands. Who was he now? He had known that the war would change him, but he could not have anticipated how much. In the beginning, like all raw recruits, he had contemplated his own death with the usual mix of fear and self-pity; he imagined his family's sorrow when they received the telegram, the consoling remarks of the neighbors, the note of condolence from a college tutor who barely remembered him. But these feelings and images, he knew, were circumscribed by convention. Esta had introduced a deeper terror into his life, one that he couldn't assimilate. Yet along with the terror came a heightened capacity to love.

That's what he had been trying to explain to Harriet that night in Tel Aviv. Unless he was confusing passion with guilt.

On the boat coming over from England, he had regarded the immediate future as a dark adventure. He remembered one afternoon, when the ship had docked in Freetown (it seemed like years ago, but it was only a few months). The troops had been confined to ship, and he had sat, oppressed by heat, on the crowded deck overlooking the harbor. A shoal of flying fish, accompanied by a pair of porpoises, had risen flashing from the water and brought him to the rail. There, the cold spray of the ocean pitting his face like small stones, he met a young woman on her way to take up a position as a nurse in Egypt. And what had he done as their conversation developed? He had led her back to his seat and read her Swinburne. He had kept her up all night with "Let us go hence, my songs; she will not hear" and "Pray but one prayer for me 'twixt thy closed lips." Irrelevant nonsense. Esta had torn through it all on the first morning that she had appeared in his office.

He raised himself up, grabbed the wheel, and turned the car back toward the road. When they bumped up, he glanced across at Esta. Her breathing was heavy and irregular. He took one hand off the wheel and ran it through her damp, tangled hair. Looking at her fingers, spread in a bony delta over her thighs, he remembered them white at the knuckles, her hands clutching ferociously at his body: the scratching and biting, the way she pinched the back of his neck between her thumb and forefinger when she kissed him, the roughness that she wanted from him—if she didn't feel things hard in the body, it seemed, she didn't feel them at all. But then, after a while, the urgency subsided in her, and she wanted tenderness. Once, she had made him cradle her in his arms all night, and he had rocked her like a child until a dingy white light filtered through the hole in the wall and he had risen to leave.

Close to the border with Palestine, he turned down a scabby

road, only to find a barrier in his way. A folding chair was set in front of some planks set on sawhorses. Nearby, over a cleared space between two crumbling walls, a camouflage net was stretched: strips of canvas and green rag fluttered from it. Rawlins slowed the station wagon to a halt. Dust rose against the glimmers of a flat pink daybreak.

A young sentry approached the car, bent his head down, and squinted; his face showed the usual ruddy, creased skin.

"Morning, Reverend. Come to lead us in a prayer? We could do with a couple of Our Fathers."

"No time, I'm afraid. We have to be in Jerusalem."

The sentry looked around the car. Esta opened her eyes and cast off her blanket. Rawlins remembered the prayer books scattered in the back; the sentry must have noticed the Hebrew lettering with the embossed Stars of David on the covers.

"Oh, I'm sorry, Rabbi," he was saying. "I didn't realize . . ."

"That's quite all right."

The sentry stared at Rawlins's uniform.

"Well, sir, hurry on up, then. If you could just show me . . ."

Rawlins, buying time, fumbled in the pockets of his tunic and came up with a black silk yarmulke. He held it up like a child magician whose trick, to his own astonishment, has gone well.

"Hold on a minute." A young soldier with a thin face, curly black hair, and glasses peered through the open window on Esta's side.

"Is Rabbi Mendoza in there? Can I have a word with him?"

Rawlins turned away from the sentry.

"Rabbi Mendoza is back at headquarters. I'm the assistant chaplain . . . Captain Weiss."

"Well, can I speak to you?"

"We're really in rather a hurry, and my companion here isn't feeling too well."

The Jewish soldier looked at Esta, registered her drawn face and cracked lips, then returned his gaze to Rawlins.

"Grossman, do you have important business with Rabbi Weiss?" the sentry was saying. "If not, get lost, sharpish."

"I'd like to speak to him"—he looked at Rawlins—"if that's all right with you, sir."

Rawlins pulled the car into a pool of weak shade offered by a large food-supply truck. He got out, and Grossman led him along a sandy path toward a rocky shoulder that overlooked the border encampment.

"I've got a problem."

"How can I help?"

"It's the food."

"What about it?"

"They're slipping stuff in."

Rawlins stared at him incredulously. What if Grossman began to talk to him about things he knew nothing of? What if he said something in Hebrew?

"What do you mean?"

Grossman, he was sure, was giving him strange looks.

"They're supposed to give a kosher ration. But someone's tampering with the package."

"In what way?" Rawlins was not sure that there was such a thing as a kosher ration. He had spent *some* time with Jewish servicemen in the mess, and he had never seen them eat anything different from his own food.

"They put in bacon rinds. They're very small. Almost impossible to notice."

For the first time in many weeks, Rawlins found himself trying not to laugh.

"Why would they do that?"

"They do all kinds of things to me."

"Only you?"

"I'm the only Jew in the unit who looks Jewish. You know what I mean. What they think is Jewish."

Grossman stared straight at Rawlins, as if Rawlins's own ap-

pearance, his green eyes and the fair stubble on his jaw, confirmed the hypothesis.

"What else has been done to you?"

"I already told Rabbi Mendoza. There was the thing with my
prayer book—maybe he told you?"

"No. What thing?"

"Well, first the torn pages, and then its disappearance."

Rawlins wanted to say, "Is that all?" but he bit his tongue.

"Not that I'm all that religious," Grossman continued. "But it
meant something to me. I used to read it at night. And I eat kosher, you see. I was brought up that way. I don't have to explain
to you, do I?"

"I'll see what I can do."

"You'll speak to . . ."

"To?"

"To Lieutenant Barnett."

"Yes. Barnett."

"When?"

"As soon as I can. When I return from Jerusalem."

Rawlins retraced his steps down the path. The pink line on the
horizon had already broadened into a shaft of blue sky; the mer-
ciless sun tipped its yellow fringe over a distant set of hills.

"Rabbi, wait a minute. There's something else."

Grossman pulled at Rawlins's arm and pressed his face close.

"I have a *yahrzeit* coming up for my father. Can you get me a
pass? I only need a day. There's a synagogue in Cairo. I should
go, don't you think?"

Rawlins didn't know what a *yahrzeit* was. But whatever
Grossman was asking, he was in no position to grant the request.

"I'm sorry, but I can't do that."

A look of disappointment spread across Grossman's face.
Rawlins tried to pull himself away, but Grossman held on. His
face took on an expression of contempt, and he whispered at
Rawlins:

"What are you up to?"

"Let go of me."

Rawlins tugged his arm free and began to walk smartly back toward the parked station wagon. He couldn't turn around. He knew that Grossman was watching him.

Rawlins reversed the car, than slammed his foot hard on the accelerator and shot forward. Grossman's attentions had distracted the sentry and, luckily, acted as sufficient confirmation of Rawlins's false identity. No one took notice as the car passed through the open barrier. Rawlins looked in the rearview mirror and saw Grossman running up the desert track, waving both his hands over his head. Rawlins continued to pick up speed. At the frontier itself, the Egyptian guards simply waved the chaplain's vehicle through.

4

They were waiting for Mendoza in his room. The whole place had been thoroughly turned over; the contents of his drawers and wastebasket had been emptied into a pile. A bulky young officer with a shock of blond hair sat cross-legged on the floor, unfolding balls of paper and trying to read them in the orange light cast by Mendoza's desk lamp. Mendoza guessed, from Rawlins's description of him, that the man seated behind his desk must be Arthur Graham.

"What on earth is going on here?"

"Calm down, Rabbi. Just a little search."

"How dare you! Under whose orders? What in heaven's name ... ?"

"Rawlins, Rabbi. We're looking for Lieutenant Rawlins. Ran out of GHQ in a terrible hurry. We hoped you might know where he was going. And by the way, you don't happen to have your car with you, do you? I might need a ride back after all this.

Is the girl with him? Or have you spirited her away somewhere else? Well, I'm going a little fast, aren't I. Getting ahead of the game. Why don't you sit down?"

Graham gestured toward the chair that had been occupied by Rawlins when he had come to ask for help. Now it was stacked with newspapers.

"I'm Colonel Graham, by the way."

"Perhaps, Colonel, you'd like to get out of my chair," Mendoza responded stiffly.

"Not necessary."

"I don't know what you're talking about. And if you want to know where I've been, I suggest you take a drive out to the front. I've just buried three very good men who stepped into a mine-field, and had another three, not so good, it would appear, requisition my vehicle without asking, to take some madcap trip, probably to the damn Berka; but wherever they've gone, their regimental commander's going to be none too pleased when they get back. If your fellow over here looks carefully enough through my papers, you might find the message I sent in to Adler reporting the bloody theft and telling him to find some way to get me the hell back to Cairo."

"Yes, we found that."

The lies stuck in Mendoza's throat. This wasn't what he had planned. He thought he would have more honor and dignity, but he was giving them what they wanted: lies.

"What is Rawlins to you?"

"I met him at Shepheard's. He came to talk to me. He has a Jewish girlfriend, and he wanted some advice. I don't believe that Jewish girlfriends are forbidden to the men, are they, Colonel? Or perhaps I'm mistaken, and the Nuremberg Laws have taken effect here in Cairo."

"Egyptian Jewess, is she?"

"How should I know?"

"Well, you said . . . you talked, discussed the problems."

"Yes, Egyptian, I believe. Her name's Renee; Rawlins didn't tell me the family name."

"No, of course not; he wouldn't, would he? Because actually her name is Weiss, Esta Weiss. She's not Egyptian; she's a Pole. She shot Waterlow."

Mendoza gave a short, bitter laugh.

"Oh, yes. You see, we have the man she worked with, Hafner, and he's spinning a very rich yarn. So if you've helped her get away, it really is rather serious."

Somewhere nearby, a toilet flushed, and water gurgled in the pipe that ran around Mendoza's office walls. The blond officer got to his feet and placed himself by the door, blocking it with his thick frame. Mendoza felt as if all the oxygen had been pumped out of the room; the air was stagnant and hot. For a moment, he thought he smelled oil and burning wood; something acrid, almost unbreathable, filled the atmosphere. Then he recognized that he was smelling his own fear.

"Such a fine record, Rabbi. How many years is it now? Almost thirty? And—what shall we say?—only one or two little incidents to be ashamed of. And they're long gone now, aren't they, Rabbi? Those young men. Perhaps Rawlins, in some way—he is, after all, a good-looking fellow—reminded you . . ."

Mendoza bit hard into his tongue. Graham was certainly good at his job, cleverer than Mendoza had imagined, dirtier. But he should have expected no less.

"I can't help you, Colonel Graham, but perhaps you can help me. Find my car. It's quite conspicuous; it has 'Chaplain' painted all over it."

"The Jews *are* having a terribly rough time. Perfectly understandable, in a way, that you should want to help. It must be . . . well, I read the dispatches myself. Hard to believe, aren't they? Hard to read."

"Have you finished here?"

"Do you remember those cartoons from the last war—I was

there too, you know. Little bodies, children, wriggling on the bayonets of the marching German armies. And then it turned out that the German soldier—they called him 'Michael' at home—well, 'Michael' was the soul of kindness, shared his rations with the waifs behind the Belgian lines and so on, and reasonable people on the Allies' side of the fight ultimately admitted that the baby-killing charges were false. Well, I want you to know I'm not one of those who say the same thing about the new claims. I think there's suffering. I think it's massive. I think it's murder. And the PM cares about the Jews. I think you know that. And it's not easy for him. Lot of opposition, not just from those fellows in the Foreign Office—we all know about that, don't we—but from your ordinary man in the street too. I was reading one of your Jewish newspapers before you came back from seeing Rawlins off. Fascinating: anti-Semitism on the *increase* in Britain. Hard to believe that too, isn't it? All kinds of nonsensical accusations: Jews crowding the stations during air raids, malpractice by Jewish traders, going round farms to buy up chicken and eggs to sell in London—it's laughable, isn't it? Jews evading military service—more rubbish; if true, why would we need you here, Rabbi? The point is, you see, I understand why you'd have all the reason in the world to think, well, why not help this Miss Weiss? She has a story of unmatchable suffering; young Rawlins is vouching for her. . . . Am I right, Rabbi?"

Mendoza was silent. He felt a yearning to speak, as if the truth were pulling like a dog on a leash and he didn't have the strength to hold it back.

"Shall we go?" Graham asked.

Phillips stood to one side and pushed open the door. Graham switched off the desk lamp. A blue light burned in the corridor. It would have been easy, Mendoza thought, to grab Phillips's revolver from its holster, aim it at himself, and squeeze the trigger. But in the middle of this ignominious departure—for Mendoza had no doubt that he was being arrested—a picture, a phrase, leaped into his mind and kept him still.

There, in his mind's eye, was the face of a rabbinical student who had sat next to him in classes twenty years ago: a boy called Rabinowitz, whom Mendoza had liked very much. They had studied together in a small, dimly lit room off the Mile End Road. The harsh, discordant cries of barrow boys hawking their wares came through the open window, along with the smell of rotting vegetables and a cidery odor of spoiled apples. Rabinowitz wasn't cut out for the rabbinate; he was too radical and impassioned, tortured by the presence of injustice in the world. Rabinowitz wanted to understand God's part in it all, to challenge him, and smoldering with the resentment of a peasant, he drove the rabbis wild.

One week, after a discussion of infanticide, Rabinowitz failed to appear in classes, and by Friday the rumor spread that he had hanged himself. The rabbi teaching the Talmud class addressed the students: "A man who takes his own life denies the Godliness inherent in his own person, just as the man who kills another denies the Godliness in his fellowman. God has given us his divine attributes, mercy and compassion. The suicide casts aside these gifts." Mendoza had thought: I will never believe in God so much as to kill myself over his failures.

All this in the half second before Phillips turned through the door. But what about his own failures: the humiliation and shame that were about to come pouring down? Wasn't it better to avoid them?

Mendoza turned to Graham.

"You won't find them," he said. "I put them on a fishing boat hours ago."

"Oh," Graham replied, "and this is your little diversion. I think you'll have to do better than that, Rabbi. Shall we move along?"

5

If anything, there were more British soldiers on the Palestine side of the border, more that were visible anyhow. Troop transports seemed to be everywhere on the road, and eventually Rawlins got stuck behind three two-tons that crawled like snails along the tarmac, leaving a trail of oil behind them. HQ of the Tenth Armored Division, to which Rawlins had once been briefly attached, was here in Palestine. There would be chaps around who knew him. He couldn't drive much further in Mendoza's car before someone stopped them and recognized him.

After about an hour, the cloudless desert sky admitted a few gray blotches, and the wind picked up a smell that Rawlins had almost forgotten: rain. The shift in the air seemed to revive Esta. She threw off the blanket in which she had sweated through the night and looked eagerly out the window.

"We're here," he said, as if they had arrived on holiday after a long drive, and immediately he felt foolish.

"Yes," she replied. "My rabbi has brought me to Palestine."

She laughed in a cracked voice that turned into a coughing bout. But her fever had broken, and her face was cool when she leaned over and kissed his cheek.

They began a steep climb behind the trucks, and soon the Mediterranean appeared beneath them, green and choppy, its whitecaps racing forward in the light wind. When they descended, Esta asked Rawlins to stop the car. She got out and walked unsteadily, her thin frame buffeted by the sea breeze, across the beach toward the water. Rawlins followed, stepping beside her footprints in the brown sand.

She had taken off her shoes, and now she waded out a little way. Rawlins sat down on the sand, removed his boots and socks, and rolled up his trousers. When he went to stand beside her, he found the water surprisingly warm. The tide was coming in, and the white line of breakers crashed swiftly around them before running up the sand.

Back on the beach, she started to shiver violently. Rawlins put his arms around her.

"I can't believe it. I can't believe I'm here, Archie. Thank you. I knew if there was trouble you would help me. Only you."

Her teeth chattered and her lips were turning blue, but she leaned in on him, pressing her face to his, sucking and biting at his lower lip, trying to wind her tongue into his mouth.

"I love you, Archie."

Her body trembled. Rawlins half dragged and half lifted her back to the car.

He wrapped the blanket around her again and proffered Mendoza's brandy bottle. Esta swallowed a gulp, and this time it stayed down.

"Mendoza said you knew where you were going."

"It's a kibbutz, Archie. It shouldn't be too far. I have a contact. Once you get me there you can turn back."

"Turn back?" He looked at her incredulously. "I can't turn back."

"But why not? You must. You have to go back to Cairo. This Waterlow murder doesn't have anything to do with you."

He wanted to say, "Does it have something to do with *you?*" but he restrained himself.

"They know that we are lovers."

Esta turned her face away from him to stare out the window.

"So tell them I seduced you. That I'm a spy, and you never realized it till now. It fits, doesn't it? First I murdered an ambassador, then I tempted an intelligence officer."

There was bitterness in her voice.

"I'm sorry, Archie. That was cruel."

"I can't go back."

Was she playing with him? Why couldn't she look him in the face?

"What else do you plan to do? Hide with me in Palestine? I won't let you do that. And if you want to help me more, go back. I couldn't bear it if anything should happen to you here because of me."

Again, she threw her arms around him, covered his mouth with hers, and clutched at the back of his head.

Rawlins broke away and turned the key in the ignition, raced the engine, then turned it off again.

"Archie, you can't stay with me. You must understand this. After I'm settled, maybe, but not now."

A jeep appeared far down the coastal road. Rawlins and Esta watched it speed forward, then slow as it approached them. The jeep pulled to a halt. There were two occupants: a driver, who smiled and waved, and his officer. The latter, a young man about Rawlins's age, with a thick head of curly blond hair bleached almost white by the sun, cast a quick glance at Esta, then looked at Rawlins and saluted.

"Up bright and early this morning, Chaplain." Rawlins picked up an Australian accent.

"Yes."

The officer noticed Rawlins's trousers, soaked up to the knees.

"Been out for a swim, sir?"

The young officer seemed delighted to have caught the chaplain in an embarrassing situation. Rawlins could already see him telling the story back at the mess.

"The nurse here doesn't feel well," Rawlins responded firmly. "We stopped to give her some air."

The driver and the officer turned to one another, barely concealing their smirks.

"Not conducting services this morning, sir?"

Rawlins realized with a pang of confusion that it must be Sunday. Should he tell them he was the Jewish chaplain or play it the way it was and hope that they couldn't see the books in the back of the car?

"Off duty today." He knew as he spoke that what he had said was absurd. No minister took Sunday off.

The two men tried to suppress their laughter.

"Well, enjoy your leave, sir."

The young officer nodded to his driver to continue. Rawlins heard a quick burst of laughter before it was drowned out by the skid of tires on tarmac.

6

They held him in a room in the Kasr el Nil barracks. There was a single window, unbarred, and Mendoza could look out past the Semiramis Hotel and the dozen or so apartment buildings that now housed Middle East Headquarters. When he craned his neck he saw the placid waters of the Nile, studded with the brown sails of feluccas.

His throat was dry and his lips were parched from the drive in the desert. He took three steps and banged on the door of the room. A junior subaltern unlocked it and poked his head around.

"Any chance of a drink?"

"I can bring you a cup of tea, sir."

"Nothing stronger than that, I suppose?" Mendoza inquired. He was ashamed, but he couldn't stop himself.

"No booze in the nick."

"This is hardly the nick."

"*You're* nicked, though, aren't you, Rabbi?"

The subaltern slammed the door. Mendoza listened to the key turn, then went and sat on one of the two narrow camp beds on offer in the room.

When the door opened again it wasn't the subaltern but Graham who entered, with two cups of tea in his hands.

"Not bad service, eh?" he said to Mendoza. "Colonel brings you tea."

Graham sat down on the bed opposite his own.

"Want to tell me where they are? Then we can all go about our business. I've spoken with those on high. Don't really want to get into a big thing with you, you know. You may not think so, but despite what I said earlier, lot of respect, jolly lot of respect. For you. For what you've done in the past. Not easy. We all know that."

Mendoza sipped at his tea, then looked up to where the sun was drawing shadow patterns on the window. Last September, before he came out, he had been in London. He remembered walking in the East End after a bombing raid. Teams of men were shoveling mounds of broken glass onto the backs of trucks. The glass sparkled and shimmered in the flushed autumn sunlight. It was one of the those terrible beauties that war threw up. He had seen most of them, in the last war and this: dark air spurting with fire, birdsong over a battlefield riddled with bodies, blazing sunsets spread over the bald head of the desert, a burned-out tank placed, it always seemed, carefully as a sculpture, to capture the best angles of light.

He looked at Graham, who sat stiffly upright, a smile playing at the edges of his mouth.

"And if I don't tell you?"

"Oh, surely you know. Court-martial. Stripped of rank. Imprisonment. I suppose your behavior does count as traitorous too, so the possibility exists—"

Mendoza interrupted. "Not if the charges against the girl are false."

Graham paused for a moment.

"Ah, I see what you're saying. No, in that case you're absolutely right. We certainly wouldn't have to shoot you. Simply a case of helping Romeo and Juliet on their way. Playing the good friar, in fact. Friar Laurence, wasn't it? Or maybe John? But you see, old chap, we're sure. Oh, there'll be a fair trial and all that. But we do have the other one's confession."

"Can I speak to him?"

"I really don't think that's a good idea, do you?"

"What about Rawlins?"

"Well, Rawlins has been very silly; *stupid*, really. He's very young."

There was silence until Graham broke it by adding incongruously:

"He's a poetry lover. So am I."

Mendoza rose from his bed and walked over to the window. Far below him, a small boat set out from the shore of the Nile and tacked away from the bank. There was a poem in Mendoza's own head now: something about a Jew who was transformed into a dog, who sniffed his way through the filth and refuse of life, but every Friday at dusk became a prince and met his bride, the Sabbath princess. He turned to face Graham.

"It's always there, isn't it?" Mendoza muttered.

"What is?"

"The possibility for betrayal. Life gives us so many opportunities."

"Sometimes the duplicity lies in *not* betraying."

"As now, you mean."

"Yes."

"I put them in the back of an ammunition lorry headed for Damascus."

"Who was driving?"

"Well, it was two women, funnily enough, paramilitary girls."

"The names?"

Mendoza took a deep breath. Graham waited patiently. A pair of flies buzzed around the teacups and landed on a sugar cube that lay brown and soaking in Mendoza's saucer.

"Look," Mendoza whispered. "Forget the women, forget Damascus. I have no more stories for you. You'll have to find them on your own. And I hope to God you fail."

Graham stood up abruptly. "Have it your way," he said. "This was the easy part."

When he was alone, Mendoza took off all his clothes and folded them on the bed. He pulled his leather belt through the loops of his trousers. There had been several suicides during his army years. Death by hanging was the most common. Mendoza had frequently been the first officer on the spot. He had cut men down. Sometimes, when the Christian chaplain was unavailable, he led prayers for the deceased. That was the rule: first chaplain on the spot; the army was ecumenical about death.

Mendoza stood on the bed, bowed his head, and turned the leather belt twice around his neck; the metal clasp felt cool against his throat. He pulled on the belt, then let it slacken. He looked around the room. There was a thick peg for clothes high on the back of the door. He walked over, reached up, and looped one end of the belt over it. Then he fetched the slop pail and up-ended it. He stood on the bucket and held the other end of the belt around his neck. He found a tight hole for the pin. He thought of the first boy he had loved, a thin boy from the rabbinical school; the boy's face blurred into Rawlins's. When he kicked away the pail, the belt snapped open and the pin caught against his face and ran a small gash across his cheek. Mendoza collapsed in a heap on the ground. He uncoiled his long body and pulled himself up. He rolled up the belt and replaced it neatly on top of his clothes, then, in the bitterness of another failure, he lay down full length on the bed and tried to sleep.

Toward dawn, the door to the room was pulled open and a figure pushed roughly in. Mendoza, woken by the noise, tugged the sheet around him. The figure sat on the other bed, where Graham had been. A thin pink bar of light appeared at the base of the black window. Mendoza roused himself and sat up.

"More questions?" he asked. "Bit early, isn't it? I suppose you haven't found them, then."

"I have no questions."

Mendoza strained his eyes and peered through the murky light.

"Who are you?"

"I'm Hafner."

Mendoza couldn't help but smile to himself.

"What does Graham want me to tell you?"

"He said *you* wanted to see *me*."

"Yes. I did. I wanted to see if I could make you tell the truth."

"I've told the truth."

Hafner shivered slightly and hugged his arms around him. Mendoza looked closely but saw no signs that he had been beaten.

"How do you know her?"

"Here? We're in a Zionist group. It's not illegal. The Zionists from Palestine visit whenever they wish. They give us lectures. There's an office in Cairo. It is only we who cannot go there."

"Why did you tell Graham that she killed Waterlow?"

Hafner paused, then rose, took three steps, and stared through the window.

"Because she did."

Mendoza was silent for a moment, then he murmured:

"You're lying. You're lying to save yourself."

Hafner turned around. The pink bar behind him had already broadened into a band. Mendoza observed Hafner's face, touched with brown marks and red around the eyes.

"Look, don't be ashamed. It's the common thing. I'm asking you to do the uncommon. Perhaps I shouldn't. No right, really. Haven't exactly been a model of rectitude myself."

Hafner didn't reply. The two men sat in silence for some minutes. Hafner sat down again and pressed his hands to his face. Mendoza lowered his voice.

"Have you been in hell?"

He regretted speaking as soon as he had done so, but he nevertheless continued.

"I mean, over there. I know you've been in hell."

Mendoza's hands were trembling. He pressed them hard against his thighs to try and still the movement.

"Did she tell you?"

"No."

"I thought I was dead. At the bottom of a pit. There were bodies all over me. They came with pistols and executed those who were still alive. I didn't see them. I only heard the shots. Mother, sister, father."

Mendoza sighed.

The door swung open again, and the subaltern on guard stepped smartly into the room.

"Right, that's it for talkies. Time to go back to the nursery."

The soldier tugged roughly at Hafner's arm and dragged him out of the room.

7

White light entered through a small square window above their makeshift bed and sent a foot-wide shaft across the room. Waking, Rawlins was startled to see stone walls, an unfamiliar fireplace, and a pile of empty gasoline cans where the six-by-three standard army table should have been. He had been dreaming, as always, it now seemed to him, of England: a country bus that took him down narrow, winding lanes, and he was on the top deck so he could see over the leafy hedgerows into green fields. It was summer, some perfect June, and he was confident that although there was no driver, the bus would take him where he wanted to go. But in the end there was always a sudden turn, a loud shift in the engine noise as the bus changed gears and countries; the noise outside his barracks woke him, and there was Harfield snoring facedown on his bed.

Only it wasn't Harfield this time, and it wasn't even the other room, her room, the smell of which had never left him, as if their lovemaking had fixed it on the surface of his body like a tattoo.

He rose, emptied a little water from the pitcher into its bowl, then splashed his face. The cold made him gasp, but Esta didn't stir. She was wrapped in the thick blanket that their driver had given her, her knees pulled up tight to her chest and her face set in a kind of frown.

He took three steps and knelt beside her on the floor. Without opening her eyes, she stretched out her arms and pulled him to her. He was still wearing his chaplain's uniform. At the kibbutz, there had been no time to change. They had pushed them into the back of a van commonly used for the transportation of chickens. It was wire-meshed on the inside, and white feathers, some tinged with blood, were trapped in the grid. While they crammed in, someone had driven off Mendoza's car. Rawlins had been amazed by the thoroughness of the preparations for Esta's arrival and the speed with which everything had been accomplished.

Now she held him tightly, as if, more than anything, she wanted the warmth of his body. But then she began to tug at his shirt.

Her body was cold. With the tip of his finger he traced the blue vein that ran from her nipple across her left breast, and then he moved his hand down to the flat of her belly. Part of him was still lost in the English June of his dream, a shuttered summer afternoon, and she might have been anybody, Claire from Shell-Mex, or the young redheaded postmistress in his parents' village, with whom he had flirted one day. He was inside the advancing light, and his hands were hungry, pushing under her and between her thighs. Only the pine scent that had risen with the dawn and intensified with the spreading light brought the subtle reminder of where he was.

The stone hut was surrounded by high pines and dark-green cypresses. The previous night the driver of the van had left them at the foot of a steep hill and indicated with a wave of his hand the direction in which they should head. Rawlins and Esta had scrambled up in darkness, grazing their hands and knees on sharp rocks.

Now, when he stepped outside, Rawlins saw a maze of narrow tracks, goat paths, running away from the hut in all directions. Below him stretched a panorama of rolling hills that, at their base, cradled the Old City. Rawlins could make out the Dome of the Rock and the ancient wall. In the far distance, mountains suffused in yellow light overhung what looked like a large body of water. Rawlins strode a few paces down the hill and then turned: even at this short distance the hut was almost invisible.

Suddenly he was startled by a set of sharp cries, followed by a tinkling of bells. A shepherd boy appeared a hundred yards or so below him, guiding his flock of black goats across the hillside. Rawlins turned quickly and hurried back to the hut.

Esta stood over the washbasin, stripped to the waist. Rawlins watched her splash water on her face, neck, and breasts. She shivered, dried herself peremptorily with the nurse's shirt that Mendoza had given her, then put it back on.

"How long can we stay here?" Rawlins asked.

"As long as we have to, or *I* have to. I told you, Archie, you should go."

At the drop-off point, they had each been given an oil lamp, a jerrican of water, and a haversack of food. Rawlins began to unpack. There was bread, goat cheese, canned vegetables, and, to his surprise, a bottle of red wine and two thick bars of chocolate. At the bottom of the pack was a change of clothes. The driver had told them that he would return in two days. Rawlins gauged that their supplies could easily last that long. Esta hardly ate, and although he was hungry, he had been disciplined by the army to run on an empty stomach.

The thing was, Rawlins thought, to act, as far as possible, as if they were not in hiding. He could not see an end of it, except a bad one—betrayal, capture—and so it was best not to dwell on the future but to behave as if this, now, were their future. Within these four walls he wanted to make something utterly domestic; he would have put up curtains if he had owned a set.

At the kibbutz, they had been given a small radio and told to turn it on only at night, but Rawlins ignored the instructions and rotated the dial to a forces music station that cranked out the latest hits from London. He kept the volume low, but the music was loud enough to let him twirl Esta round the floor.

The radio played "You'd Be So Nice to Come Home To" and "You Made Me Love You." Rawlins pressed Esta close to him and sang the words of the ballads softly into her ear. He hadn't danced with anyone like this since his last night in England, when he had taken Claire to the old Drury Lane Theatre and they had moved in slow circles around the dance floor set up over the front orchestra seats. Three or four times during the evening, Rawlins had been embarrassed when the band suddenly shifted pace and he didn't know how to jitterbug.

Now he was surprised to discover how easily Esta slow waltzed to the songs. She followed his lead, as if they had been partners for months, and coyly put her head on his shoulder, like a teenager. He had forgotten that she wasn't always a refugee, that she, too, had a life before the war, with music and boyfriends and dancing. She was less than a year younger than he, and before everything collapsed around her, she must have taken her own excursions into pleasure and foolishness.

As the pace of the music quickened, Esta began to breathe heavily and cough a little. At first Rawlins paid no attention, and when a break came, he pulled her down to the bed and tried to make love to her again, but she was weak from the dancing and didn't respond when he pushed up her shirt and began to kiss her breasts.

Touching his lips to her forehead, he found that her fever had returned. He propped her up on the empty haversacks, squeezed water onto a cloth, and wiped her face and forearms. Her skin was pallid, but there were raised red marks on her cheeks.

The radio crackled and spat: bad news from the desert, worse from Europe.

"I have something to confess."

"Not now."

Rawlins pressed the damp cloth to her temples. Whatever she had to say he didn't want to hear. What use would it be at this stage to learn that he was the fool of fools?

"What I told you in your office. That story. It's true. But it isn't mine."

"What do you mean?"

"It's Falik's."

Rawlins glared at her until she closed her eyes and turned away from him.

"The grave? The children? You didn't see them?"

"*He* saw them. I saw other things. Does it matter? Which of us saw what doesn't change a single fact."

"You weren't in Poland?"

Esta shook her head.

"I was in Vienna."

"That's impossible. You told me . . . You mean you lied. That day in my office. All lies?"

Rawlins felt the old rush of confusion that had attended all his dealings with her. For a few hours, on the previous night and when he had held her this morning, his bewilderment had vanished. But now the truth was warped and twisted again: a rail bent out of shape all the way down the line.

"Why should I believe you now? What were the 'other things' you saw? What were they? Maybe you didn't see anything at all. Maybe you've been in Cairo for ten years. Maybe you've been in *Palestine* for ten years."

Esta coughed hard and spat up a small mass of green phlegm, streaked with blood. Rawlins stared at her for a moment, then rose and brought her water from his canteen. She drank, and her coughing fit subsided.

"I don't want to tell you now."

"You told me Hafner's story, didn't you." Rawlins heard Phillips's interrogatory voice in his head and felt a moment's shame.

Esta raised her thin arms, stretched them, as if she was pushing away an invisible presence, then let them fall in her lap.

"In the beginning—I'm talking about right after the Anschluss—the storm troops came and rounded people up on the streets. It was a Saturday, at the end of April. The Germans had been in Vienna for six weeks. They collected a whole group of Jews, hundreds of us. They drove us out to the Prater. It's an amusement park. It was spring, you know, Archie, and I was in the back of this lorry with my mother, and I remember how blue the sky was, and there were birds swooping over our heads."

Rawlins watched intensely how the Jerusalem sunlight flickered on the stone walls of the hut, as if images from Esta's mind might suddenly appear there, like a magic lantern show. Her voice was trancelike, almost without emotion, as it had been on that first time in his office. Again, Rawlins was transfixed.

"First they stood over us and made us eat the grass. We were animals, you see. They stood on our hands with their boots and cracked the bones. Then they put a blue ladder against the trunk of a tree and made us climb into the lower branches. We had to twitter and croak like the birds."

Here Esta tucked in her elbows, and Rawlins saw her as a bird. He wanted her to soar, to be the red hawk that he had watched riding the air at dawn, when he peered through the hole in the wall.

"They took my mother with some older people and strapped them into the scenic railway. My mother begged them: 'I have a weak heart, please, please.' They said, 'You're going for a "pleasure hour,"' then they sent them around and around at top speed, an hour, maybe more, until the people fainted. The rest of

us were made to run in circles until we dropped. Then the beatings began."

Rawlins couldn't find a way in. He groped for Esta's hand, but
even as he gripped it he felt hopelessly distanced from her. He
knew he couldn't cross the chasm that separated them, not even
when he was in her and she tore at his body, like a lioness into
a hind.

"What happened to your mother?"

"She was dead in the railcar."

It seemed to Rawlins that a long time passed before he
whispered:

"Why didn't you tell me?"

Esta turned to him, and Rawlins saw, for the first time since he
had known her, tears on her cheeks. He gestured toward her, but
she averted her face and spoke in a voice that was hard and
matter-of-fact, adopted, he felt, to keep him from comforting her.

"It was already known. No one was denying: beatings, tor-
menting of Jews. All this was known for a long time. Even you,
Archie. You probably read about it. Those poor Jews in Germany
and Austria. Look what they're suffering now. They have no
shops, they can't go to restaurants. The storm troops beat them
up, sometimes they kill them. And then you turned the page.
Maybe you went out to dance."

Rawlins grimaced. He had long ago ceased to hear the radio,
but now the music came through to him in the form of one of his
favorite tunes: "That Lovely Weekend." The melody, which before had always moved him, now struck him as trite; the lyrics,
hopelessly false and sentimental. The singer purred, "Those two
days in heaven you helped me to spend." Rawlins thought of
Lensbury and Claire, how she had romanticized everything. Everyone was doing that; it was a style of behavior. It was good for
morale if you had a girl to come home to, and on their first weekend, Claire pretended that she would be that girl. The music, he

now realized, worked the cause, was an employee of the government. They wanted you to think you had a loved one, "Faithful For Ever," sitting by the fire, knitting socks, listening to "your song" on the radio. And that's who you were supposed to be fighting for: the patient, virtuous Claire, who waited for you to walk in the door. But half the time you never walked through the door again, or if you did, someone was wheeling you, or maybe the girl was in bed with someone else. There were no songs about that. Suddenly Rawlins realized that this whole train of thought, and the way that he had let it go on, was an indulgence, a diversion, because perched at the front of his mind, a dark figure that could not be erased, was Esta in the tree, gibbering in order to stay alive.

Rawlins rose abruptly and turned the radio off. To push the woman-bird away, he said:

"Tell me about Hafner."

"I didn't meet him for a long time. Somehow he had escaped from Poland to Vienna. We were hidden together on a barge in the Danube. The river froze. We stayed almost a month. He was very sick. I fed him. I kept him warm."

Rawlins felt a spurt of jealousy; his cheeks reddened and, horribly, horribly, he wanted to slap her.

"In that situation you hear everything. You *tell* everything. He was in the grave, the Nazis thought he was shot, and at night he climbed out. He tried to tell your officer. But you know what happened."

"Do you know where he is now?"

"No. Do you?"

Esta's quick response startled Rawlins. He had to collect his thoughts, to remind himself that she couldn't possibly know what he had done. Even Mendoza didn't know. It hurt him, because he thought he was on the side of the truth now, but he would have to continue to deceive her.

"I was supposed to meet him and some of the others—you remember, I told you the night before you left—but I never got there. The rabbi came as I was about to leave. He took me to the house of a friend of his, Abbas, a young Egyptian. He was very kind. He hid me until we knew that you were back."

Esta began to cough and spit again. She drank from the canteen, but the water only set her off on another round of coughing.

"You need to see a doctor."

"I'm all right."

Rawlins wasn't sure that they could wait the two days till the driver returned. What if she should worsen in the night? He blamed himself for not insisting that she see someone while they were on the kibbutz. But everything there had happened so fast, and in the last hour or so of their drive, Esta's condition seemed to have improved. Whenever he asked her, she said she was feeling better.

"I'll go back to the people on the kibbutz."

"You can't do that, Archie. And I don't want you to leave me now. Soon, but not yet. Don't worry, I won't die on you."

Esta tried to laugh, but the laugh bubbled into a cough.

"Tell me where I have to go."

"Don't be ridiculous. It's a long way from here. You know how long we drove. We'll wait for them to come. In the meantime we'll drink wine and you'll read me poems."

Was she teasing him?

"My books are in Cairo."

"Then you'll have to recite."

He sat next to her with his back against the wall. Esta rolled on her side, facing away from him.

"Come on, Archie. A beautiful English poem."

He began with Keats. He knew why. At school, in his final year, he had won a prize for recitation, and "To Autumn" had been his set piece. He had received the Palgrave's *Golden Treasury* as his award.

An ivory sunlight spread through the window and blocked the room. Rawlins intoned, "Season of mists and mellow fruitfulness." Esta stayed motionless on her side. Her shoulders hunched, birdlike, in a way that he knew would always make him uncomfortable. In the second stanza he stumbled and skipped a couple of lines. But he recovered the third, and the end came in a rush of memory. He was standing before the whole school: his housemaster directly in front of him, the judges to one side, the boys massed in rows. He had been instructed to look beyond the audience and its inevitable distractions, at some arbitrarily selected fixed point. He chose the honors board that listed in gold leaf the names of the school's war dead. He concluded with all the "expression" that he could muster: "The redbreast whistles from a garden croft;/And gathering swallows twitter in the skies," and was greeted with the derisive whistling and ironic cheers that followed any such performance until the masters quieted the throng. Now, in this hiding room, he barely whispered the last lines.

He leaned over Esta. She was asleep, her thin chest heaving with the effort to breathe. Her body trembled. Rawlins wrapped himself into her. Her hair was sweaty and malodorous from their journey in the chicken van. He crushed his face into the mass of her dark curls and breathed deep.

8

"Would you mind if I ended my prayer?"

Mendoza turned back to the window and stared out. Graham, who had entered the room smartly, as if he meant business (this time not holding a tray), tapped impatiently on his calf with his swagger stick.

"If you must. But I'd appreciate your attention."

Mendoza prayed in an undertone.

"Guard my tongue from evil and my lips from speaking guile. Open my heart to thy Law and let my soul pursue thy commandments. Let the words of my mouth and the meditation of my heart be acceptable before thee, O Lord, my Rock and my Redeemer."

He finished and continued to stare out the window. He wasn't sure that the words meant anything to him any longer. He prayed out of habit, not conviction. In the past, adversity had strengthened his belief. But the events in Europe had changed all that.

Outside, the Nile was coming alive; its riverbanks were crowded, and the water, always calm, was thronged with lateen sails.

"Look, I don't want to waste any more time. We picked up that Egyptian boyfriend of yours. And I'm afraid that when it comes to divulging secrets, your batman's less reticent than you. So it's all over. We know she was there. He even showed us the bed she slept on. Now where the fucking hell are they?"

Mendoza didn't respond. He saw that Graham was the kind of man who hated to lose his temper. He was proud of his self-control. He liked everything neat, and his cruelty, like everything else about him, needed to be contained if he was to feel secure.

"Do you know there's a bloody war on? Do you know that? I'm running around chasing after your fucking Jewess. Do you know we lost a brigade in that balls-up at Cyrenaica? And now we've got a whole fucking coastal road jammed tight between Derna and Tobruk. Movement Control tells me—"

Graham stopped in midsentence, as if he had suddenly remembered that Mendoza was someone who could not be trusted.

"They're in Palestine, aren't they?"

"It certainly would be a good place for a hunted Jewess to be."

"Don't be clever with me, Rabbi. I'm not in the mood."

Graham walked over to the door and swung it open. Mendoza heard his steps echo down the corridor. Two subalterns entered quickly and closed the door behind them. Mendoza took the first blow full in the face. There was a sharp crack, and a gush of blood from his nose. He swung back wildly through the pain, but his flailing fists met nothing but air.

9

"Why didn't you send for me earlier?"

The voice of the kneeling man was angry, impatient.

"She didn't want me to leave. I had to wait for the driver."

"And you listened to her."

"I didn't . . . I mean, I thought . . ."

"You thought what? That a person with pneumonia can sip a little water and pull through?"

"You're *English*."

The young man turned and removed his stethoscope.

"I *was*," he replied, "although that's hardly what matters here, is it?"

Rawlins blushed. Esta lay close to unconsciousness. There were heavy beads of sweat on her neck and down the cleavage of her breasts. The young man delicately folded back the lapels of her shirt, undid a button, and replaced his stethoscope on her chest.

He had arrived soon after dark and immediately set about tending to Esta. His crouching figure threw a huge shadow on the wall. He had turned her from side to side, then pounded on her chest. Esta had responded by coughing up wads of green sputum, then she had fallen back, exhausted, on the floor.

"You'll have to light a fire. This room has to be warmed up, and we're going to have to boil some water. She needs steam."

"We can't. I mean, we could be spotted."

The young man turned toward Rawlins. He spoke forcefully, as if talking to an obstinate child.

"The British army's not going to rush over every time they see a wisp of smoke on this hillside. Why do you think we chose it? There are shepherds' huts here, you see."

Rawlins was about to defend himself, to say, "They instructed me on the kibbutz . . . ," but the look of frustration in the young man's eyes brought him up short.

"Is she going to be all right?"

"If you could collect the wood, that would be a help."

Rawlins stepped outside. The moon had barely risen over the pines. He watched it move negligently through dark tracts of space above him. A cool breeze had begun to blow from the east, carrying a faint scent of jasmine and violet from the desert. Rawlins walked off the goat paths and into the forest, bending every so often to pick up cracked twigs and small broken boughs. The night seemed to him deceptively quiet, as if a trap was waiting to be sprung. But he heard no steps or voices. When he returned, the doctor was putting away his instruments.

"Let's get that fire going."

Esta tossed restlessly on the bed. The young man snapped shut the bag that he had brought with him. Rawlins set a match to the wood. Some of the twigs were green and didn't catch. The doctor came over and began busily poking at the fire, snapping off twigs and adjusting the position of the branches. Rawlins watched him, feeling awkward and embarrassed.

"How is she?"

"Not good. She should be in hospital."

"Is there a place? I mean a safe place?"

"Maybe. But not tonight. I can't move her now."

Rawlins held out his hand. "I'm Archie Rawlins."

"Yes. I know who you are."

The young man turned his palms to the flames. When he spoke, he looked away from Rawlins and into the fire.

"Lewis Marks."

"How long have you been in Palestine?"

"I left London ten years ago."

Marks continued to stare into the fire. Rawlins looked at his short, compact body, conservatively dressed in a broad-collared white shirt and gray trousers. He had spread his jacket over Esta as an extra blanket.

"You met her in Cairo?"

"Yes."

The red-blue flames reflected in the lenses of Marks's glasses.

"Listen." Marks lowered his voice. "She may not make it."

Rawlins nodded. He had been standing, hovering awkwardly between the bed and the fire, as if a step in either direction might upset some delicate balance in the room, which held Esta steady. Now he moved toward Esta, squatted beside her, and took her hand. Her face was colorless, and her breath came in short, sharp gasps; the air in the room eluded her.

Rawlins sat with her for what seemed to him a long time. With his free hand he stroked her hair back from her forehead. Marks busied himself heating a bowl of water; occasionally, he glanced over toward the bed. At those moments, Rawlins became aware, with a sick feeling in his stomach, that he began to overdo his solicitousness to Esta, to append an exaggerated tenderness to the gesture of his hand on her head. Was it because he wasn't a Jew that he felt he had to demonstrate the sincerity of his feelings for her?

"All right, it's ready."

Rawlins lifted Esta under the arms and raised her into a sitting position. Marks covered her head with a towel from his bag, then bent her forward over the enamel bowl.

"We have to mobilize the secretions," he said. "That's what the pounding and the turning's all about."

Esta lolled forward, open-mouthed. Marks whispered encouragement.

"That's it, try to breathe, you're doing well, that's it."

When the steam had evaporated, Marks set the bowl down and laid Esta gently back on the blankets. He bolstered her head with the towel. Slowly, Esta's breathing grew less desperate, and she settled into an uneasy sleep.

"You'll repeat the process throughout the night. Did you see earlier how I pounded on her chest? And don't forget to turn her, every half an hour or so; it's very important."

"You're going to leave?"

"Shortly."

"But surely, if she needs to be in hospital, then you should at least . . ."

"I would stay if I could, but I'm afraid it's impossible." Marks hesitated before adding, "There are other patients whom I only see at night."

"But I can't . . . I'm not at all qualified."

"Look, to be honest with you, the only reason to have her in a hospital is because of the nursing. I'm sorry, but I've shown you all that I can do. There are no medicines, I'm afraid. No magic cures for pneumonia. Tomorrow I'll try to set something up. But it may be that she's here for the duration of her illness. If so, you have to make her as comfortable as you can." Rawlins stared at Esta, then turned quickly away. He grabbed Marks by the arm and pulled him toward the door of the hut. Marks, taken by surprise, did not resist. Rawlins shoved him outside.

"She's going to die, isn't she? She's going to die tonight. And there's nothing you can do. That's what you're really telling me, isn't it?"

Marks pushed Rawlins's hand away from where it clutched at his shirtsleeve.

"You haven't been listening to me, have you? I don't know if she's going to pull through or not. But there's a chance, and that's not always the case. She must have been ill for days. Why didn't you do anything, you damn fool?"

Rawlins began to stutter a few words of excuse but then stopped.

"Yes," he said, "you're right. It's my fault."

Marks shivered. A cluster of stars had wheeled into view over the heads of the trees.

"Listen, I'll get back as soon as I can. I'll come by day. It's a risk, but I suppose we don't have much choice. Expect me at the latest by midmorning. If I absolutely can't come, I'll send some-one else. In the meantime you know what to do. Make sure you stay awake."

He turned back into the hut. Rawlins waited a moment, taking slow breaths, sucking the cool air deep into his lungs as if some-how he might be able to hold it for later transference to Esta, then he followed Marks back inside.

Marks was standing over Esta. He gently lifted his jacket off her sleeping body and draped it over his own shoulders. He looked around the hut for a replacement blanket. Rawlins inter-cepted his gaze.

"I'll keep her warm."

"See that you do."

Marks picked up his bag and took two steps toward the door.

"What happened, Rawlins? Why did you get involved?"

"I didn't think about it."

The doctor seemed oddly satisfied with this answer, as if it confirmed a general impression that he had developed of Rawlins as someone inept and neglectful.

Marks stepped outside. In the open doorway, he turned and thumped his fist on his chest as a last demonstration of how Rawlins should proceed.

At intervals throughout the night, Rawlins was sure that Esta was going to die. For long periods she coughed dryly and her chest heaved in a desperate struggle for breath. He beat on her and forced her to discharge the green pus and blood-threaded mucus from her lungs. She barely spoke, except when she needed his help. He held her from falling while she squatted over the chamber pot, and when she shivered violently and demanded more blankets, he lay next to her, pressed his lips to her burning skin, and encircled her with his arms.

The fire dimmed, and the room turned a sulfur yellow. Rawlins waited for Esta to fall asleep, then rushed madly into the forest to collect more wood. He tripped over roots and bumped into the trunks of trees. He moved like a deranged man, scurrying on all fours. His mind raced: If the fire died, then so would she. Got to heat the water; more steam. Mustn't forget to turn her. He had never in his life committed himself so wholeheartedly to a single task.

Toward dawn, overcome with exhaustion, he fell asleep near her on the floor.

10

Mendoza lay bleeding on the bed. He ripped off a piece of sheet and held it to his nose. There were large swellings around his eyes, and his head throbbed ceaselessly. He tried to lift himself, but his body ached too much, and he slumped back down. He could feel the heat of the day rising. His shirt was soaked through under the arms; sweat mixed with blood ran down his face. He turned on his back. The sun, locked into the window of the room, screened by a delicate veil of dust, sent a shaft of sand-brown light across his body. Mendoza touched a hand to his face and groaned softly.

In London, five years before, he had been savagely beaten, set upon by a group of Mosley's Blackshirts as he stepped from a synagogue in Stepney, where he had been visiting one of his former teachers. He had fought back, but to no avail. Mendoza remembered lying on the ground as the kicks came in; the sky was the color of lead, the air bruised with clouds, the cobblestone street glazed and slick. He had been rescued by two Jewish taxi drivers emerging from a pub, tough brawlers who had given the young Fascists a hiding. Afterward Mendoza felt, strangely, that the violence had made him supple, heightened his vision and the intensity of his experiences: as he walked to the tube, the city's gray-brown hues were thrillingly vivid, the noise from the street rapturous and symphonic.

His reverie was broken by the return of the subalterns.

"Wakey, wakey. Someone wants to take you for a drive."

They pulled Mendoza from his bed and half marched him down two flights of stairs, along a corridor, and into a washroom.

"Better spruce yourself up, Rabbi. A little bit of cold water now. You've got a nasty bump. Hasn't he, Norm?"

"A few nasty bumps."

"That's right, a few nasty bumps."

The windows of the bathroom were flung open, and as they were lower down in the building, Mendoza could hear the shouting and bellowing of street merchants, hucksters, and beggars, all punctuated by the high screech of a donkey driver's demand for passage. He reached for a towel. Once, he had seen a blind man walking down an alley in the souk and hooting like an owl in order to warn people out of his way.

They led him through a maze of corridors and out to the rear of the building. He was thrust into the back of a car. One of the subalterns got in beside him. A driver was already in place and set off as soon as the door slammed.

"Where are you taking me?"

"Trip in the desert. We're handing you over to Rommel, and he's going to give us Cyrenaica in exchange."

The car moved slowly as the ever-present crowd of Cairenes pushed and stumbled their way forward. Mendoza sat upright in his seat, gazing through swollen half-closed eyes as the miraculous theater of the street spilled its cast of characters out before him: ice cream vendors rattling brass cups, lemonade merchants jingling silver bells, hashish peddlers, money changers, scribes, half-naked camel drivers, English soldiers in tropical uniform, a priest with a parasol and a cylindrical hat, men with red fezzes and green turbans, a man in a spotlessly white burnoose, with a hood lying in folds around his neck and shoulders; all wandered indifferently among the clangorous traffic.

The car headed out of the city and was soon speeding on the black, undulating, sand-fringed road that linked Egypt to Palestine. After several hours, they approached the spot where Mendoza had abandoned Rawlins and Esta. The car did not stop. Mendoza thought now that the runaways must have been captured. But why bring him all the way out here?

It was nightfall by the time they halted. The subaltern escorted Mendoza into a four-man tent, where a bench, a small table, and two chairs had been set up. He handcuffed Mendoza to one of the chairs, then left him alone. The room buzzed with mosquitoes, and Mendoza was powerless before their assault. It was a relief when Graham entered, accompanied by two men, and ordered Mendoza uncuffed.

Graham sat down at the table and immediately addressed the younger of the two men.

"You know who this is?"

"Rabbi Mendoza."

"And you've had dealings with him?"

"Yes, sir. It was about my prayer book, sir. You see, I come from—"

"Yes; all right, Grossman. Perhaps you'd like to tell the rabbi about his assistant."

Grossman sat down, then turned in his chair to address Mendoza. He was making small nervous gestures, twisting a strand of hair above his ear and blinking.

"You all right, Rabbi?" he whispered. "Don't look too good."

"Never mind that, Grossman," Graham interjected. "Just repeat what you told me."

Grossman began, hesitantly, to sketch the details of his conversation with Rawlins. Mendoza listened impassively, occasionally nodding his head as if to assure Grossman that it was in order to continue. When Grossman finished his story, Graham told him that he could leave, but Grossman remained in his chair. He looked uneasily at Graham, then back at Mendoza.

"Is it big trouble, sir?"

"Yes."

"I didn't mean no harm. Look: You've always been very fair with me. And to be honest, I have tried to pull a few. And it's not just that. I mean"—Grossman lowered his voice—"stick together and all that."

"It's all right, Grossman."

"My father's *yahrzeit*, you see. I wasn't making that up. I always respect his memorial. I asked your assistant if I could go to Cairo. He didn't know what I was talking about. I knew something was up. I thought maybe he'd stolen your car."

"I gave it to him."

"You'd have given me that day off, wouldn't you, Rabbi? I mean, what rabbi wouldn't?"

"That will be that, Grossman. Please leave."

Grossman stood, wiped his right hand on the front of his trousers, then extended it to Mendoza.

"No hard feelings, sir. Had no idea, really. Simply told them the story." He looked round quickly at Graham and Harfield, then turned his back to them. "You know how it is."

Mendoza grasped Grossman's hand. "Yes, I know."

"Return to your duty." Harfield lifted the flap of the tent.

As he was on his way out, Grossman's nervousness evaporated and his old cockiness returned.

"Any chance of rest of the night off, sir?"

"Get out of here."

Graham shuffled a sheaf of papers on the desk.

"Well, cooked goose, wouldn't you say?"

"Why did you bother to bring me here?"

"I wasn't sure that you would believe me, and I thought you'd like to hear it from the horse's mouth. And oh, sorry about yesterday, but you did rather bring it on yourself. In any case, when this is over tonight, we're sending you on."

Graham had regained his composure since the previous day and was clearly pleased with himself for having done so.

"Sending me on?"

"A real prison, I'm afraid. But it's in Palestine, old fellow, so in a way you'll be among friends."

"You haven't found them."

"We're closing in. Chap you saw last night, very eager to help, gave us the names of his Palestinian contacts. In code, of course, but it won't be long now."

"He wants to live."

"We all want to do that."

Graham looked around the tent, a tight smile on his face. Harfield grinned back.

"Can I ask you something? I'm a little confused. Been going over your record. Can't quite understand something in the background. For my own benefit, really. Want to get the picture straight. Your father was a baker, correct?"

Mendoza nodded.

"But the rest of your family, rather well off. Bankers, I understand."

"My father's second cousins and their children run a merchant bank."

"Yes. *Second* cousins. And they're people of some influence."

"What are you getting at?"

"Oh, nothing at all. But you yourself, you were a scholarship boy. Isn't that right?"

"I went to Owens."

"Owens? Yes. So you *acquired*, in a way, position and, perhaps, accent? While your cousins, your *second* cousins, were more— how shall we say?—integral?"

"I'm as English as you are."

"Are you? Yes, of course you are. Much to be admired. A lot of struggle involved."

"Are you worried, Colonel Graham?"

"What on earth do you mean?"

"I see my powerful cousins have you a little alarmed. Is someone you know in debt to them? Or are you simply one of those who think that Jewish bankers run the show? If so, no need to trouble yourself. We're not close."

Graham slapped his hand twice at the back of his neck, then inspected the small red stains on his fingers.

"Do you know, someone showed me your little prayer book the other day—perhaps it's the copy that chap Grossman lost. Wrote most of 'em yourself, didn't you? You know, I was moved. Truly. I've got it here somewhere."

Graham patted the pockets of his tunic and, having found the right one, extricated the square pamphlet.

"Do you . . . no, you wouldn't . . . have a copy with you, that is?"

Graham extended his arm.

"To take with you. Something to read in the cell?"

Harfield laughed, but Graham cut him short with a look. For a moment, Mendoza thought that the endless and familiar irony that layered Graham's conversation had fallen away. But perhaps he was mistaken. He reached out and took the prayer book.

"Well, this is it for now. Everything ready, Harfield? Why don't you check?"

Harfield exited the tent.

Graham rose and approached Mendoza.

"I understand, you know. Don't approve, but I understand."

Graham glanced toward the opening of the tent. Mendoza thought that he was going to offer his hand, but in the end he merely shrugged and walked out.

11

Rawlins woke in a panic. In sleep he had twisted and turned, and now his head was close to the dead fire. His hair was tinged with ash. He scrambled over to Esta. The room was still dark. He groped for her body in a frenzy under the rumple of blankets. She wasn't there. He looked up and saw her crouched over the chamber pot, a blanket hung loosely over her thin shoulders.

"I'm here, Archie."

He went and knelt beside her, kissing her hands and face. Her skin was still burning, but her eyes seemed to have lost their feverish glow of the previous few hours.

Rawlins took the pot and emptied it outside. It had begun to rain, in heavy, fat drops that pocked and splattered the earth. How could he collect more wood? Everything would be soaked. He went back to Esta. She was propped on her side. At least six times in the night he had forced her to turn; the crease down her back that deepened through her buttocks was now as familiar to him as the central artery on a much perused map. He knew her thighs, the thin columns of her legs, the dark curlicues of her pubic hair, her heart pounding behind the bars of its ribs.

She coughed, and he roused himself again to pummel her chest. But she held him off.

"No, Archie, I'm O.K. Wait. Only hold me."

He felt her flimsiness, and when she shook, he gripped her and leaned on her like a weight, heavy and quiet. Without him, he felt, the wind rattling the window would burst in and blow her away like a piece of paper.

"I want to see my father."

"The doctor said you shouldn't move."

"You can bring him here, Archie."

Rawlins rose from the bed. He pretended to adjust the window latch. If her father came, he would tell her about their meeting. But how could he refuse?

"Where is your father?"

The question dropped from his mouth; an anchor unwinding from his heart and stilling its movement.

"In Tel Aviv. I'll tell you the address. I have to see him."

She made an effort to sit up, with her back against the stone wall.

"I don't want to leave you. Someone else should go."

"Archie, please, today. You must understand. Look at me."

He saw her pallid cheeks and split lip, the rough sores at the rim of her nostrils; heard the desperate rasp of her breathing.

"Wait for Dr. Marks to return. He'll arrange for your father to be picked up."

"Archie, I don't want to wait. The doctor may not come for a couple of hours, and who knows how long his arrangements will take. Besides, they may not want him here, another person knowing where we are. I *can't* wait."

As if to emphasize her predicament, she fell into a prolonged coughing fit.

A thin light penetrated the murkiness of the hut. Rawlins listened to the rain fall hard on the roof; a few drops splashed down the chimney, impressing small round stains in the ash.

He could have argued with her, pointed out how it was dangerous for him to travel by day, how it was likely that he would lose his way, how everything would be quicker if Marks set it up. But while the hazards of the journey were real, he knew he had no choice. Bringing her father was part of making things right.

"I'll wait until the doctor comes, and then I'll leave."

"No, Archie; go now. He'll come. He's trustworthy. He helped me."

"You know he's English."

"English!"

For the first time in days, Esta made an effort to smile.

"Then he *must* be a good man, isn't that right, Archie?"

Rawlins moved the remainder of the food near her bed, wiped

her down, and rearranged the blankets around her. He stripped off the uniform that Mendoza had given him and put on the blue shirt and trousers that the kibbutz had provided. Esta told him her father's address, and he pretended to commit it to memory.

"What if he's not there?"

"Try, Archie."

He kissed her on the head, then made to move away. She held out her arm, took his hand, and pushed it down under the rough blankets, between her legs.

"Feel," she said. "Feel how sick I am."

Rawlins felt the hot, feverish sweat on the lips of her cunt. He tried to pull back his hand, but she held him there. He was embarrassed; she was breaking the rules, violating the relationship he had set up between the caring nurse and his dying patient.

He tried again, halfheartedly, to pull his hand away, but she resisted, and he inserted first one, then two fingers inside her. Esta closed her eyes. He slid his fingers out and began to masturbate her; she lay still for a while, then squeezed his wrist to stop him. She raised herself up in the bed. Rawlins remained kneeling next to her. She pulled at his belt and undid the buttons of his fly. She reached in and curled her fingers around his penis, but she released him almost immediately and fell back exhausted on her side.

Rawlins leaned over her. She was on the edge of sleep, and her breathing seemed lighter, although Rawlins thought perhaps that was simply because he wanted it to be. He rose, buttoned his trousers, and walked over to the fire. He cleared the ashes in the grate, so that their dust would not disturb her breathing.

He told her to keep wrapped up, to drink, to try to spit. Halfway through his litany of instructions, he realized that he was repeating the phrases his mother always used when he was ill and home from school and she left him to go out shopping.

He had almost forgotten his own family. He hadn't written to them in weeks. They probably thought he was dead. He imagined a frozen moment: arriving at his parents' house with his Jewish war bride. His father emerging from the long drawing room that showed oak trees in the west. His mother looking Esta up and down, appalled by her skinniness, her accent, her wild hair.

Rawlins leaned over Esta.

"When you fall asleep, I'll leave."

12

The rain flattened his hair to his head. He scrambled down the side of the hill, sliding on rocks and through the yellow broom that grew in broad, unruly bushes at the side of the road. The sky was stamped with blue-black clouds. The rain slanted into his body, stopped suddenly, then began again. A single-engine plane droned invisibly above him.

He had not slept more than two hours, his eyes stung and his muscles were numb from the cold floor. He walked as fast as he could in the direction of the city. A scent of rosemary lingered in the air. When he had gone about a mile, the rain suddenly stopped and the mist that hung over the far valley began to clear. Rawlins felt drained and confused. The sparkle of sunlight on the city's rooftops, the emergence of the purple-brown hills behind them, the intoxicating scents that rose from the plants and vegetation beside him, began to lift his spirits and distract him. But he knew that what he experienced, the raw beauty of the landscape and the harmonies that it implied, was false: nothing in the natural world could ever move him again as it had once done.

On the bus to Tel Aviv he fell asleep. When the vehicle hit a bump or took one of the sharp curves on the Seven Sisters Road, he jolted awake, to glimpse the bright corner of a yellow field, men stripped to the waist at work in an irrigation ditch, an ambulance halted by a roadside accident. The images merged into his restless dreams. He laid his head forward on the cool metal bar of the seat in front of him. An irritated passenger rudely pushed him back and shouted at him in Hebrew. A woman in an embroidered dress, with a live rooster on her head, stood over him and smiled; Rawlins wasn't sure if he saw her in dream or reality.

At the bus station, Rawlins was the last to leave his seat. He looked through the open window beside him, trying to reorient himself to the city. Four Tommies stood by a corn stand, biting into white-yellow cobs and letting the coated butter drip down the sides of their lips. Two more patrolled under the sign on a building that read RESTRICTED AREA. Three young officers stood smoking under a jutting balcony whose white plaster face flaked in long strips. Rawlins observed them with suspicion, but then his unease turned to envy. He, too, could be on leave, leaning nonchalantly against a wall, watching the parade of pretty Tel Aviv girls. Couldn't he still turn back? Take a train to Cairo. Explain. Begin again.

The bus driver yelled something. He wanted him off the bus. Rawlins stepped out into an interminable racket of motor horns and klaxons, a dense brown fog of exhaust fumes, black smoke rising from a hot-food stand that had overheated and caught on fire. The driver climbed up on the roof of the bus, unstrapped the luggage, and began to throw it down to the passengers below. Rawlins passed anonymously through the crowd of travelers, his eyes fixed on the ground.

By the time he arrived, Ezekiel Street was beginning its afternoon siesta. A lone mechanic, in clothes more or less identical to Rawlins's own, lowered the metal shutters of his workshop and snapped its padlock. As Rawlins passed, he shouted across to him. Rawlins didn't understand and kept walking. The man pointed at his wrist, then tapped it.

"Two-fifteen."

"Two-fifteen," the worker repeated, making the words sound like arbitrary figures in a math problem. He smiled uneasily at

Rawlins, trying to understand the strange amalgamation of his language and his appearance.

It was hotter in Tel Aviv. Lines of sweat formed on Rawlins's brow; his feet felt tight in his boots. He walked hatless and wished that he owned the mechanic's flat cap, to protect and disguise him.

He skirted a squat pillar of discarded tires and turned into the lobby of the building that housed Esta's father. He rang the upstairs bell and waited. Inside, the toilet flushed; the noise of the water muffled a yell issued in Rawlins's direction. A moment later, the door opened half an inch.

"Who are you?"

"I'm Archie Rawlins. Don't you remember me?"

"I don't know anyone by that name."

Rawlins remembered with a chill that during their last meeting he had called himself Phillips.

"I'm the British officer that you met. We discussed your daughter."

"Yes, yes. What, you think I forget so fast? Come in."

Weiss pulled open the door, and Rawlins followed him into the kitchen.

"Do something useful. Make some tea. That's right. The matches are over there. So what about my family? Do you have news?"

Rawlins busied himself with the kettle and turned his back to Weiss.

"Your daughter is in Palestine."

Rawlins heard the chair screech back. Then Weiss had him by the elbow.

"What are you saying? She's here. My Esta. You know this for sure? Where is she? Is she with her mother?"

"She's alone. Listen, she's not well. I've seen her. She's in Jerusalem. I can bring you to her."

Weiss stared at Rawlins; his mouth dropped open a little. The blood drained out of his face. He looked as if he needed to sit down, but he continued to stand, gripping Rawlins by the arm.

"What's wrong with her? How did she get here? You're sure this is my Esta? Esta Weiss."

"She's in hiding."

As before, Rawlins felt that he wanted to hurt Weiss, but this time with the truth rather than lies. He wanted to frighten him, make him see what trouble his daughter was in and know how he, Rawlins, had saved her. The dark knowledge he carried, that Weiss's wife had been murdered, failed to soften him.

He explained about the Waterlow murder. Weiss sat down at the kitchen table and in a futile gesture of despair picked up his straw hat and placed it on his head.

When he had finished his story, Rawlins expected Weiss to cry, or bury his head in his hands in despair, or perhaps rush them out of the apartment and back to the bus station. Instead he thumped his fist on the table.

"Why would she do a thing like that?"

"What do you mean?"

"Get involved with people like that. Zionists."

"Surely you don't believe . . ."

"Is someone else fighting the Nazis apart from the British? Tell me that! We should give them whatever we have. Boots, tobacco, chocolate, soap, bandages, typewriters, mattresses, shovels, horses, railroad equipment—whatever they want! To shoot the British? What's the point? To shoot a Nazi I can understand."

Rawlins listened in astonishment. Weiss was giving him a version of the "ingratitude" speech that he had heard so often in the mess.

"There's plenty of boys here enlisted in the British army. From Day One. They understand. I've got a friend, Birnbaum, his son works over in the university. He makes serums for the British army medical corps. Helping, you see. Who else do these smart

Jews like my daughter think will help them? The Arabs? *They'll* come in marching behind Rommel in a big long line. And you're telling me my daughter shot an ambassador. What a dumb fool!"

Weiss ended his tirade, tipped his hat back on his head, and placed his thick fingers on his temples. When he spoke again, his tone had softened.

"So sick, you say. How sick? And in terrible trouble. A shooting, my God. What do they do to a person who shoots?"

"They won't find her."

"What makes you so sure?"

"Will you come with me?"

Weiss lifted his eyebrows and shrugged, as if to say, "What else?"

"And listen. I didn't say she shot anyone. I told you that's what she'd been accused of. I think it's a trumped-up charge. I think Esta's being used. They need a scapegoat. They don't know who did it, so they might as well blame it on the Jews. They need something to tell them back in London, you know. A Zionist cell in Cairo is just the ticket. Never mind that all these poor people wanted to do was get into Palestine. They'll work it out, find some evidence. It's not too hard. Get London off their back. This wasn't just anybody who got shot; it was a man with a lot of connections. Esta's a person without any connections. Apart from yourself, of course. And the rest . . . the rest of your family."

Rawlins's voice trailed away, but the familiar way in which Rawlins had spoken his daughter's name alerted Weiss.

"And what's all this to you? Why do you know where she is? What happened to your uniform?"

"Are you going to come or not?"

Weiss looked around the kitchen, a look of bewilderment on his face, as if everything solid and familiar was now loose and obscure.

"My poor Esti."

He began to cry.

"And my Rina, where's my Rina?"

"Perhaps your daughter can tell you."

Weiss rose from the table and shuffled toward a cabinet. He took out a jar of birdseed and emptied it into two small metal containers. He sniffed and wiped his eyes.

"Open that cage, will you. Can you clean that out?"

Rawlins hesitated but then flicked the latch on the cage and reached in. The birds whirred and flapped; Rawlins felt the tips of their wings brush against the backs of his hands. He removed the encrusted sheet and held it out to Weiss.

"Don't give it to me. Throw it away. Now put this in. That's right. And the food. Clip it on there. And this water. Now we're ready to go."

They walked back down Ezekiel Street. At the corner, outside the café where Rawlins had first met him, Weiss stopped.

"Hold on a second. I have to use their toilet."

He headed through the door. Rawlins stood in the shade of a small acacia, recently planted and sheathed by a wire cage. When, after a few moments, Weiss failed to reappear, Rawlins followed him in.

Weiss was standing at the counter, drinking a cup of lemon tea and talking between sips. The café was empty save for the proprietor and an old man sitting at a table in the corner. As soon as he saw Rawlins, Weiss switched to English.

"Here he is. I told you. He found my daughter. She escaped! Escaped Hitler, can you believe that? She's alive!"

Rawlins took two steps toward him. Weiss held his hands up as if in surrender.

"All right, all right, I'm coming. What? I shouldn't tell my friends that my daughter's come home? And maybe my wife as well."

When they were back on the street, Rawlins dragged Weiss roughly against the tree's wire cage.

"Are you crazy? I told you she's in hiding. Do you want her to be found? Do you want her dead?"

Weiss extended his short, strong arms and pushed Rawlins back.

"Ach. You're a fool too. I should have known. There's people you can trust and people you can't. Should I trust you, for instance? You come out of nowhere. Three times I see you, you're drunk and telling me stories. How do I know where you're taking me? Maybe I should call the police on you."

"Don't you want to see your daughter?" Rawlins spoke in a restrained howl. "She's dying, for God's sake, she's dying of pneumonia. And all you can think about is your fucking glass of tea."

Weiss's hand moved fast, and his hard slap caught Rawlins full in the face.

"Don't tell me dying."

Rawlins trembled. His impulse was to hit back, but he kept his fists clenched at his sides. An open truck rounded the corner where they stood, its wheels screeching. Further down the street, a metal shutter clanged open.

They continued on, Rawlins slightly ahead, Weiss stepping in his shadow. They crossed vacant lots where half-built apartment houses struggled out of the ground; steel rods angled skyward and sideways from stark concrete blocks. Wherever possible, Rawlins hugged the shaded side of streets or looked for shelter under the lines of ficus trees that bordered the wider boulevards. Weiss panted, stopping every few minutes to remove his hat and wipe his brow with the back of his sleeve. Rawlins waited for him: he felt exhausted, but he could not really distinguish between his physical exhaustion and the dread and fear that lay somewhere inside him like a lump of granite.

When they reached the bus station, Weiss insisted that Rawlins purchase both tickets. Rawlins pulled a worn five-piaster note from his diminishing supply of money and offered it at the booth. A bus had just left, and it was a forty-minute wait until the next one.

The two men sat on a long bench, shielded from the sun by a streamlined concrete roof. Before long they were joined by a range of travelers: thickly bearded Orthodox Jews in heavy dark suits and broad hats; Arab and Jewish women, their baskets spilling over with vegetables and fruit; an attractive young woman whose long tangled curls, thin legs, and flat chest for a moment reminded Rawlins of Esta; and two young soldiers. The Tommies were the last to join the line; as they did so, Rawlins glanced quickly at their uniforms and picked out the insignia of the Tenth Armored Division. He didn't dare look at their faces.

Weiss started talking with the person sitting next to him, an old man with a white beret and a herringbone apron tied over his shirt and trousers. Rawlins didn't know what they were saying, but in midconversation Weiss suddenly turned to Rawlins.

"How long is this going to take us?"

"Shut up," Rawlins hissed at him, trying to turn his face away even as he spoke.

"What?"

"Don't speak to me."

Weiss made a little whistling sound through his lips, intended to express his exasperation.

Rawlins quickly scanned the bench. The soldiers looked like fresh recruits; their faces were youthful and not yet tanned. One held something in the flat of his palm and showed it to his friend. Rawlins thought it was probably one of the dirty postcards that could be purchased in the bazaar. They were relaxed and laughing. Why shouldn't they be? Palestine was far from the front. Until he met Esta, Rawlins, like everyone else at GHQ, had thought of the place as a leave center.

The bus pulled up. Rawlins held Weiss back until the soldiers had taken their seats. He watched them move toward the back of the bus, as he knew they would (schoolboys at heart, he was sure), then took his place further up on the same side so that only his back and not his profile would be visible to them. Weiss squeezed in next to him, removed his hat, and held it in his lap.

The bus lurched suddenly forward, and Weiss was thrown sideways onto Rawlins. He righted himself but inadvertently kept his shoulder leaning into Rawlins. Rawlins felt the coarse cloth of Weiss's shirt rub on his arm. He hated Weiss's proximity, the birdcage smell that came off his clothes, the small, damaged teeth that showed when he opened his mouth to drink or eat and which, despite Rawlins's effort to disassociate the father and daughter, reminded him of Esta.

Rawlins shifted in his seat; laying his head against the window, he felt the vibrations from the bus's journey pass through him. Weiss threw his head back, let his jaw slacken, and began to snore loudly.

They approached Jerusalem at dusk. Rawlins could see the hills around the city, rose colored, with mauve pockets where the shadows were falling. Above the massive silhouette of the Dome of the Rock, a slight silver haze surrounded two stars. Most of the passengers had left the windows next to them half open; a cool breeze filtered in, bringing, at first feebly, but louder as they approached the city, the insistent call of the muezzin.

As they passed the Damascus Gate, Weiss awoke with a start. Rawlins stared out the window. The bus had stopped in traffic, and a donkey took advantage of the jam to relieve itself. The urine spattered over a row of flat bread loaves that a baker's assistant had spread on the edge of the roadway to cool. The donkey's owner remained indifferent, munching on a pomegranate and spitting out the seeds, until the bakery man struck him from behind. He turned and fought back with a fury. The bus driver leaned out his window and shouted at the top of his voice. A policeman emerged from the crowd of merchants gathered around the gate and sauntered into the street.

Rawlins looked at the sky and realized with a shock that it

would soon be dark. If they didn't move now, he would lose sight of the landmarks he needed to guide himself back to the hut. He roused Weiss from his seat.

"Here. Let's get off now."

He half dragged Weiss to the front of the bus and twisted the handle to unlock it. The driver began to remonstrate with him, gesturing back to the seats in the bus. Rawlins continued to pump the handle, which appeared to be jammed. He looked toward the soldiers in the back row. At present they were uninterested in the commotion. Weiss said something to the driver, put his hand to his chest, and began to breathe deeply. The driver left his seat, pushed Rawlins aside, gave a quick jerk on the handle, and the doors flew open. Rawlins grabbed Weiss's arm and tugged him into the street.

They walked for more than an hour. The moon had risen, and the first pale-blue stars, unblurred and enormous, seemed to hang above their heads like clusters of grapes. At first Rawlins retraced his steps with ease, keeping far to the right of the palatial white building that housed the British high commissioner. They descended through terraces of weather-beaten olive trees and along a hedge of spiked cactus and thornbushes that led to an Arab village. As they approached the first home, Weiss stopped.

"We can't walk through here."

"Why not?"

"If you're a British, maybe you can, but me?"

"Nothing will happen to you."

A hundred yards away, a woman was preparing a meal outside on a makeshift brick stove. She looked toward the two men but quickly glanced down.

Rawlins proceeded. The houses on both sides, constructed from mud and stone, were windowless, and the front doors had been left open to let in the dying light. In the morning, on his way into Jerusalem, Rawlins had been surrounded by ragged children. They had pushed forward one of their number, a tall girl with velvety blue eyes and a red cotton sash tied around the waist of her soiled dress. She must have been about thirteen. She was drooling from the mouth. They had begged him for baksheesh, and it wasn't until he got through the village that Rawlins realized the children had been offering her to him. But now, apart from the solitary woman, the street was deserted. The harsh aspirations of the muezzin could still be heard cutting the air, and Rawlins guessed that the men of the village were at prayer.

Weiss hurried alongside Rawlins, eager to get to the end of the street. From the time that they had left the bus, he had pestered Rawlins for information, urging him to explain more fully the role that he played in Esta's life. But Rawlins had fended him off with vague replies. Now Weiss began again.

"And who's been looking after my daughter today?"

"A doctor."

"A doctor? Well, that's better. Why didn't you tell me this before?"

"I forgot."

"You like to play worry games. If we have to go much further, that doctor will have two sick people on his hands."

At the foot of a steep hill, where Rawlins thought he recognized the gap in the wild broom, he turned off up a narrow goat path, only to find himself immediately lost. Weiss's forearms and face were soon scratched and bleeding from the bushes they cut through on their aimless wandering. Rawlins caught his foot in an extirpated root and tripped. The pain in his ankle, which had subsided during his last days with Esta, intensified again.

From his prone position he saw thin tendrils of smoke rising in two or three places high on the hillside, and when he got up he headed in their direction.

A small stone hut came into view. Weiss stood still and heaved a sigh. But Rawlins veered off again into the trees. He struck a meandering path, hacking through bushes, and after ten minutes of walking he knew exactly where he was. Weiss called after him.

Rawlins ran the last fifty yards to the hut and beat on the door with his hands. It swung open to reveal an empty space. The ashes of a dead fire filled the grate. Rawlins's own blanket was spread on the floor. Esta was nowhere to be seen.

PART
THREE

PART

THREE

JERUSALEM

1 9 9 1

I searched the old man's face for certain features: a bump in his nose, a drag in his exposed eye, a shadow above his thin lips. As a child, I was always told that I looked like my mother; even strangers would sometimes stop us on the street and remark on the likeness. I had her thick curly hair (it's thinning now), small stained teeth, and dark-brown eyes. I accepted the correspondence between our faces as something unsurprising and inevitable—who else could I possibly resemble? But at university I had a girlfriend, Penny Duncan, who minored in fine arts and liked to use me as the model for her life-drawing exercises. In her charcoal sketches, I saw my features tugged, stretched, and exaggerated; another face emerged, as in a palimpsest, one that altogether evaded my mother's looks. Sitting on my narrow dormitory bed, turning the pages of Penny's sketchbook, I saw, for the first time, the possibility that I also carried someone else's features: the slight deviation in the line of my nose might have begun as a bump, the almost imperceptible slowness in my right eye could be the weak inheritance of an overstated paternal feature.

I realized that my mother, who had never uttered the quasi-affectionate admonishment that I heard so frequently in the homes of my friends—"You're just like your father"—had laid a kind of claim on me through both the superficial similarity of our appearances (did she intentionally leave my hair unbrushed?) and, with the exception of an occasional allusion to my height, her stubborn refusal to indicate those areas of my being, outer and inner, where a genetic insistence from the other side had made its mark.

But if the old man standing before me was the coauthor of my face, he gave no indication, when I announced myself, that an authentic intimacy existed between us. There was no hug, no gasp of surprise, no Hollywood embrace powerful enough to transform a grown man into a weeping boy.

He ushered me into his house with the courtesy due the friend of a friend rather than the demonstration of profound affection that I had wildly imagined might come my way.

The room we entered, though larger and more refined, resembled those that I had seen when peering through the windows in the Orthodox quarters of the city. A rectangular wooden table, with some chairs, stood in the center, and another, smaller table against the wall. An armchair, its flowery fabric discolored and frayed, sat beside a reading lamp and opposite a surprisingly large television set with a VCR mounted on top. On the wall, above a bookshelf heavy with volumes, hung two framed photographs: a family portrait of an Edwardian family gathered against a backdrop of velvet curtains, and an aerial view of the Old City of Jerusalem. The one patch of color was provided by a shoulder-high, bright-yellow glazed tile stove.

The blinds in the room were drawn, but the early-summer light was strong enough to penetrate, and narrow white shafts lay across the furniture. My host offered me tea and, without waiting for my reply, shuffled into the adjoining kitchen. I didn't quite know whether to follow him or remain where I stood, so I hovered uneasily between the two rooms, listening to the clink of cups and saucers. He returned with a kettle, set it on the yellow stove, then fumbled with a box of matches. His hands shook, but when I offered assistance he waved me away.

"Have to learn to do these things."

Finally, with the stovetop lit, we sat down at the larger of the two wooden tables.

"You must be Daniel, then."

"And you?"

"Ah, then you don't know me."

Although he must have been in his late eighties, his voice was still strong and supported an unfashionably edged upper-class English accent, the kind one hears rarely nowadays outside the most entrenched aristocratic circles, and even there it always sounds contrived and parodic. The kettle let out a series of shrill whistles, followed by a prolonged scream. I got up quickly and removed it from the heat.

"Not mentioned, then."

"I found your letter in my mother's correspondence. I'm afraid I couldn't distinguish the signature; only the address."

"Her correspondence?" He sighed. "She's gone, then. It's almost everyone now. Sad. I hadn't heard from her in a while. So, naturally, at our age, you begin to wonder. She was younger than me, of course, but even so, past seventy, you wonder."

"I brought her here. She's buried in Jerusalem."

"Here?" He circled the cup of tea with his hands, as if its warmth might still their trembling. "Appropriate, really. Her choice or yours?"

"Hers."

"Yes, of course; must have been."

The sun's rays darted between us on the table, like white scepters.

"And you are?" I murmured.

"Oh, I'm terribly sorry. Still haven't introduced myself. I'm Gerald Mendoza."

The name meant nothing to me.

"And you knew my mother well?"

"Oh, old friends. Although we never actually spent much time together. Mainly an epistolary relationship. People don't have those anymore, do they?"

"And my father?"

I felt my heart pounding inside me.

"Your father?"

Mendoza turned his gaze around the room and seemed to become distracted by the movement of light on the frames of the old photographs.

"Didn't know him. Londoner, wasn't he? Someone your mother met in London at the end of the war. Got rid of him rather quickly, as I remember. We were out of touch, you know, for a number of years. I was, well, out of touch with everyone. Then a mutual acquaintance hooked us up again. What was he like?"

"I also didn't know him."

"Yes, as I thought. A bad egg. Your mother never mentioned him much. You look like her, though."

"I was born in 1942. February 1942."

Mendoza seemed to take in this information very slowly, as if, before it could drip, glacially, into his consciousness, it had to permeate a stratified rock of memory where nothing had shifted for decades.

His body quivered, and his head twitched to one side, almost as if he were avoiding a blow.

In the deep stretch of time, almost half a century, that I had imagined my father, and despite the proximity of my mother, who carried his memory like the flickering shadow of a bird as soon pointed to as gone, I had never come closer than at this mo-

ment to sensing his palpability. I was reminded of those best moments in my work, when, editing some director's vagrant video, I
would manage, after a long struggle, to distill ten hours of film to
a punchy, intense fifteen minutes. The satisfaction that I felt at
such times paralleled the emotional impact upon me of Mendoza's reaction. If, for a documentary covering my lifelong search
for my father, I could have chosen one image to represent my
hopes and illusions, it would have been this: Mendoza trembling
before his apprehension of the significance of my birthday. I did
not believe that the tremor of Mendoza's hands, and the small
spasms that jerked his head, signaled possession—the arrival of
my father's spirit, whether diabolical or benign—but rather I felt
his physical reaction, to what I sensed were painful memories,
draw me powerfully into the orbit of their as yet undescribed
catalyst.

And what happened when I found myself in this magnetic
place? Oddly, the last question that I would have expected to pop
into my head did so with an insistent hammering: Why do you
care so much? In the last weeks, it had occasionally occurred to
me in the eruptive flare of this ancient city that my quest was misguided, the adventure of a dull narcissist (this was something my
former wife had also accused me of), for whom history and politics were only a fading backdrop to the exaggerated drama of
personal life. I was "American," my wife said, in my psychologi-
cal intensity. With her airline exec she talked about *everything*—
the outer world, politics, real events—and she had been released
from our endless and tedious discussions of motive and blame
and their relative styles.

Her words came back to me when I walked, with the other
tourists—mostly Christian pilgrims from Germany and Scandi-
navia—through the crowded alleyways of the Old City and, with
them, saw the spray-painted graffiti curling in Arabic characters
over pink stone walls. The content of the messages was unavailable to me, and I reacted to the green-red scrawl as a kind of ab-

stract art, one that came to represent a discrete expression of my failure to respond to anything but the sensual or decorative aspects of the place.

In talking to Mendoza, I realized with a shock that ever since my arrival, the struggle of two peoples for the same small area of land had almost entirely passed me by. I was lost in the way the half-light refracted in the small square colored panes of the glassed-in porches of Nahla'ot, in the stink of goat shit outside the city walls, in the rosemary, in the melon rinds rotting in the gutters, in the entire sensual/sexual fiasco of the place: lost, too, to the tug of blood inside my veins, to the people whose creative force was responsible for my own tiny parcel of existence. I felt ashamed.

But on the other hand, wasn't it precisely because my own parents had been the playthings of history that I found myself lost in the throes of my obsession? I hated history, for uprooting my mother, destroying her family and her childhood. But I was also grateful to it for flinging her, however destitute, in the path of my progenitor. I was a product of upheaval, confusion, and conflict. How could I entirely ignore or disdain the great and terrible swings in the smooth motions of people's lives if their end result was to fling strangers together from odd corners of the globe and hold them in an act of love? This was, I knew, a dreadful, ignorant thought. But I sensed then, I believe, that what this old man knew could tell me not only who my father was but what in the world had made him what he was. And that if I did not understand the latter, the former would be the empty gift of a name, an identity bracelet hung loosely on a skeleton's wrist.

"Nineteen forty-two, nineteen forty-two." Mendoza repeated the date like a mantra. "February, you say." He paused and then straightened in his chair. "Would you mind very much," he finally asked, "bringing me to your mother's grave? I'd like to pay my respects. And perhaps we can talk better there. I need to collect my thoughts."

He held my arm and we walked out to the street, where a dusty green Subaru was parked in the shade of a cypress tree.

"Haven't driven since my eye operation. And a good thing too, probably. Have you seen the way they drive here?"

He pulled a set of keys from his pocket and handed them to me.

I guided the car, following Mendoza's directions, on the drive to the cemetery. The main streets were heavy with traffic. We jolted from light to light, the cars behind us honking as soon as the green flashed. Mendoza remained oblivious to the noise and stared concentratedly through the open passenger window.

"Haven't been getting out much," he said, more to himself than to me.

We pulled onto the side street that led to the cemetery and had to swerve to avoid crashing into an army jeep that screeched to a halt in front of us. Two soldiers jumped out and sprinted over to an Arab taxi that was parked half up on the curb. They pulled out the occupants at gunpoint, pushed them against a nearby wall, and began to search them. Mendoza sighed and shook his head despairingly.

"Terrible situation," he said. "Don't like to see this."

I maneuvered around the jeep and parked next to a set of black wrought-iron gates. We got out and walked slowly past neat, well-tended rows of pink and yellow flowers. On our narrow path through the graves, he seemed to relax. He stopped to breathe deeply and point out the pomegranate and fig trees. He revealed some pride, as if he were showing me his own garden, and it seemed to me then, as we approached the marker of my mother's grave, a hopeful sign, as if he had reached an accommodation with death that was, as yet, beyond my imagining.

At first, as we stood at my mother's graveside, Mendoza offered polite expressions of regret for her passing. Then he added a few instructional comments on the history of the cemetery and brief allusions to his life in Jerusalem since the establishment of the state—I was surprised to learn he was a rabbi.

He plucked a spray of lavender from a nearby bush and twisted it nervously, rubbing the ends between his thumb and forefinger before pressing them to his nose. Above us a flock of starlings wheeled and landed in unison on the high branches of a dust-laden carob tree. Mendoza watched the birds descend and settle.

"Tell me about my father."

"Yes," Mendoza replied. "I believe that time has come."

TEL AVIV/ JERUSALEM

1 9 4 1

1

At the end of every dream there was a room with white walls that seemed to rise like steep cliffs toward the vast blue clarity of the sky. Sometimes the room was empty, as if no one had been or ever would be there. This morning, two buzzards circled, their wings extended and still, magnetized to one another. She was in awe of their grace and their power to hover without falling. She watched them from the safety of the tree. The thing was to fly up and out, but this could happen only when her harsh, discordant bird voice turned to birdsong, and then she would leave the branch, swooping in great hoops, buoyed by invisible currents.

A noise of aircraft split the blue, and Esta tumbled awake, leaning half out of the bed, the ceiling back in place on the coffee-colored walls, the oversize men's pajamas that they had given her damp under the arms and at the crotch.

She reached for the glass of water on the floor beside her and took quick swallows. She was lying on a narrow trestle with bright crossed metal supports and small rubbery wheels. A narrow window was half open. She thought she could smell the sea. A blue stool stood at the end of the bed, and someone had set a round vase stacked with wildflowers on the seat.

The feeling of illness was still there, frozen inside her body, but something was different. She was breathing more easily. She sucked in air and found, for the first time in days, that she could fill her lungs and exhale without coughing or spitting. There was a small mirror on the far wall. She got out of bed, walked over, and stood before it: her hair was terribly tangled and seemed to show more gray than she remembered, but her face had some color.

When they came to get her from the hut she hadn't wanted to leave, but in the end she'd had no will to resist. The doctor had carried her in his arms, swaddled in blankets, like a sleeping child. There had been a blast of chill air, a delirious swirl of treetops, and then the long, bumpy ride. She fell in and out of sleep, her head resting in his lap. He held her the way she used to cradle Falik in the barge.

She heard the noise of a motorcycle grow loud and then cut sharply somewhere outside. Moments later, the door pushed open and Marks entered the room. She turned, and he looked at her with surprise.

"I'm better."

"I see. But let's check, shall we."

He motioned for her to return to the bed. Sitting on the edge of the mattress, he unclipped his stethoscope from around his neck.

"Would you mind . . . ?"

He gestured to the buttons on her pajama jacket. She undid them, feeling, for the first time since her illness had begun, awkward and disconcerted, but at the same time realizing with a kind of joy that her embarrassment could only mean that she was healing.

Marks moved the endpiece over her chest and listened carefully.

"Yes, a significant improvement. Not yet perfect, but much better."

"You thought I was going to die."

"At one point I did, yes."

"I thought so too."

There was silence while he removed the instrument and re-placed it in its case. He seemed nervous. Now that she was more of a person and less a patient, the fundamental awkwardness of adult human relationships had reasserted itself.

"Where's Archie?"

"Rawlins? We don't know, I'm afraid."

"He was supposed to come back—" She was going to add: "with my father," but she stopped herself. She wasn't sure why she was reluctant to mention him. Perhaps it was because his palpable existence, the possibility of meeting up with him, and all the imaginable consequences of that meeting, still seemed so remote. It was tempting fate to outline his part in her plans.

A suspicious look passed over the doctor's face.

"Where was Rawlins when we arrived? I thought I told him to stay with you."

"We ran out of fuel for the fire. He said there was an Arab village nearby. He went to try and fetch some wood."

"The fool."

The color rose on her pallid cheeks. Marks saw that he had aggrieved her. He softened his tone.

"He'll show up."

"But the soldiers were going to the hut. You told me I had to leave. Didn't you say they were catching up with me? You said yesterday that they knew about the hiding place. What if Archie arrived at the wrong time?"

"You need to rest."

"How can I rest?"

"I'll make inquiries. I'll come back."

"I want to get up now. I want to go back. I have to find Archie."

"You can't. You simply can't."

"Where are we?"

"Givat Rambam. It's a village not far from Tel Aviv. This is a vegetable farm. Do you want to see?"

She rose from the bed, a little shakily this time. Marks held her by the arm and brought her over to the window. Esta looked out over small, neatly tilled fields; close by, a tractor bounded along the lanes, and in its dusty wake a line of workers bent and picked potatoes, then flung them into a wooden bin. Fifty yards from the window, outside a corrugated lean-to, a truck labeled "Admoni Potash Company" was parked.

"You should be safe here. We couldn't bring you before. There was someone else in the room."

He tried to lead her back to the bed, but she pushed his arm away and continued to stare out the window at the blue haze and the wasps hanging in the air.

"You should lie down."

Two wasps caught in a stupor of sun were crawling up the pane, their bellies exposed to her. Esta tapped on the window, and they started into flight.

She felt hopelessly alone. It had been like this ever since the incidents in the Prater. Only once, with Archie, one night during their first week together in Cairo, had she felt that someone was truly with her. She had carried him, by the sheer force and reck-lessness of her lovemaking, to that place on the edge of the bough, where fear ended and the terrible understanding began. But then she had seen, by the look on his face, when he pulled out of her, that she had been mistaken, because Archie was scared and confused. She had bitten him hard in the shoulder; her toothmarks were visible where she had broken through the skin, and a thin skein of blood ran down his arm.

Marks stood quietly beside her.

"Are you afraid? Don't be. I told you they won't find you here."

"I'm not afraid."

"You should get back to bed."

"I've already spent too much time there. I need this window."

He turned toward the door.

"I'll come back tonight. You're on the mend!"

"What about Archie?"

Marks hesitated a moment by the door.

"I'll do what I can."

Esta removed the vase from the blue stool, placed it on the floor, then dragged the stool over to the window.

"Who brought these flowers here?"

Marks blushed. "I did."

"That was kind of you."

He nodded and quickly left the room.

When he had gone she sat for a long time, her eyes fixed on the ragged line of farmworkers following the tractor. They worked fast and didn't stop to drink until the tractor halted and the driver got down. Something in the driver's build, his barrel chest and heavy approach, made her visualize her father. She imagined him coming across the field to greet her, squat, impatient, stopping to wipe his brow. He slid in the ruts, fell and cursed, then stumbled forward, his trousers stained clod brown, the hat that he always wore planted askew on his large, round head. When he arrived, panting, and stood before her on the other side of the window, she didn't know what to say. She wanted to run outside and embrace him, but something held her back: her anger, the accusations on the tip of her tongue that she didn't want to release. "My mother's dead," she mouthed at the window. "Go away."

The tractor started up again, drawing Esta out of her reverie. The workers remained stretched out in a rough circle, passing a container of water from mouth to mouth. The driver yelled something at them, and wearily they roused themselves.

Esta rose and turned away from the window. She replaced the bowl of flowers, in the direct path of the light. The last time she had seen her father, she was fourteen. They were standing on a station platform. Her father was hugging her. She was already nearly as tall as he. All the way to the train he had been complaining about his back, and in the end it had been her mother who carried his bags the last half mile or so. But now he lifted her, seemingly without effort, and swung her around the way he used to do when she was a small girl. When she landed she remembered feeling that she had arrived on the other side of an invisible threshold, that he was already in America, and that as soon as her feet touched the grimy platform she and her mother were back in the family kitchen, frozen in a strange, permanent quiet. And then, within half an hour of his final, steam-shrouded, storybook wave, they *were* back, and she found herself recalling the sharp tap of his soup spoon on the bottom of the bowl with the Chinese pattern, which meant that he wanted more, or the rasp of his paring knife as he removed the skin of an apple in one long spiral.

In those first weeks, more than anything else about him, Esta missed her father's *physical* presence: his bulk, the way he took up space at the dinner table. When he left, there seemed to be an empty area in the room, one that neither the personality of her self-effacing mother nor the awkward endowments of her own character could fill.

He wrote: brief notes lacking in description, mainly reports on his financial situation, and once actually *requesting* money from Uncle Leopold. He was doing better or worse (usually worse), he had fought with his landlord, he lived in a cold-water apartment, the Americans were ruthless cheaters and thieves, even the Jews, he should never have left Vienna. He mentioned Esta only in a quick phrase or two at the end of each letter. Her mother explained that he didn't say more because it was too painful for him to dwell on her absence from his life. Because, as Esta knew, he loved her more than anybody in the world.

Through all his endless self-pity (which at the time she never recognized), through the litany of broken promises that *next* month he would be sending for them, Esta remained committed in her love for him, writing, at least twice a week, long descriptions of her school and social life, and dreaming of America. Her mother, meanwhile, grew increasingly anxious and bitter. Every shopkeeper was slighting her: pickles from the bottom of the barrel, day-old bread, rotten fruit; even her friends could not be trusted, they talked about her behind her back. It was *him*, of course, who was letting her down. But her mother would never admit it. And in a horrible way it was almost a *relief* when the persecutions began, because her mother could direct her invective elsewhere and the vicious monologues that accompanied every meal finally found an appropriate target.

She went and lay down on the bed. A brilliant summer light permeated the room; her head felt heavy, as if it could not sustain the weight of her memories. The light sliced through the glass bowl and across her body in a pattern of false execution, sharp yellow nicks severing both her and the flower heads at their slender necks.

Toward evening Marks returned as he had promised. She sat up in bed and ate with relish the meal that he had brought her.

"Appetite's returned, then."

"Did you find him?"

"He's not at the hut."

"Why didn't you leave a message to tell him where I was."

"That would have been foolish. Suppose someone else had got to it first."

Esta pushed the tray away from her.

"Listen," Marks said. "I'm going to tell you something that I don't think you'll want to hear. We're not sure about him."

"I am."

"He's a British officer."

"So, I believe, are some Zionists."

"Yes, but they're Jews."

"He's risked everything for me."

"Maybe."

"You don't know him at all."

"No, but I know his type. I grew up in England."

"And what did you learn there about Archie's 'type'?"

"They hate us, and they fear us."

"Isn't that the Nazis?"

"That's different. At least the Nazis are recognizable. They're out in the open."

"You don't know what you're saying."

"No, Esta, I do. In England there's a knife behind the smile."

It was the first time that Marks had called her by her name, and it rocked her a little.

"Not with Archie. He's too sad to smile."

The corners of the room had sunk into darkness. The evening breeze puffed lightly at the diaphanous curtain that she had stretched over the window before falling asleep. She heard cicadas begin the nightly battering of their wings. Marks leaned forward in the brown-violet light and kissed her gently on the lips.

"You're going to be fine now," he murmured.

2

Weiss stood behind Rawlins at the door, breathing rapidly, his hat tipped back on his head.

"No one here. We come all this way, and no one here. I should have known better than to trust you. You sure this is the place?"

Rawlins peered through the darkness. The visitors, whoever they were, had taken everything except a single blanket. He got down on his knees and crawled around the floor, looking for a note, something dropped or left behind, anything that might give him a clue as to where she was or who had taken her. Near where the bed had been he sniffed like a dog, but the chill in the room had dissipated the odor of her sickness.

"What are you doing? You tell me you're bringing me to my daughter, we travel for hours, you take me to an empty hut."

"She was here."

"Where? I don't see her."

Rawlins stood and absentmindedly slid the toe of his boot through the ashes in the fireplace.

"A doctor was supposed to come. He probably took her to a hospital."

"She wouldn't have told them to wait a little? Her father's coming, right; she hasn't seen him in eight years. According to you, she sends you to fetch me. So she's not going to wait? What are you, a crazy person? Did you bring me here to stick a knife in me? Your daughter's alive, your daughter's sick, your daughter's in Jerusalem, your daughter's nowhere to be seen!"

He slumped suddenly against the wall, clutching his chest, then sat down heavily, his short, sturdy legs splayed in front of him.

"I can't breathe in here."

Rawlins stepped back out of the hut. He had already run through all the possibilities in his mind. Most likely the doctor *had* taken her. Rawlins didn't trust Marks, but he saw that he'd wanted to save her; that, at least, had been clear. There was always the chance that the army had searched them out. If so, she was already on the way back to Cairo or in detention somewhere. But he doubted that she had been captured. He saw how the Jews had handled things on the kibbutz. They knew what they were doing, and for reasons that he didn't want to think about, she was important to them.

He rummaged in the pockets of his trousers, as if he might come up with a card printed with her name and new address. Far down the hillside he heard a screech of brakes, followed quickly by the sound of car doors slamming; Rawlins froze, but then the shouts of two men arguing in Hebrew wafted up on the light breeze, and he relaxed.

Rawlins shivered a little. He felt light-headed, confused by her absence. Was it possible that he was relieved? Without her, he felt, his old self began to reassert itself, but the feeling was strangely somatic, as if aspects of his personality—his immaturity, hopefulness, or diffidence—that were eclipsed when she was around were now embodied in a set of nervous tics: the way he pushed his hair back from his forehead, or tugged at his earlobe, or rubbed under his left eye.

Once before, in the first days of his posting to Egypt, he had experienced a similar sensation. Two drivers had been assigned to escort a group of the new officers out to familiarize them with desert terrain. They traveled fast, in jeeps that just broke the crusty surface of the sand. The shells of white desert snails crunched under the tires. Then, suddenly, the floor of the desert broke into steep-sided valleys and little plateaus studded with gravel and pink rock. They stopped and got out. Rawlins wandered a couple of hundred yards or so away from the group, climbed a dune, and found himself entirely alone. When he looked back at the desert behind him, it seemed to have turned ice blue, as though the sky had spilled over the horizon and across the sand. He felt, for a moment, utterly effaced, erased by the brilliant, sun-blasted spectacle. He heard the other officers calling his name, urging him to get back to the jeep, but he remained rooted to the spot, as if he had lost the ability to identify himself as "Rawlins." He was in a state of near panic, when McIntyre, one of the young lieutenants, appeared at the foot of the dune and yelled up to him. The sight of the other man set him in motion, but it wasn't until he climbed in next to the driver that "Rawlins" returned.

That day, upon his return to Cairo, he crossed Bulaq Bridge and visited, for the first and only time, the Church of England cathedral on the banks of the Nile. He entered the modern, yellow-brick building with only the vaguest sense of what had drawn him there. A service was in progress, and he knelt in a pew alongside a pair of army nurses. The vicar's voice was high and rather nasal, but had a comforting familiarity in the way that it bounced off the cathedral walls and surrounded him. And suddenly Rawlins recognized what he was there for. In England he had always felt that he knew who he was, his slot had been determined before birth, all he had to do was arrive to fill it. The service—the prayers and hymn singing, even the slow torpor of the sermon—gave him back a little of this old certainty, and by the time he returned to his barracks he had more or less forgotten about the moment in the desert.

But then Esta had appeared in his office and issued another, even stronger, challenge to his identity, one that he couldn't divert with a quick visit to church.

"Well?" Weiss called through the door.

Rawlins went back into the hut. Weiss had picked up the gray blanket and wrapped it around himself. Rawlins left the door open, and Weiss affected an exaggerated shudder.

"You might as well go back," Rawlins said.

"Back? You mean you don't want me to spend the night here? You can unfreeze me in the morning."

"We won't find her now. But she will find you."

"Good. I'll go home and wait for the doorbell to ring. Maybe one of your fellow officers will come and take me on another hike."

"You'd better leave, before it gets too late."

"And another thing. You told me your name was Phillips. *Captain* Phillips, wasn't it? You think I don't remember these things? Now all of a sudden you're Rawlins. What's going on here? You're her boyfriend, aren't you?"

The word "boyfriend" seemed so unsuitable that Rawlins almost laughed. It conjured up a world he had hardly known before it had disappeared, a teenage world of dancing, flirting, and teasing, heart flutters and disappointments. He hadn't even thought of himself as Claire's "boyfriend."

"I'm Esta's lover."

Weiss screwed up his face in disgust and spat on the ground.

"She's got a 'lover,' " he said derisively, more to himself than to Rawlins. "Where'd she find you?"

"We met in Cairo."

"All lies. Everything you told me."

"Not all."

"Where's Rina?"

Rawlins looked away.

"My wife. Where is she? Maybe she's got a lover too?"

"She's dead. The Germans killed her in Vienna. Your daughter escaped."

As soon as he spoke, Rawlins was appalled that he had done so. He had no right.

Weiss pulled his knees up to his chest, shut his eyes, and dipped his head; he raised the blanket up and covered himself with it. He looked like a small boy who tries to hide because he has done something wrong, but at the same time is afraid to leave the room that his parents are in.

"I'm sorry."

Weiss let out what sounded like a string of cries but were actually deep, long, openmouthed intakes of breath.

The moon threw a meager light through the smoke-yellowed panes of the hut's square window. Rawlins squatted beside the enshrouded figure. Weiss rocked back and forth. Twice, he banged the back of his head hard on the stone wall behind him. Rawlins grabbed him by the shoulders and tried to hold him steady. He could feel Weiss's whole body tremble.

"My fault. All my fault."

"You didn't kill her."

"Then who?"

He began to sob. Rawlins pulled away but then, with a great effort, forced himself back to Weiss's side. Weiss stretched his hand out from beneath the blanket, and to his own astonishment Rawlins grabbed it and held on to it. He felt Weiss's warm, plump flesh and the fine hair on the back of his hand.

"I'm an old man," Weiss said. "I need help."

He was still shaking. Rawlins stretched out his leg and kicked the door closed.

They sat in darkness. After a few moments, Rawlins let go of Weiss's hand and leaned back against the wall. Weiss was still crying, but the sobs had diminished to whimpers.

Rawlins closed his eyes. He was coming from a cinema in Piccadilly Circus into the inky blackout of the street. Everyone carried pocket torches, and the shadowy unlit world was broken by fragile beams extending a pale imitation of the crisscrossing searchlights above. In parts of the Haymarket it was so dark he had to grope his way down. The taxis that passed were all fitted with Hartley lights and illuminated only as much of the street as was needed to drive by. He stopped in a shop doorway for a smoke. A woman appeared from nowhere and slipped her arm through his. When she spoke he saw that she was missing her upper teeth. But that wasn't why he remembered her now. It was because of what she'd said. As he'd detached himself from her grip and started down the street, she had shouted after him: "Don't worry, dearie, I won't jew you. I'll give you yer money's worth."

He opened his eyes. Weiss had stopped crying and was sitting up straight, staring into the gloom. Rawlins felt that he should say or do something to alleviate the man's grief. But all that came to mind was to make a Weiss a cup of tea, and the empty room annulled the possibility. He thought of Mendoza, of the formulas that men like him must learn to console the bereaved. There must be prayers, Jewish prayers, that Weiss was supposed to be saying. Mendoza had given him that book. He still had it with him; perhaps he should give it to Weiss. Although in this light he wouldn't be able to read a word.

Rawlins stood up.

"We have to go."

He tugged at Weiss's arm. Weiss resisted at first but then got slowly to his feet.

"What are you doing?"

"I'll go with you back to the bus station."

"It's too late for a bus. I'll stay here."

"You can't. There's no fire, no food."

"Not *here*. In Jerusalem. I've got a friend. You think I haven't got friends? I know people. I'm not so bad I don't have friends. Just walk me through that Arab place."

Halfway down the hill, Weiss stopped to catch his breath. He leaned against the trunk of a pine tree and with his free arm held on to Rawlins.

"Esta told you about her mother. Is that right?"

"Yes."

"Was she there?"

"I don't know."

"They shot her. Did they shoot her?"

"I'm sorry, I don't know."

"She'll come to me."

Rawlins didn't respond.

"You said she'll come to me, find me. But not tonight. Tonight I'll stay here. When she finds me I'll explain. I tried, you know. You think I didn't try? It's not so easy to get someone from one

country into another. They couldn't have come here. Not now.
You know what it takes to get around the rules? A thousand
pounds in a British bank, per person, then maybe they give you
a visa."

"I'm sure you did your best," Rawlins replied. The words
came out muffled and dry.

Weiss continued mumbling to himself, formulating excuses,
explaining his actions, and intermittently asking his dead wife for
forgiveness. He had grown indifferent to Rawlins's presence.

They passed through the Arab village and continued a mile or
so on the road toward Jerusalem. When the Dome of the Rock
came into view, silhouetted against the star-loaded sky, Weiss told
Rawlins that he wanted to go on alone.

"I'll walk with you."

"I don't need you."

"Do you know where you're going?"

"I told you, a friend. You want to know if it's a woman friend?
All right, it's a woman friend. I'm not ashamed. She's a friend.
Who else should I turn to at a time like this?"

"I don't care who you go to."

"There you are. You don't care. So I should stay with you?"

Rawlins waited until Weiss's stooped, thickset figure had disappeared around a corner, then he turned back toward the Arab
village.

He walked quickly past the first houses. He was looking for the
place that the children had burst out of in the morning. The unpaved street was lit by a murky orange light that emanated from
small braziers and crept through narrow slits left between the
doors of the mud-and-stone huts and their windowless walls.

Rawlins found the house he was looking for, walked up, and
knocked on the door. There was a sound of shuffling feet, a
nervous cough, and then a teenage boy appeared. He looked
apprehensively at Rawlins but then broke into a smile. He

pulled the door open so that Rawlins was standing in the full glow of the brazier. Dust and wisps of thin smoke rose and coiled around him.

Rawlins looked past the boy and into the room. A woman, perhaps his mother, sat cross-legged, holding a pot by its blackened handle and stirring it over the heat. Beyond her, in the dimmest corner of the room, sat the retarded girl whom Rawlins had seen in the morning. She was wearing the same threadbare dress, but the sash had been removed. The boy said something to her, and she giggled. He held out his hand to Rawlins.

"Baksheesh."

"No. Only to sleep."

The boy stared quizzically at Rawlins. Rawlins placed his palms together, tilted his hands, and leaned his head to the side. The childish gesture indicating sleep made the boy break into a bigger smile. His palm remained outstretched.

Rawlins felt in his pocket and produced a handful of coins. He pressed them into the boy's hand, took two steps forward, and lay down with his face close to the coals. The girl pushed herself forward across the floor and began to play with his hair.

"No," Rawlins said, pushing her hand away. "Only sleep."

The older woman finished stirring the pot and poured coffee into three small cups. She spoke for the first time, to the boy. He picked up a thin blanket and laid it on top of Rawlins.

3

If she was well, then she should be able to leave. She had been telling this to Lewis every day for the last week. Almost a month had passed since her arrival at the farm. The pneumonia and its lingering aftereffects had almost disappeared entirely. But the doctor kept coming. He didn't examine her anymore; he simply sat in one of the room's two upright chairs and talked. Sometimes he came late and when night fell the two of them walked through the fields, keeping away from the main roads and the flare of headlights. Whenever she asked about Archie, Lewis always had the same reply: "No news."

When they walked, he slipped his arm possessively through hers. He talked to her about everything that was on his mind: the latest developments in the war; the future of Zionism (despite the precariousness of the current situation, he was optimistic); his own future; the medical school he had attended in London; the various slights and rebuffs that he had experienced as a Jew in England. He asked her very few questions, and pleased by this, she offered almost no information. Occasionally, he stopped, and on the pretext of pointing out something arresting in the landscape—the monumental silhouette of an upturned plow left abandoned in a field, or the way the moonlight glazed the ancient tell behind the farm—he grabbed her hand. He bent his face toward her, and a nervous tremble entered his voice beneath the rush of words.

Esta waited for the moment when she would have to resist him, but so far it hadn't come. She was too lonely now to tell him, "You're wasting your time," and she was grateful to him for nursing her back to health. In any case, in the foreground of her mind there was Archie, his face when he had left, distorted by the revisions of her delirium into some strange creature with huge red eyes and hard yellow spikes of stubble on its face. The creature scuttled around the room, trying desperately to light the fire, and her whole body and heart went out to it. In the back of her mind was something else: her secret knowledge that the prototype of a man was not a caring lover, or a protective father, but a murderer. And this could not be spoken.

Esta stared out the window; an old horse with ulcerated skin was tethered nearby, on a long, frayed rope; beyond him the farmhands were at work. The potato crop was in, and the workers had moved into the artichoke field. The sun blazed down, but

they worked with relentless energy, the men stripped to the waist
and the women in khaki shirts and shorts. Esta knew their rou-
tine, the time of their breaks, the groups they liked to form into.
At the end of the day, she watched them file down to the shower
room, less than fifty yards from her room. The men and women
went in together, casting their work clothes in a grimy pile outside the door. She heard their laughter and joking, and watched
in admiration as, unembarrassed, they emerged naked from the
shower and stood in the hot late-afternoon sun, pulling clean
shirts and shorts over their glistening bodies. This was the ease
and openness that Lewis had bragged to her about: the new society, equal and harmonious, without corruption or inhibition.

Lewis brought her books to read, but she couldn't concentrate,
except on one, *The Birds of Palestine*, by Azaria Laon. She went
slowly through the pages. She was interested in everything: the
colors of the birds, their wingspans and natural habitats. She tried
observing through the window of her room, waking early to
catch the dawn chorus and the first darts of color across the
brightening sky. She asked Lewis to bring her a pair of binocu-
lars, and after a few days he turned up with a weighty set of British field glasses, "appropriated from the enemy our friend."

At first Lewis was excited by her preoccupation, but he was
visibly disappointed when she told him that she didn't make notes
on her sightings. He seemed to find it disturbing that she wanted
only to watch, as if there were something perverse in scrutinizing
nature without cataloguing it.

She couldn't tell him, because she couldn't tell herself, that it
was all a preparation for sleep and the dreams she had to face.
Somehow, she knew, her daytime observations would help her
during the night. When the time came to escape, and the time always came, she would rise from the bough, imitating the quick,
flashy beats of the hoopoe or the languid strokes of the large
birds of prey.

Lewis came in through the door. He was smiling but seemed

edgy. His face was red, and his wavy black hair glistened with sweat. He looked as if he had been running.

"What is it?"

"Sit down."

She ignored him and continued to stand by the window.

"I have to tell you something."

He offered her a Turkish cigarette, and when she declined he lit one himself. He threw a copy of the *Palestine Post* onto the bed. Esta glanced at the photograph on the first page: a column of tanks crossing an expanse of arid black lava. She read the head-line: "Wilson Crosses into Syria." It meant nothing to her.

"About Archie?"

"Yes."

She picked up a hairbrush and began to pull it through her hair, tugging at the knots and wincing as she did so.

"We think he's the one who gave you up. They've been hold-ing Hafner all this time in Kasr el Nil."

Esta closed her eyes and ran her finger along the thick, almost unbroken black line of her eyebrows.

"How do you know this?"

"How do we know anything? We have reliable sources."

"Where is Archie now?"

"Nobody knows. He did his dirty job, and it was all a mess-up anyway, and now they've sent him off somewhere else."

"It's ridiculous. He could have had me arrested a hundred times—even at the border crossing."

"We think he was planted to try to get information about us as well."

"Well, why didn't he hand me over in the hut?"

"How do you know he didn't try to, for God's sake? Suppose we hadn't come early that day? He left you there, didn't he? He knew we were coming. How do you know he ever went anywhere near any damn village. Maybe he left to tell the others where you were."

"You told me that they already knew that. And anyway, I forced him to leave; he didn't want to. I was cold."

Marks paused. "That's as may be. But it's true about Cairo."

"I don't believe you."

"What?" Marks looked utterly bewildered. "I'm telling you we think he betrayed you."

"No, Lewis, he saved me."

"And what about Hafner? They're probably going to shoot him. And it could have been you. It could easily have been you. It still could be."

Esta turned from him and stared out the window. The sun had set, leaving a faint red line on the horizon and a few crimson-stained clouds strung along it.

"Falik told me he was being watched. He had known that for weeks. Ever since he first went to talk to them. Somebody there hated him. It has nothing to do with Archie."

"You don't want to believe it." His voice was developing a hysterical pitch.

Was it possible? On their last night in Cairo he had questioned her about the meeting place. But what she remembered most was his tenderness, how clear he had been in his lovemaking. He had drawn her in, so that for the first time she felt as if she was not simply trying to wipe out the past through the wild exertions of her body but the act was an actual expression of love. Marks was wrong, he had to be, otherwise the whole world was a grotesque lie.

"Archie loves me. He's not my enemy."

Marks took a step toward her. At first she thought that he was going to hit her, but instead he pulled her roughly to him and tried to kiss her. She turned her face to the side. Suddenly he pushed her onto the bed and pressed himself on top of her. She fought him, pushing at his shoulders and squirming beneath him.

"No, you can't do this."

He reached down and tried to unbutton his fly, his fingers working maladroitly while she flailed at him with her free arm.

"He's a bloody murderer."

He gave up with his shorts and held her pinned to the mattress. Esta stiffened her body. He undid her blouse, but when he had revealed her breasts and lowered his face to kiss her nipples, an awkward embarrassment overcame him and he loosened his grip.

"I'm sorry," he said.

Esta lay on the narrow bed. She pushed her skirt down and buttoned her shirt. Marks had rolled off her. He sat on the edge of the bed, with his back to her and his head bowed.

"I wanted . . . well, you're Jewish, for God's sake."

"Yes."

"Well, doesn't that mean anything to you?"

Esta looked at him with revulsion.

"You know what it's like to feel like a foreigner in your own bloody country, don't you?"

"Until the war started I didn't feel like that."

"Well, I damn well did. My whole bloody life. People like your Mr. Rawlins, some snide remark behind your back: three Jews committed suicide by jumping off their wallets; not in this club, I'm afraid, not in this school, or this college. Half the interviews I went to I was out of the door as soon as I told them my name."

"I don't understand."

"I was Markowitz. That was my family name. I had to change it, *had to*, otherwise, you know, the opportunities close down. Do you think if I'd gone into a hospital with my qualifications and my name had been Smith, or Rawlins, they'd have passed me over? I don't think so."

Esta rose from the bed and walked toward the door.

"You think this is all petty, don't you? All right, it doesn't compare to your suffering, of course it doesn't."

Marks stood up and barred her way. He was trembling slightly. Then he came at her again, more violently this time, shoving her against the wall. He held one hand over her mouth and tried to push the other between her thighs.

"I'm sorry," he murmured again, "I'm sorry," but he didn't stop trying to force her. She used all her strength to resist him. He took his hand from her mouth and tore at her shirt. She tried to scream, but her voice froze in her throat. She scratched at his back and kicked him in the leg. As they struggled, the bowl of flowers on the stool fell to the ground and the glass shattered. Marks held her with one arm and this time managed to undo his buttons. She felt him rubbing against her, and then, before he could enter her, it was all over. She felt the spurt of his come on her skirt. He stood back, panting, still repeating his apology. He started to cry.

"You won't see me again, will you? Not now."

Esta didn't respond. After a few moments, Marks buttoned his fly and left the room.

She waited until she heard the sound of his motorcycle fade into the distance, then she gathered up her few belongings and stuffed them into her bag.

She took a serpentine path between the wrinkled furrows of a vacant field and the columns of artichoke plants. The moon had risen, steeping the fields in a fall of green light. When she reached the roadside, Esta put down her bag and waited for a car to appear.

Eventually a jeep pulled up and two British soldiers let her into the back. Almost immediately, they started to flirt with her, laughing and joking about their sexual deprivation. One scolded the other:

"Cut it out, Norman; you're a married man."

"Everyone has his needs," Norman replied. "Isn't that right, miss?"

They drove past orange groves fenced off on either side of the road; electric pylons stood over them like giant scarecrows.

"Where are you from, miss?"

"Back there. The farm."

"Doesn't look like a farmer, does she, Norman?"

"Well, maybe she's the farmer's daughter? Are you the farmer's daughter, miss?"

They were still playing, but the faintest hint of menace had crept into their voices.

"I work in the fields."

"Been in Palestine long?

"Yes."

"I suppose you must have been. Unless you snuck in, that is. Where'd you come from?"

"Vienna."

"Nasty business going on over there. Bet you're glad to be here."

The driver interrupted his companion.

"Know where I was last week?"

"No, where was you?"

"I was up at Lady bloody Gorgon on Mount Canaan."

"What? Morgan, you mean, the viscount's wife?"

"That's what I said, didn't I?"

"Rifle Brigade?"

"That's right."

"What'd they send you up there for?"

"They wanted someone to drive the kitchen boy back to Tel Aviv."

"You're joking. So you had to go. A regular driver. What a bloody waste."

"Her brother's a lieutenant in the RB."

"Bloody waste of time."

"So I get up there, and the kitchen boy's pumping water into a tank on the roof of the house. Only he keeps on pumping after it's full, and there's a bleeding waterfall coming down the side of the house. Gorgon, the viscount, comes out of the house—which is a bloody palace, by the way—walks right under it, stands there like he's taking a shower. Starts talking to me like nothing's happening. 'Oh, Gibbs. You're here. Would you mind very much . . . ,' and so on."

"They are fucking clowns, aren't they?"

"Do you know what I heard? Wingate likes to stand stark naked and stroke himself with the bristly side of a hairbrush."

"Who told you that?"

"His batman."

"You're joking."

"Straight up."

"And they're the ones giving out the orders. Bloody joke, isn't it?"

The soldiers started to laugh.

"No, but wait," Gibbs said. "You haven't heard the end. I go in the drawing room, where I'm supposed to pick up said passenger after he gets down off the roof, and there's Her Ladyship, sitting round with a bunch of refugees in shiny suits, nattering away in German. It's a little tea party—scones, miniature cakes, everything. They're all muttering, *Dankershern*, *Bittershern*, any kind of *shern* you can think of. 'Oh, Sergeant Gibbs,' she says when I come in. 'These gentlemen are helping to improve my language skills.' As if I care what they're bloody doing. She's quite a piece, mind you, and I wouldn't mind a helping or two myself."

It seemed that they had forgotten about Esta. But then Norman turned to her and said:

"You'll hear it all here. We don't hold nothing back."

He began to whistle a tune that Esta didn't recognize. Gibbs gave him a look and began to laugh again.

"And where can we take you to on this beautiful summer night?"

"Tel Aviv."

"Got a boyfriend there?"

"No."

"Hear that, Norman? She's all alone by the telephone."

"Well, maybe she'd like some companionship. Like to go dancing, miss?"

"No, thank you."

Esta stretched out, exhausted, across the seat.

"How about something to eat, then. Or isn't that kosher?"

They laughed. It was strange to be out in the world: to hear stories and jokes, to be treated as if she were any young woman hitching a ride.

A second jeep cut in front of them and flagged them down.

"Bloody hell," Norman said. "Look who it isn't. Haven't they got anything better to do?"

Two military policemen got out fifty yards up the road.

"Sorry, miss, best if you slip out the back here. Not supposed to be giving rides, I'm afraid."

Esta was already climbing out of the rear seat. She moved quickly into a clump of trees and stood hidden by the side of the road. She heard Norman remonstrating about something, his voice loud and indignant. A few moments later, both vehicles drove off.

She looked out from the side of the road. In the far distance she could make out the silhouettes of a city's low buildings; she assumed it was Tel Aviv. A warm wind picked up, and the blown trees in a nearby eucalyptus grove made a screeching sound.

After half an hour, a bus came speeding toward her, its wooden sides clattering. She moved out into the glare of its headlights and waved for it to stop. To her astonishment, although there was no bus stop nearby, the vehicle came to a screeching halt. She clambered on and began to fumble for coins. The driver started to yell at her to hurry but when Esta came up empty-handed from her search he broke into a smile, winked, and indicated that she should move down the aisle.

Esta was surprised to find herself in what seemed like a clamorous social gathering. Everyone on the bus was engaged in conversation. After her weeks of confinement, the sound of human voices was blaring and shrill. Someone had a radio, and when a series of blips signaled the hour, the passengers fell silent. She listened to the Hebrew and thought that she caught the names of some European cities, but almost as soon as the news had begun, the talk started up again: loud, impassioned, and indifferent.

Tel Aviv was blacked out and sleeping. Esta got directions to Ezekiel Street from the bus driver but almost immediately took a wrong turn. By the time she realized that she was lost, the streets were deserted and there was no one around to ask.

After an hour or so of aimless walking, she found herself at the seashore. A cool breeze blew in light gusts off the water, banishing the warmth from the air. She sat on the sand and watched the waves rise and crash. She had to get past the feeling that what happened to her now was of no consequence. When she was ill, she had wanted to live, but now she wasn't sure where that desire had come from. It was an instinct, not a want: the same instinct that had kept her in the tree, doing her captors' bidding. Without it she would have thrown herself at them, tried to grab a gun, shot until they killed her.

But the impulse to live had sprung, unbidden, when she was most threatened—by the storm troopers and by her sickness—and when it arose it had been uncontrollable. Now, she felt, she was in a better position to master such feelings. She could walk into the sea, and then she would never have to face her nightmares again.

But what about Archie? It was ridiculous to hope; she would never see him again. And Marks had planted a seed; she couldn't ignore it, and she kept going back in her mind, trying to recall every nuance of their relationship: she remembered the odd, insistent questions he'd asked her, the time she felt that he had been looking through her address book, his anger with Falik, and his jealousy. But in the end she had to believe that Archie was honest. The betrayer, the real betrayer, was here in Tel Aviv. She wondered now if she hadn't got lost on purpose, if, after all this time, she had delayed meeting her father because she knew exactly what she wanted to say to him, but knew, too, that she would not say it.

She lay down full length on the sand, her arms folded behind her head. Dark clouds scudded across the moon. It seemed to her that she had arrived at the last of her hiding places and that the only thing to do now was to act like a free woman until the moment came, if it ever came, when she was caught. Once, Archie had told her about a superior officer he had heard of, a colonel, second in command of a brigade, who had been killed while standing up in his tank and shaving under fire. That's what Archie had said, "shaving under fire," and they had both laughed, just like the soldiers in the jeep, because his death had seemed so aristocratic and absurd. But now she understood very well the impulse to thumb your nose at death, and the colonel's action didn't seem so foolish to her anymore.

After a while, she left the beach and wandered in an area of small hotels. Here, although a semiblackout was in effect, the city came to life: there were dimly lit pavement cafés and soldiers on leave making street-corner arrangements with groups of dark-haired women. Dance music blared from a range of radios, and in each café two or three couples danced erratically, banging the sides of tables and knocking the chairs.

Esta chose the least crowded place and sat at a corner table. The waiters ignored her for a long time, but eventually one shuffled over with a glass of water and requested her order. She asked if she could just sit for a while. He shrugged his shoulders.

A listless sea-rippled breeze blew in her face. The talk from the other tables flowed around her. Moonlight illuminated the radio masts on top of the concrete apartments that abutted the café. The buildings' balconies were cluttered with junk: old paraffin heaters, twisted bedsteads, broken chairs; metal vegetation spreading in all directions. Some residents appeared to have spilled the entire contents of their closets into these tiny areas: buckets, brooms, clothes, and rolled-up carpets competed for space with beach chairs, flowers sprouting from discarded white enamel sinks, and cracked flowerpots.

When she had drunk her tumbler of water, she asked the waiter if he could direct her to her father's address. He told her that he lived near it, and if she waited for him to finish work he would walk her there.

She waited while he stacked the chairs and received his distribution of the tips. He was an older man, with a broad, fleshy nose and a monk's fringe of gray hair on his otherwise bald head. He moved with slow, deliberate movements. When he had removed his apron, he beckoned to Esta and offered her a cigarette. For some reason, although she had never smoked before, she took one. He lit it and she tried to inhale. The smoke burned her lungs and induced an immediate coughing fit.

He led her through dark, unpeopled streets. Occasionally, a car passed, its headlights dimmed and painted. The air warmed as they turned their backs to the sea, and it seemed to Esta to be tinged with a scent of orange blossom hung over from another season. The waiter smiled and nodded at her but spoke only once, when they reached her father's block.

"City of Jews," he said, waving his arm to encompass the entire metropolitan area.

She walked down the narrow street, her lungs still smarting from the aftereffects of the cigarette. She found number 6 and entered the building. After struggling with the Hebrew letters on the mailboxes, she managed to make out the name Weiss. She climbed two flights of stairs and banged on his door with her fist.

There was no immediate response, but when she knocked again she heard someone grumble and shuffle across the floor.

"Who is it?"

"Esta."

At first she thought that he hadn't heard her. The door didn't open right away, and she was about to repeat her name when it swung back and she saw him. Tears were running down his broad face and across the gray stubble on his cheeks. Esta fell into the room, as if she had tripped and tumbled into a dark pit. Her father held her. She was taller than he now, and his face pressed into her neck. She smelled the sweaty odor coming off his pajamas; it mingled with the sour smell of the room itself and the too sweet orange blossom that she carried from her walk. His skin chafed against her neck. They stood together in a green pool of phosphorous light.

4

Rawlins wore the grimy, loose-fitting striped galabia that they lent him, ate the food the woman made—a broth, usually, but once horse or donkey meat—and slept in more or less the same position by the fire every night. He gave the boy all his money and the kibbutz clothes.

He hardly ventured out of the hut except to relieve himself in the rocky field that fell away in a sharp slope behind the last home in the village. His straw-blond beard was quite thick now, although the hair above his lip was wispy, a boy's mustache.

His eyes had adjusted to the permanent semidark of the room. At night he watched the girl curl into a corner, rock and moan. Sometimes the woman spoke sharply to her; at other times she ignored her completely. The boy, whose name was Asad, was more solicitous. He helped to dress her in the morning, pulling off the soiled nightshirt that she slept in and replacing it with the equally soiled dress with the red sash. It was the boy, too, who brought water from the well. Rawlins washed first—they would have it no other way—then Asad, followed by the mother and, finally, the girl.

One night, three village men came to the door. The woman refused to let them in. She opened the door an inch or so, then unleashed what sounded like a string of invective. They shouted back. The argument went on for a long time. He knew that it was about him. Eventually the boy removed some of the money that Rawlins had given him from a small purse hidden inside a coffee-pot, and handed it to his mother. She selected three of the small tin coins and extended her hand through the door. The men went away.

Every morning the boy took his goats out to graze, and at night Rawlins heard him bring them back in. After a few days he could recognize the bells that signaled the passage of Asad's ani-mals. He liked to listen to the long caterwaul of the muezzin; it passed with ease through the walls of the hut and sent the girl into uncontrollable giggles. Sometimes she approached him and made a series of grotesque seductive faces; Rawlins simply shook his head.

His plan was to wait a week or two and then go to Tel Aviv in the hope that Esta had shown up at her father's place. But he had lost track of time. He had no idea how long the woman would continue to put him up or how many nights he had bought. She visited the market daily, and he had the feeling that she had long since spent the money he had given her. They were keeping him now. He was ashamed. But somehow he would make it up to them.

Rawlins sat in the doorway of the hut and watched the woman approach. She stepped slowly down the rocky path, her purchases in a basket that she balanced on her head.

There was nothing for him to do. He read Mendoza's little prayer book with the attention that he used to give to the *Golden*

Treasury. The prayers were a strange mixture of the biblical and the homespun. Mendoza would often begin colloquially: "My mind is full of the sweet memories of home, and I am dreaming of the dear ones I love who wait patiently for the day when we may once more be united"; but then he would bring in his "thy"s and "thou"s and lines from the Psalms, which Rawlins recognized. In one prayer the speaker was "surrounded by the horrors of war," but, Mendoza had written, "thy rod and thy staff they comfort me."

The boy noticed Rawlins constantly with the book and asked him, in broken English, if he was praying. Rawlins said that he was.

By drawing in the dirt, he indicated to the woman that he wanted her to buy him pencil and paper. For several days she returned from the market with food only. Rawlins thought that she must have misunderstood him. He didn't want to make her uncomfortable by explaining again. But then one day she came into the hut and unpacked her vegetables from the basket, to reveal a thick school exercise book. She had stuck the pencil in her hair like a bobby pin, and now she extricated it and handed it to Rawlins. She brushed away a pair of flies that had landed under her right eye. The girl rocked quietly in the corner.

He wrote poems. He saw that they were awkward, amateurish, first attempts. The lines didn't work in the way that he wanted them to, and they kept turning sentimental. He wanted to produce something honed and hard, but his language kept betraying him. Nevertheless, he filled the notebook with a thick, forward-leaning scrawl, licking the end of the pencil when it blunted, the way that he had done at school. He wrote late at night, in the red glow of the brazier. Sometimes the girl would wake up. As he read over what he had written, she mimicked his muttering, turning his barely audible English into squeaks and clicks of her tongue.

He asked the boy if he could accompany him on his shepherding. He had lost the fear of being found and caught. The boy didn't seem to understand, so Rawlins went along anyway. The first time he did so, all the children in the village followed him. They laughed and tugged at his galabia. Their bodies were stick thin; some had open sores on their faces, while the eyes of others were clouded by trachoma, like the half-starved children of the poor he had seen begging on Cairo's most wretched streets. Only the girl lingered behind, tying and untying her red sash, then rubbing it provocatively between her legs.

At the foot of the first terrace, the children ran back to the village, and Rawlins was left alone with Asad. By day, the sky was steel blue and the sun burned down. The boy led the flock down to a long wadi where a rivulet of brackish water ran not more than two feet wide. On one bank stood a dilapidated stone house. The goats moved in and out of its empty, roofless rooms. Rawlins sat in the shade of one of the walls. The boy picked up a handful of stones and began to throw them at the branches of a carob tree in order to knock the fruit down. In the dry, windless heat, the stink of goat shit was overwhelming.

One day, there was a wedding in the village. Rawlins watched from his customary position, squatting cross-legged behind the half-open door. The groom approached on an old white horse, its head bent and its flanks scarred. Behind him a man walked, stretching his arm to hold a yellow umbrella over the groom's head. Behind them in the procession came a slew of celebrants, clapping and shrieking. The bride was on a donkey, surrounded by women, her face veiled in white.

A feast was held in the dusty lane between the houses. A smell of roasted meat hung in the air, and musicians played on reed pipe and drums. Late in the night, Asad's mother returned to the hut. For the first time, she tried to communicate with Rawlins. Through a quick play with the rings on her fingers, she asked if he was married. Rawlins shook his head from side to side.

That night he was cut with a feeling of excruciating loneliness.

He had given himself up to his fate, accepted the consequences of what he had done, and his acts had brought him to this hut and its poverty-stricken inhabitants. Up until now he had tried not to let the past, and all its might-have-beens, overwhelm him. But tonight his resistance vanished. He was desperate for English conversation; in memory, even the stupid chitchat of Harfield and Phillips, their ceaseless gibes and complaints, their rudeness and bigotry, seemed appealing. He lay by the brazier and tried to sleep. Half dreaming, his mind flooded with images from his childhood: He was trimming the hedge outside his house on a warm May night; his father let him hold the shears but carefully guided his hands; when they cut near the stem, the scent of privet was subtle and bitter; then he was back inside, leaning over the radio, turning the wand through the lighted dial that illuminated the great cities of the world. When he found some music that he liked, his mother came into the room, lifted him up, and began to dance with him, swinging him around, his feet not touching the ground. A heavy scent of lilac poured in through the open window. His mother wore a blue dress with large white polka dots. Suddenly Rawlins found that he was weeping. Asad woke up and crawled over to him.

Rawlins wiped the tears from his eyes with the back of his sleeve. Asad stared into his face. Rawlins realized that he didn't even know how old the boy was; he guessed at eleven or twelve, but perhaps he was much younger. That morning Rawlins had helped him search for a lost kid. They had split up and wandered among the rocks and bushes of the wadi, calling out and whistling. Finally, they traced a weak bleat and found the goat, its hindquarters trapped in an old sump hole behind the abandoned house. Rawlins had helped Asad to pull it out. There were swollen blood balls on the kid's back end; its black-purple tongue lolled in the gap of its mouth.

The boy tucked himself in against Rawlins's long body. Rawlins smelled the goat musk on his flesh and knew that he shared the same odor. All he wanted now was to sleep and wake between clean sheets in some place where the war had not begun. If Esta was there too, then his life would be perfectly reconstituted.

He was up throughout the night. His mind tracked a hazy path through the past, a ragged chorus of voices and a parade of familiar faces: school friends, teachers, and relatives. In a brief snatch of sleep he was on the troopship, the water widening from the dock edge. He climbed to the very top deck. From there he could see the whole congregation of his acquaintance massed in a large group on the riverbank. His most intimate friends and his parents stood apart on a boat jetty, waving white sheets. Rawlins held a large white towel in his hands and waved back until they were out of sight.

Toward morning he rose and exchanged his galabia for the kibbutz clothes that the woman had neatly folded and placed in a corner of the room. He took off his watch, engraved "AR 17/1/40" on the back—a present from his parents on his twenty-first birthday—and laid it on the ground at the tip of the boy's outstretched hand.

He left the family sleeping and walked out of the village shortly before the sun rose. The sky already held a premonition of dawn, and the morning stars lay dull and flat against the brightening darkness. A cock crowed, and Rawlins heard what sounded like an invisible flock of birds take off all at once, their wings whirring, a chorus of high-pitched notes flung in ripples across the sky. He didn't know which way he intended to head, west to Tel Aviv or south and back toward Egypt.

He walked about a mile. In the distance the sun rose over Jerusalem behind the Mount of Olives, in a great fan of light pulsing up from the east. Swifts flew screaming through the air, cutting it like darts, tearing above the stony flanks of the valley and off toward the ocher-brown walls of the distant city.

Rawlins reached the main road and decided without difficulty which way to turn. He noticed two figures approaching him. It was a man and a woman. He recognized Marks and broke into a smile; he called out "Esta" to the woman and ran toward her. She lifted her face, and he saw that it wasn't Esta but a dark-complexioned woman with a cap pulled over her eyes. Marks raised his arm and pointed. The woman took aim and fired. The first bullet hit Rawlins in the stomach and the second in the shoulder; his assailants scaled a terraced wall and ran into the olive field at the side of the road.

For a long time Rawlins lay bleeding by the roadway. The pain was intense until he drifted into a state of semiconsciousness. The trees around him became a mobile orchard circling above his head. Then he was sitting at the edge of a swimming hole near his house, where he used to go to stare at the girls. There was one, with green eyes, who kept beckoning him to dive in, but he was afraid to go. He knew the wound in his stomach would hurt if he went in the water. He was tired, and his eyes and clothes were full of sand. He saw an Arab woman kneel beside him, muffled and shrouded in the cold air. He tried to stretch out his hand.

5

Esta was charmed, or else she was a ghost. That was it, she was a ghost. She moved through the heat-scarred streets in full daylight, crossing the paths of British soldiers, who stared right into her face. She cut her hair short, to within an inch of her head, but that was her only genuflection to fugitive status.

She went into shops and used her own name. No one reported her, nothing happened. She walked along the promenade and stood for long periods of time, watching the waves kiss the shore. The sea breeze blew through her clothes. When you are a ghost you are free. You can walk anywhere, listen in to private conver-

sations, observe the most intimate acts of strangers. She didn't
want to do that. She wanted to contain some of her powers; for
the present, she was happy to drift alone and pass unnoticed in
the city.

She was exhausted almost from the moment that she woke up.
Her recuperation had been so long. Now the muscles ached in
the backs of her legs. When she walked, she felt as if her body
were loaded with a heavy liquid; her fingers *were* swollen. She
couldn't pull off the silver ring that her mother had given her as
a present when she was sixteen.

The city's heat was inexorable; a hard white light blazed down.
As if to challenge it, she took to crossing town in the middle of
the day, urging herself forward under shuttered balconies, past
peeling walls, drawn by the lightest of breezes, until she reached
the sea. Her head throbbed; once, a passerby told her to put on
a hat.

The birds in Tel Aviv were white; those in Jerusalem, black.
The white birds suited her mood, which was spectral, appari-
tional. She watched the gulls hover in the wake of small fishing
boats, then fly in low through the salt spray above the shoreline.
They landed and walked thin-legged and undisturbed among the
sunbathers on the beach. No one seemed to notice them.

In the apartment, at night, she sat on the balcony and tried to
ward off sleep. She saw the neighbors prepare for bed, then
watched them as they lay in dimly lit rooms with the windows
thrown open, tossing on their thin mattresses, slapping at mosquitoes. She felt entirely alone: a small boat, obscure and black,
rocking in the transparent blackness of an immense harbor.

On the first night, her father had held her hand, cried, and
begged her and her dead mother for forgiveness. She noticed that
although he cupped her face in his hands, he had trouble looking
into her eyes. He brought out a chocolate box, and she almost
laughed because she thought he was going to give her sweets, but
inside were photographs that he had brought with him from Vi-

enna. They pored over the reproduction of her mother's face: taut, unsmiling, the stiff pose she always adopted. Then there were images of herself, aged twelve or thirteen, skinny and short for her age, hair drawn back, lips slightly parted; she stood in the doorway of their house on Rathaustrasse, or leaned against a sun-dappled tree in the street outside. In one picture she was five years old, in a velvet dress and white knee socks, a bow in her hair; her father held her on his lap.

Her father looked back and forth from the photographs to her own face. Then he began to cry. He said, "Where's my little girl?" She tried to comfort him. She didn't know where the little girl was either.

He asked her what happened in Vienna, but almost as soon as she began to tell him about the events in the Prater, he stopped her, saying, "Mother's dead, that's all. Those bastards, those bloody bastards." He didn't want to hear any of the details. That was for the best. If she had begun to talk about the scenic railway, and the tree, she might have been led to talk about her dreams, and she wasn't ready to do that. In any case, he couldn't follow her there; no one could, not even Archie.

She didn't know how long she would remain a ghost (the stranger who had told her to cover her head disturbed her), and so she gave herself daily tests. She approached the highest-ranking officer whom she saw on the streets and asked him for directions to Allenby Street or Rothschild Boulevard or the bus station. She liked to ask the way to her father's house. She would repeat back the instructions that she received and say, "Thank you," emphasizing her address. "I'm going to number six; that's what I'm looking for, six." If they had been able to see her, they would have followed her home, or arrested her on the spot. She thought that next week she might try wearing a particularly striking hat, one with feathers, perhaps.

This morning, she woke in a heavy sweat, stumbled into the toilet, and, as on the previous three days, vomited into the bowl.

Then she returned to the living room. Her father was asleep on the sofa, snoring loudly. The previous night, he had told her a confused story about how Archie had come to fetch him and he had recognized him from a previous visit. Esta thought he must have been mistaken; he had spoken between sobs, flustered and disoriented.

He had been volatile ever since her arrival. When she pressed him for information about Archie's whereabouts, he flew into a rage: Archie had tricked him, lied to him, dumped him in a hostile Arab village, God knows where; it was lucky he was alive to be here when Esta arrived. If it hadn't been for a very kind friend in Jerusalem, whom Esta would meet, hopefully soon, she would have two dead parents. And then he had broken down again, sobbing, apologizing, saying that he was speaking that way only because he was upset. She thought she would wait until he settled down before she queried him again.

She went into the kitchen. A pale light penetrated the blinds and clarified the objects in the room: glass plates, four cups and saucers neatly stacked (by her) on narrow shelves. Two pots and a frying pan hung on nails over the sink. There was an expensive clock, looking overlarge and out of place on the cracked kitchen wall. He had taken it from their home in Vienna, leaving her and her mother to cope for a few days in a timeless world. The birds sang weakly in their cage. She fed them and changed their water.

She pushed open the small kitchen window and leaned her face outside. She felt like vomiting again. She couldn't get rid of the stale smell of mold and bird droppings. She went back into the other room. Her father opened his eyes and took in her presence with a wild stare. She sat in the chair beside him. He continued to gaze at her. He looked as if he might begin to cry again, as he did every morning. But this time he spoke to her instead.

"A cup of tea would be nice, Esta. I haven't had anybody make *me* a cup of tea in a long time."

She returned to the kitchen and lit the gas.

"A little later, Esta," he shouted after her, "you can help me with a few things. It's not easy, you know, living alone the way I do. This is a hard country. The people are hard."

He had a hundred little chores for her to perform: shirts that had needed ironing for six months—he couldn't do them himself because of the arthritis in his hands; trips to the post office to purchase stamps; official letters that had to be hand delivered because "you couldn't trust the mail." He was always running out of "refreshments," and he sent her to bring drinks and *bourekas* from the local grocery. He instructed her never to pay but always to run up the tab; at the end of the month he would take care of it. The owner of the store, a small man with a Charlie Chaplin mustache, turned sullen and hostile when Esta came in. In the mornings, his shop was always crowded, and his two young children were busily employed: they clambered on a rolling ladder and threw produce down from the highest shelves. Esta felt the customers freeze when she presented her shopping list. Yesterday, because her father's back was hurting, she had helped the iceman carry a block up the two flights into their kitchen.

Esta waited for the water to boil. She still felt faintly nauseous and worried that she was getting sick again. She opened her lungs and took two deep breaths. Her breathing was fine. No cough, no pain.

She brought her father his drink: tea with a slice of lemon. She watched him lift the rim of the cup to his lips. In the years since she had seen him, his body had thickened and he had grown almost completely bald. There were small tufts of white hair in his ears and at the edges of his nostrils. In Vienna he had groomed himself meticulously before he set off for work. She remembered sitting on the covered toilet in the bathroom while he stood barechested, shaving before the mirror. He pulled the razor in long, careful strokes; she liked the way it glided through the lather to expose areas of his smooth red skin.

Weiss didn't care that she went out. He had already told her that Archie was a madman, a drunk, a deserter with no home. Nothing he said could be trusted. If Esta had told him, as she had, that all this assassination talk was rubbish, then what was there to worry about? Rawlins, Phillips, whatever his name was—the man couldn't tie his own shoelaces.

Her father put down his cup and began to talk about his friend Birnbaum's son. He wasn't a doctor, but he worked in a laboratory. He assisted in the manufacture of serums. Perhaps he could talk to Esta: wasn't it biology that she had begun to study at university? Yes; she had written to him about it. He had shown the letter to his friends in New York. Maybe young Birnbaum could help her find a job. She couldn't walk around all day being a refugee. Everybody was a refugee, everybody had problems. Who knew what would happen in this war? Jews were dying to get into Palestine, literally dying. She was one of the lucky ones. And he was nearly sixty; no one wanted to give him a job. They couldn't scrape by on his income. Sure, he did a little business here and there, he always had, small investments of one kind and another—he had a little piece, a very little piece, of that coffee shop on the corner—but it would never be enough.

The humidity in the apartment was unbearable. While he was talking, sweat formed in heavy beads in the crevices of Weiss's forehead and rolled down his nose and cheeks. He patted at his face with a crumpled handkerchief. Esta felt the nausea spread through her body again. She needed air.

"All right," she said. "I'll go and see your friend's son. I'll write to him and make an appointment."

"That's not how things work here. Just show up. Believe me, he'll be pleased to see you."

Esta stepped languorously down Ezekiel Street. It was not yet eight o'clock, but the sun was already hot on the road. The scrawny mongrel that had taken to accompanying her on the early part of her walks trotted out from behind a broken fence, barked, and fell in beside her.

In the small body shops at the side of the road, the mechanics were hard at work hammering and welding; they did not look up when she passed. In any case, she was already old news: the first brazen attempts of some of the younger workers to attract her attention had drawn no reaction, and they had quickly given up.

She was halfway down the street when she heard her father call out to her from the balcony of his apartment.

"Esta!" he yelled. "Don't forget the refreshments on your way back."

The laboratory where Birnbaum's son worked was not far from Tel Aviv's fruit and vegetable market. Once she was in the vicinity, Esta had to make her way through a large, jostling crowd of shoppers, who elbowed and forced their way to the front of stands, bargaining with the stall owners at the tops of their voices. On another day, she might have been excited and cheered by the animated bustle and variety of the market—the cacophonic voices, the scent of ripe melons, the radiant black at the heart of the bunches of yellow tulips on display—but this morning she was overwhelmed by the rank smell that rose from the rotting and discarded vegetables in the gutters. If she had not already emptied the contents of her stomach, she would have vomited again; even so, she found her way into a shadowed back alley stacked with crates and retched silently.

A man appeared around the back of a van, wheeling a dolly stacked high with boxes of parsley. He tracked unevenly down the alley, and Esta had to straighten up and move to avoid him. As he went past, his elbow caught her hard in the stomach. She winced, lost her breath, gasped for air, and, as she did so, was struck, suddenly and inescapably, with the knowledge that she was pregnant.

Esta leaned back against a warehouse wall. A thin stream of foul-smelling water ran beneath her shoes and across the scattered debris of the market: orange rinds, broken crates, stripped lettuce and cabbage leaves, all soaked and blackened in the rancid stream. Further along, the alley was littered with old newspapers and bruised fruit; a few mangy stray cats prowled a fly-ridden, overflowing garbage bin.

It didn't seem possible that she could carry a child. She had missed her period, but she had thought that was a side effect of her illness; not bleeding had seemed to her a confirmation (almost a happy one) that she was out of life.

Now the air around her seemed charged, electric, violent; she heard the noise of the crowd emanating from the market as the pent-up cries of a frenzied mob. She felt, for a moment, horribly violated, as if she was being hauled back into the world against her will. Ghost by day, bird woman by night—there was no space there for the concerns of motherhood. And then, to her astonishment, because she thought that she had lost the capacity to do so, she was sobbing hard, as though the entire reservoir of her pain, changed to liquid, were emptying through her eyes; but the sockets weren't big enough to contain the flow, and she felt as if her tears had to find another outlet on her body. She squatted down and picked up her skirt, afraid to lift it high; as she urinated, she felt the edges of the material dampen against the back of her legs.

She rose and stumbled out of the alley, almost bent double by the ache in her stomach. When the pain faded, she found a bench near a bus stop and sat down. Where was Archie? How long was it since he had been inside her? Before she was sick, while she was sick? They had made love in the hut, but her memory of the event was weakly perceived, hallucinatory. She remembered the roughness of his beard on her cheek, so that she had turned on her front and he had reached from behind under her body and cupped her breasts in his hands. The stone walls of the hut seemed to lean in, like trees over water.

A bus came, and a mass of passengers descended and flowed around her. The driver shouted at her to hurry and waited for her to get on, drumming his fingers on the steering wheel. She looked at him without moving or speaking. He shrugged and slammed the door. A woman with a full shopping basket sat beside her and began to complain in Yiddish about the harsh light of the sun, the sand that had got into her shoes, the fly-filled heat. She should never have come here, she said. She took off one of her shoes and spilled out the fine silver dust.

Esta got up from the bench. The sun burned down. She walked slowly, stopping occasionally in the shaded areas of the street when she felt that her nausea was about to return. She checked her father's directions, written in pencil on a scrap of paper. At the bottom of a narrow, twisting side street, she came to a small brick building, set back and out of place among the flat-roofed white blocks that surrounded it.

She entered through the wooden door into a reception hall. The woman at the desk directed her into a small room with a tiled workbench, a few glass receptacles, and about twenty standing flasks and test tubes. A few moments later, Birnbaum appeared.

"Miss Weiss?" he said. "I've been expecting you."

He saw Esta glance around the room.

"No, no, don't worry." He laughed. "This isn't where we work. The building was once a school. This is the old chemistry lab. No one's got around to clearing it up."

He led her down a corridor and into a stifling, windowless office. He was a small man, a few years older than she, with a chubby face and horn-rimmed glasses. He wore a white lab coat and sported a bow tie that seemed an incongruous symbol of decorum in the heat and chaos of Tel Aviv. He invited Esta to sit in the only chair, while he swung himself up on the desk.

"What took you so long?"

Esta shrugged.

"My father called here half an hour ago. He meets your father every morning for breakfast at that café. What's it called? Cosmo, short for Cosmopolitan." Birnbaum laughed. "He told me you were on your way."

"I got lost."

"Lost? How long have you been in Tel Aviv?"

"I don't know. Weeks. Three weeks."

"Only three weeks. Goodness. How did you beat the blockade?"

Esta stared at Birnbaum. Why was he talking to her in this way? As if she were a normal person.

"Would you like to drink something?"

Birnbaum opened a small cabinet and brought out a bottle of orange juice.

"It's warm, I'm afraid."

Esta took the drink and gulped it down.

"My father tells me you're looking for work."

Birnbaum explained the way the laboratory functioned and the nature of his research. The British army depended upon them, he said, and there was a good supply of money for development and materials. Esta tried to concentrate, but Birnbaum's words slid past her and out of reach. There was a travel poster on the wall showing the Sea of Galilee and in the distance a green valley enclosed by gentle hills. A brown hawk hung in the air, watching the earth. Esta knew the stasis in the poster was deceptive; the bird could drop like a stone from the sky onto its prey and up away again in a flash. It could come out and claw at her stomach, rend it with its talons until it had torn the fetus from inside her. She folded her hands across the flat of her belly and imagined that she felt a slight swelling there. Birnbaum was still talking.

"The kind of position we might offer you would depend, of course, on your experience. But if you're willing to take anything—I mean, even answering the phone just to begin with—well, I may be able to work something out. Now, where can I contact you?"

"I'm sorry, I . . ."

"At your father's?"

"I have to leave."

Esta stood up and almost keeled over. Birnbaum moved forward and caught her.

"Thank you. I'm all right."

"Are you sure?"

"I'm feeling a little nauseous. The room."

"Yes, I'm so sorry; I should have thought. It's very stuffy in here. Full of smoke too. We can't light up in the labs, so everyone comes in here. Here, let me help you."

He guided her back down the corridor, past closed doors with opaque windows, and out a side exit into a small courtyard. A couple of white clouds were scattered over the blue midday sky, but otherwise there was nothing to protect them from the searing heat. Esta looked across a dilapidated fence: an old house had recently been demolished, and the ground was covered with gray roof tiles, chunks of broken plaster, doors ripped off their hinges, and, situated on top of a pile of rubble, a blue china teapot, oddly intact except for a broken handle.

"Do you feel better?"

"Yes."

"Take some deep breaths."

Birnbaum left her side for a moment but soon returned with a glass of clear water. He handed it to her. She drank it. She was sick of being nursed and helped, fed up with having people dance attendance upon her. But that wasn't his fault.

"Are you all right now? It's so hot out here. I'm not thinking clearly. I've brought you from the fat into the fire."

"I'm sorry," she said. "You've been very kind, but I have to leave."

"Can't I help you?"

There was a jar full of dusty pink geraniums in a corner of the courtyard. The color of the petals struck Esta as extraordinarily intense, as if they had been painted. She took two steps, bent, plucked off a stalk, and tucked it into her waistband.

"I must go now."

Birnbaum escorted her to the front door. She knew that he was looking at her strangely, but there was nothing she could do about it. It was impossible to explain. The person whom he was talking to wasn't there, was hidden. She felt like one of the Russian dolls that she had played with as a child: inside her shell was another, smaller Esta, and there was another inside that, and another, tinier and tinier. And all the Estas could be broken in two, until you arrived at the fetus that she was holding in her womb, which she and Archie had created, and whose being, like the wooden doll at the heart of the nest, was inseparable.

She walked home on a different route, thinking at first to avoid the tumult of the market, but then, impulsively, she changed direction, turned down a narrow alleyway, and was back in the heart of it. She sat on the curb outside a refreshment parlor, with a phonograph going full blast behind her. A child stood in front of her, sucking at an overripe fig. She gave herself up to the noise and clamor. Her nausea came in waves, rippling through her body, and more than once she thought that she might vomit into the street. She sat for a long time, watching the give-and-take of bartering; the faces of the customers and the stallkeepers grew red and swollen with the heat of their arguments, which were carried on in hoarse, guttural expletives. She watched the porters stagger under heavy loads and let out their jackal yells. All the voices around her seemed to rise to a crescendo, and the hands in the crowd flew out as if they had taken on a life of their own.

She sat until a strip of yellow gold appeared on the edge of the sky where the sun had dropped, and the cut flowers in the stall opposite her seemed to lose their courage and close up. The fruit and vegetable stalls began to shut, and pockets of gray shadow appeared on the street. Esta rose and walked past a meat stand, where the blood of a slaughtered chicken congealed on the pavement. A thousand flies buzzed over the refuse and offal that was slowly being swept aside, and Esta saw a barefoot olive-skinned boy pick through the waste and emerge with a handful of bruised cucumbers.

By the time she arrived on Ezekiel Street, she was exhausted. A British army jeep was parked half up on the curb outside the corner café. She paid it no attention. She needed to sleep. She felt so tired that she had to fight the impulse to lie down in the dusty street, move a stone under her head for a pillow, and stretch out between the rainbow pools of oil that spilled beneath the shutters of the workshops. She dragged herself the last hundred yards.

She mounted the stairs. The door of the apartment was ajar. She pushed it open. A man in uniform knelt with his back to her, examining the photographs that her father had left scattered on the floor. He turned at the sound of her footsteps and murmured her name.

6

The dark shape in front of the brazier was the woman, and the darker shape in the corner was the girl. He remembered that there had been a boy too, but that was a long time ago. Perhaps the boy had been him. He thought he had seen him fishing; he was standing with the minnow trap that he had made by knocking a hole in the bottom of a bottle. He watched the boy in the red sweater and Wellington boots put crumbs inside and lower the bottle on strings into the chalk stream that ran by the village school. He weighed the strings down with heavy stones. As soon as the minnows swam in, he pulled up the bottle and emptied the fish into his jar.

The woman had bandaged his stomach with strips of torn clothing, but the blood oozed through. He couldn't move his right arm, and his shoulder was bandaged and bloody. The brazier glowed red in the middle of the room. A thin glaze of starlight filled the gap between the door and the wall. At home there were planes taking off from Manston and Deal, Lympne and Gosport. He watched from the garden with his father. He explained how to pick out the Defiant; smaller than the Hurricane, it was a two-seater, with a turret behind the pilot. In the turret there were four Browning machine guns, which were aimed and fired all together by the second man. His father seemed impressed. He said, "Hitler had better watch out for you."

The woman tried to put something in his mouth. He couldn't swallow. She pushed the spoon back and forth in quick jerks, like the tongue of a lizard, trying to catch him with his mouth open. She whispered all the time. He knew she was encouraging him. The girl laughed in the corner, then she crawled over and touched her hand lightly to the bandages. Her mother pushed her away. The girl smeared her hand on the floor; it left a reddish-brown streak. It was the beginning of October in Sherbrooke, and the air was sharp with the scent of the sycamores and the chill of autumn, but despite the coolness in the air he was sitting outside in the garden with his chest bare. He was shivering. This time his father was planting spring bulbs. He asked Archie to help; he was quite insistent and called him "Archibald," the way he did when he was angry. It seemed like such a waste of energy to put in the bulbs if you were never going to see them flower. It was better for Archie to conserve his strength. Why didn't his father recognize that if he had to bend and dig, the pain would be too much for him?

The boy appeared before him. He remembered his name: Asad. His lank black hair was swept back from his thin face, and his eyes were full of fear. There were tears on his cheeks. Archie tried to tell him not to cry. He had no idea if he had succeeded, because when he spoke his voice seemed to bubble and spit, and he couldn't hear what he was saying; but the woman talked to the boy, and he wiped his eyes. He remembered her name, too, now: Yasmin. She was heating something in a pot; the air in the room filled with a bitter scent. The embroidered pattern on her black dress looked like lines of writing: messages in worn pink thread that he couldn't interpret.

At first he experienced unbearable pain, but now it had subsided. He could stand it as long as he didn't move. Asad knelt beside him and held a cup of water to his lips. He closed his eyes and waded across the river near the church. He wore his uniform, and a machine gun strapped across his back. He was showing his parents, and everyone else in the village, what he had learned in basic training. Everyone was there, his friends and teachers, even the redhead from the post office. She stood at the front of the crowd with a big smile on her face. Every so often he would raise the gun, wave, and smile at them. It was a perfect moment. They were all so terribly proud of him. Then someone fired at him from the belfry. The crowd on the bank dispersed in a panic. He was alone in the river; a bullet grazed his shoulder and he bled slowly into the water. Phillips leaned out of the belfry tower and shouted at him: "It was a secret mission. You should have removed your cap badge and insignia. Then nobody would have known who you were."

Yasmin was changing his bandages, lifting the strips of cloth from his stomach as delicately as she could, although the blood had clotted near the hole and she had to tug to free the fabric. The pain came back, and Rawlins swung the trunk of his body sideways with a scream. The girl screamed with him. Her mother was tearing up her day dress, then soaking the strips in the boiling pot. The red sash went in, too, and emerged bleached pink. Rawlins saw Asad staring at the hole in his gut; he moved his left hand down to cover himself, blood ran over his fingers, then Yasmin came and applied the bandage.

Every so often Asad would go to the door and peer out. Whoever they were expecting did not come. Now that she had finished boiling the water, Yasmin let the brazier die. It was a warm night, and the room was hot and stifling. The girl sat with her fingers in her mouth. She had started to rock again, never taking her eyes off the strips of her dress that circled Rawlins's waist.

Esta was running through the Cairo streets, a look of panic on her face. He was chasing her, calling out to her to slow down; he yelled after her that there was nothing to worry about, he had taken care of everything. She had a good lead on him, and he ran as fast as he could to catch up. He pumped his arms for extra speed, the way that his PE teacher had instructed him, but the searing pain in his ankle hobbled his progress. Esta disappeared, and he began to call her name. The street was a whirling carousel of noise and color: rope makers, basket weavers, rug dealers, a stall of dyed wools hanging crimson, deep blue, bright yellow, and black. Then Lewis Marks's face rose up before him, and the face of the woman with the gun, whom he had never seen before. They emerged from behind a tram, with their backs to the Nile; the sun sparkled on the water.

Rawlins began to shout again. Yasmin moved closer to him and began to wipe his forehead. At the touch of her hand he felt a great sense of relief. After a while, he opened his eyes.

Asad and the girl were both asleep. They lay curled in opposite corners of the room. Yasmin sat cross-legged a foot or so away from him. When he looked at her she nodded and spoke to him. He felt an immense gratitude to her. She was trying to save his life. She could easily have left him in the dust by the roadside. He was an absolutely expendable stranger. No one knew who he was or where he was from or what his allegiances were. It might have been dangerous to get involved with him. Obviously, she didn't care.

The pain worked steadily in his stomach. That day in Jaffa, when he had gone to the bar, Livock had told him all kinds of stories: chaps left to die for hours in the desert, great gaping holes in their stomachs, and if some scrap of shell had only ripped a little hole, Livock had said, you could survive for days. It wasn't the wound that killed you but the infection, peritonitis; if no one got to you in time, bloating set in; once that happened, you were gone.

Rawlins wondered if Asad had been out looking for a doctor. They couldn't be planning to take care of him themselves. But he had been there all day, and no one had come. He stared hopefully at the warped wooden door. When it finally opened, it was his mother who came in. He had been trying not to think of her, but here she was anyway, wearing the familiar sensible walking shoes that bulged out at the sides because she had wide feet. She was in the blue-and-white wide-skirted polka-dot dress that he liked and a thick knitted white cardigan, which seemed horribly inappropriate for the khamsins of the Middle East. He didn't say anything because he didn't want to upset her. There was no hiding the wound, however, and his mother turned pale when she saw it. He tried to explain. "It's all right, Mum," he said. "I've got the sleepy sickness." At first this seemed to satisfy her, but then she hid her hands in her face.

He told her to make a cup of tea, to calm down, that everything was going to be fine. The gas jets danced on the stovetop. He watched the blue flames curl back and flatten when his mother set the kettle down. Two boys holding a cricket bat and a worn tennis ball came to the door and asked if Archie could come out to play, but his mother said that he was ill and sent them away. Then she was alone in the kitchen, reaching behind her back to untie her apron, and Rawlins felt an unutterable sadness because he could not speak to her or touch her. He wanted to stand behind her and throw his arms around her legs the way he had done when he was two or three years old and his mother would laugh, shuffle forward, and drag him around, his feet sliding on the tiled floor, his face buried deep in the back of her skirt. But he was still in the room, lying in the corner, his face hanging in the shadows like an ashen moon.

There was a sour taste of blood in his mouth, and he could

smell the fetid odor of his own body. He was going to die, and it was terribly unfair, because his whole life up until this time had simply been a preparation to begin. For twenty-two years he had jumped hurdles, that was all: first at school, then at university, and finally in the army. All the pale, cold days of testing had brought him here to the mud floor and putrid, bloodstained bandages.

As he lay in the darkness, straining to make sense of what had happened to him, all Archie could come up with was the list of requirements that he had written in a letter to his mother from base: razor blades, sea boots, new drill slacks, baby powder. The last item stuck in his mind. His skin had grown raw and coarse from exposure during the long days of tank gunnery training at Lulworth, and his hands were callused from the chores that he had been made to perform, most of which had no purpose other than to demean: scrubbing out the lavatories, shit shoveling in the stables. And so he wrote to his mother with the list. What softness had he been dreaming of? The fresh sheets on his bed after his mother had washed and ironed them, or the white powder on Claire's neck where she had overdone her makeup and the softness of her breasts pressing into him as they danced. He didn't know anything then about the other—terrible—dance, the one that Esta was doing in Vienna, flapping helplessly to the tinny, wild music of some broken merry-go-round, waving her arms, then flopping her body down off the branch and waiting to die. But *he* was the person dying. It wasn't right. He was much too young. If only there were some way to explain that he was just a boy; it was what all the parents said: "They're only boys," so it had to be true.

He woke, startled by pain, to feel a man's fingers probing his stomach. Yasmin stood behind the kneeling figure, and when Rawlins cried out she spoke harshly to the man, moved forward, and wiped Rawlins's brow. The man had a bushy gray mustache and thick-rimmed black glasses. He wore a loose-fitting pair of drawstring trousers and a white shirt that exposed his bulky chest. A string of amber beads dangled from his neck and brushed against Rawlins's skin as he leaned over him.

The man stood up, turned to Yasmin, and shook his head. She unleashed a stream of rapid sentences, gesticulating and pointing at Rawlins. He let her finish and then knelt again by Rawlins's side. He stared into Rawlins's eyes. Archie guessed that the man was looking for death, trying to ascertain how long Archie had, whether or not he was worth helping. Finally, he shrugged, turned, spoke to Yasmin, and left the room. She seemed satisfied and began tidying up the girl, pulling a comb through her hair and helping her to wash her face.

Rawlins heard a donkey bray, then the door pushed open and a brittle morning light poured in. He could see the hindquarters of the animal hitched to a cart; its large red back wheels were pulled up on the dusty path as close as possible to the hut. The man with the mustache returned. He gathered Rawlins up in his arms and lifted him, like a bride over the threshold, toward the back of the cart.

As in his first days, when he had gone into the pasture with Asad, the village children came out to watch. They stood in a small group, barefoot in their tattered galabias, chattering among themselves. Asad ran toward them and tried to scatter them with shouts and movements of his hands; they did not move but fell silent.

The pain in Rawlins's stomach (he didn't even think about his shoulder), exacerbated by the sudden movement, was intense, and he had to bite his tongue hard in order to stop himself from crying out. As carefully as he could, the man laid him down in a corner of the cart and propped him against the corner slats. Then Yasmin got in beside him with Asad, and finally the girl clambered up, grimacing and gesturing at the other children.

They covered Rawlins with thin goat-hair blankets and placed a white kaffiyeh on his head, bound with a leather agal. The square of cloth was long enough to be pulled across his face like a veil, but Rawlins let it hang where it was. He stared at the narrow goat path that ran through fields sparsely covered with thistles and grass. The sky was wide and blue, although a dim pink stain held for a moment on the horizon, then seemed to dissolve before his eyes.

The driver whistled and cracked the reins; the donkey labored forward. Rawlins jolted sideways, the pain slicing through him, but the girl's body was there to protect him and keep him from falling. One or two of the younger children waved at the cart. The rest watched, expressionless, until it had disappeared from sight.

Esta was in her room. Rawlins stood on the sturdy wooden ladder that his father used when he had to fix the cottage roof. He could easily see her through the hole in the wall. She had her back to him. She was naked, and he was hoping that she would turn round. He wanted to look at her breasts and the dark triangle of her pubic hair. He was afraid to call her name or do anything that might attract her attention. He didn't want her to catch him looking. He was embarrassed, too, because of the wound in his stomach. It didn't hurt him anymore, but the stench was overwhelming. He hoped it wouldn't filter into the room. For a long time, everything she did was with her back to him: she knelt to write in her address book, folded the blankets on the bed, pulled dead petals off the anemones. When she leaned forward her thin buttocks arched, and he glimpsed the dark slit of her vagina. He was aroused, but he still wanted her to turn around. It was hard to keep silent for so long. The sun beat down on his head, and his hands were sweating so much that he worried he was going to lose his grip on the ladder. He almost fell asleep. Toward dusk, the peal of church bells and the cry of the muezzin began simultaneously, but even the sudden noise filling the air failed to distract her. Finally, he could no longer bear to wait, and he called her name. She turned, looked directly at him, as if she had known all along that he was there, and pierced him with a cruel stare. Her body was as he remembered: thin breasts, flat, almost concave, belly, her ribs visible beneath her taut white skin. But her head—sharp eyed, with hooked beak and slate-gray feathers—was that of a predatory bird. She flapped her arms and let out a series of abrupt, whistling cries.

The bird swooped and tumbled above the cart, cutting a swath in the blue air, which seemed to close behind it as it flew. The donkey plodded forward. The twin domes of the city grew closer, then dwindled again, as the donkey turned in a different direction. They had been climbing at a slow pace for hours, it seemed, but now they began a steep descent, and the driver, trying to alleviate Rawlins's discomfort, slowed the cart almost to a halt.

From time to time, a car, a truck, or an army vehicle approached or overtook them. On a particularly narrow stretch of road, a patrol car got stuck behind them, and its driver began to honk incessantly. Rawlins looked at the markings on the vehicle and mumbled the specifications to himself: "Chevy WB, thirty hundredweight, R Patrol." It was an LRDG vehicle. What were those chaps doing here? Must have driven it all the way in from the desert for a spot of leave.

"Move, you stupid buggers, move."

A soldier in a black beret was standing up in the passenger seat and yelling at them. He seemed to take in Rawlins with a glance, but if that was so, his face failed to register anything strange. Rawlins supposed he could do something: shout or wave his arms for help. But even if he announced who he was and demanded their assistance, they might not give it to him. These soldiers were drunk and angry: they wouldn't want his blood congealing all over their seats: nasty mess, and someone would have to clean it up. In any case, he trusted the people in the cart. He had no idea where they were taking him, but they were surely moving him for his own good.

The road broadened, and the patrol car pulled up alongside

the cart. There were two men in the front and two more in the back, perched high on what looked like ammunition boxes; but this far from the action, they probably weren't. The rifle mounted on the steel bridge across the body was wrapped in cloth.

The driver of the car decelerated to the pace of the cart. He was grinning. The two men on the ammunition boxes, who had been sucking on oranges, threw the rinds and pulp at the occupants of the cart.

"Why don't you take your bloody time?"

"Get off and milk it."

"Put the woman in the harness and let the donkey in the back. Poor bugger, he's *exhausted*."

They were laughing hard. The soldier in the passenger seat took a swig from a brandy bottle, then held it out at arm's length.

"Here you go, Abu. Take a swig of this."

The bottle was almost empty.

"What? Don't you want it? Don't want to drink with us? Well, fuck you, mate."

A bus, approaching from the other direction, forced the driver to pull away. As the patrol car veered in front of the cart, the soldier in the passenger seat pretended to bite the pin from an imaginary grenade. He turned and lobbed the brandy bottle back toward the cart; it arched through the air and smashed in front of the donkey, causing the animal to come to a standstill. The driver pulled on the reins, tugged the donkey's head sideways, and maneuvered him carefully past the broken glass. Rawlins watched the patrol car speed downhill, leaving a miasma of exhaust fumes in its wake.

The sun had almost reached the zenith of its heady climb through the empty sky, and the heat in the back of the cart was intense. Rawlins groaned and tried to turn on his side. Yasmin leaned forward and spoke to the man. A little further down the hill, he turned the cart off the road onto a terrace of gnarled olive trees, which offered welcome but insufficient shade. Far beneath him, Rawlins could see the stone houses and red slate roofs of a village. A high tower, which looked as if it might belong to a church, rose from the cluster of small buildings. The driver encouraged the donkey a little further, then nudged him to a halt under a tree with thicker branches. Asad stood up and plucked at the tree's jade-colored fruit: he burst its sticky, glistening skin with his thumbnail and spilled the white feathery pith onto his hands.

The driver swung down with a bucket in his hands and disappeared over the terrace ridge. The girl, who had been drowsing sullenly in the opposite corner from Rawlins, now roused herself and crawled over to him. She stretched out and nestled her head carefully against Rawlins's good shoulder. Her mother said something to her, but the girl responded with a sharp shriek and her mother relented.

Rawlins liked the weight of her head pressing into him and the pungent smell of her hair, which seemed to mingle sweat with the smell of the earth and the rosemary that grew wild in the fields that surrounded her village. Her mother pointed at the girl.

"Alia," she said. Rawlins looked at her quizzically, and she repeated again, "Alia, Alia."

And then Rawlins realized that she was telling him the girl's name, and he felt suddenly and inexplicably happy, as if a great gift had been bestowed upon him.

"Thank you," he replied. "Alia."

The girl lifted her head, tilted it sideways, then laid it back down on his shoulder. He was overcome with a strange tenderness, a feeling almost cloying but that somehow he believed to be authentic, and this despite the fact that the words of an appallingly sentimental song had drifted into his mind, and he found himself pretending for a moment that the retarded Arab girl with her head on his shoulder was *his* girl. He wanted to half whisper and half sing to her the words of "I'll be with you in apple-blossom time," in the hope that the lilting melody, even if it was produced by his own cracked voice, would evoke the same feelings of sweet nostalgia that he had experienced whenever he heard the song on the radio, months before he went into the army, when he was already imagining with pleasure the pangs of longing and pains of separation that would be his as long as he had a girl to come home to.

The driver returned, lit a cigarette, and stood smoking, while the donkey lowered its head to the water bucket. Yasmin removed two bruised pears from the pocket of her dress. She offered one to Rawlins, but when he declined with a shake of his head, she handed them to her children. The girl ate lying down, chewing noisily; the juice from the pear, mingled with her saliva, dripped down Rawlins's arm.

After a while, when the donkey was rested, they drove back onto the road again and began their sluggish descent toward the village. Rawlins stared at the bare brown shoulders of the hills, which seemed to bump against the sky. The turns in the road grew sharper and the air heavier, and soon his view of the hilltops was obscured by a thick pine forest. The scent of the pines was pleasant and soporific, and suddenly he felt that he didn't want the journey to end. He was happy to revolve in this hot, vertiginous crucible, listening to the ponderous clip-clop of the donkey's hooves, while the girl leaned into his side. Even the pain wasn't bothering him so much anymore; when it came, it seemed to slide evenly through his body and exit smoothly, leaving him physically drained but with his senses oddly sharpened, so that the greens of the forest and the red of the approaching village rooftops were intensified. But at the point when he had given himself totally to the dizzying effects of the light on his downward spiral and the world had become a kaleidoscope of color, the cart came to a halt.

Alia didn't want to get down, and her brother had to tug at her arm in order to pull her away. The donkey was drawn up by a wooden door set in a long whitewashed wall. The driver rang the bell, the door swung open, and Yasmin and the driver disappeared inside.

The children stayed close to the cart. Asad sat in the narrow block of shade thrown by the long wall, while the girl squatted next to one of the wheels. Rawlins propped himself up on his elbow. Across the street, in a small garden, an old woman was feeding a couple of scrawny chickens. She was surrounded by flowers sprouting in every kind of makeshift pot: old kettles, tin baths, a cracked terra-cotta window box. White butterflies fluttered around her head as she mumbled and spat, dropping tight handfuls of grain on the ground in front of her.

Rawlins heard a faint buzz in the air, like electric wires in an approaching storm. He thought he would like to go home now, to lie in his old bedroom while the rain streamed on the windows. Esta could sit by the side of the bed; perhaps she could read him some poetry, the way that he had recited for her when she was sick. She would have to take meals downstairs with his parents, and he would have to warn her to close her ears to anything she heard, especially from his father, who might well come up with something untoward after he'd had a couple of drinks. She should know, though, that it wasn't just Jews that he snubbed, but all foreigners, and despite everything he had a good heart.

His mother served dinner, and Rawlins could see now that they were all getting on quite well together; Esta was polite but straightforward as always, and his parents, who were taciturn people themselves, didn't seem to mind that she fell silent for long periods of time. A place had been set for him, but of course he couldn't be there. He felt uncomfortable and frustrated, and he called down to them from the bedroom, but no matter how loud he shouted, they couldn't hear him. It seemed ridiculous that his illness, which had begun innocently enough as a child's bout with influenza, had turned into this isolating sickness. He wished that Esta would come back up the stairs. He wanted to tell her that when they moved to London, nobody would bother them at all: it was a cosmopolitan place, *the* great city of the world, in his opinion, and anything went there. He would look for a job, although doing what, God only knew. He realized that he had never told her that he had studied history at university—medieval and modern—which, as she could see, had prepared him well for any eventuality. He touched the tips of his fingers to her lips. She leaned forward and kissed him, then rose from the chair at the side of his bed and drew the curtains across the bedroom window.

He opened his eyes. The whitewashed wall seemed higher than before and surrounded by tall cypresses. He could see through the door now to a patch of land covered with wild geraniums. A lizard was poised on a round stone, taking the sun's rays and working its swift tongue. The scent of rosemary was overwhelming; he couldn't tell if it came from some nearby bushes or had lingered in his memory from the girl's hair.

7

Esta almost didn't recognize Mendoza. His graying curls had been shaved close to his head, and his cheeks were sunken. The skin sagged around his eyes, and it was flecked with small white blemishes.

He stood up and let the photographs that he had been holding drop to the floor. He took two steps toward Esta and held out his hand.

"It's good to see you again."

She nodded and shook his hand.

"You look much better. Can I take it that you're completely recovered?"

"I'm all right."

"Your father." Mendoza looked around the room as if Weiss

might materialize out of thin air. "He popped out for a moment. I expect he'll be back."

"I expect so."

Mendoza smiled at his own awkwardness, then gestured toward the armchair.

"May I?"

Esta nodded, and Mendoza sat down. He extricated a packet of cigarettes from his shirt pocket and began nervously to fumble with the wrapping.

Esta sat on the couch.

"Archie?"

"I don't know, I'm afraid."

She took a deep breath and clasped her hands together.

"But listen: It's over. They're not looking for you anymore."

Mendoza held his unlit cigarette between his fingers and felt in his pockets for matches.

"Over?"

"Yes. . . . I'm sorry, do you . . . ?" He gestured helplessly with the cigarette. Esta rose and walked into the kitchen. Her legs were heavy; she felt as if she were wading through a swamp. She found the matches and gave them to Mendoza.

"Wrong lot. You and your friend. They had the wrong Zionists"—Mendoza smiled again—"then they found the right lot. Cairo based, somewhat militant, not simply interested in a trip over the border. Maybe you heard of them? Chap called Rentz and a few followers. At any rate, the Waterlow evidence against them was strong. They called off the search for you. And they'd found where you were. On the point of picking you up, in fact. But they haven't been looking for, oh, a fortnight or so. Waste of time and people. I'm happy to say they've lost interest entirely. Affairs of the heart are of no concern to them. They even gave me your address, can you believe that? They'd still like to get Rawlins back, though. Probably want to give him a good thrashing. Prison, I imagine, but it might not be for too long."

"And Falik?"

"They let him go."

Mendoza struck the match and lit his cigarette. His hands shook.

"You wouldn't have . . . This is terribly rude, but does your father keep . . . something to drink, perhaps?"

Esta went back into the kitchen, opened a cabinet above the sink, and produced a bottle of whiskey and a small tumbler. When she turned, Mendoza was standing behind her.

He half filled the glass, added a little water from the faucet, took one sip, downed the rest of the shot, then poured himself a refill.

Esta felt a sudden pang in her stomach and slumped down on one of the kitchen chairs.

"Are you all right?"

"Yes. Your news."

"A great relief, isn't it? You've been through so much. And you're . . . well, you're here!"

They sat in silence. The birds chirped fitfully in their cage, probing the kitchen's stale, exhausted air. Esta stared at the flypaper that hung from the ceiling; it was heavy with the bodies of summer flies. The moment of nausea passed. Mendoza looked at her. She thought that she caught a flash of disappointment in his eyes. She couldn't be elated, or even pleased, not while Archie was missing. And even if he was found, she wasn't sure that she could come back, be a person who got up, dressed, ate, went to work, talked to other people. She imagined covering her face with white makeup until all her features were obliterated. She could still hide, even if they weren't looking for her. Why should she stop? She raised her eyes to look at Mendoza.

"And what about you?" she asked.

"Dishonorable discharge. It all happened very fast. They were happy to get rid of me. I shouldn't even be wearing this uniform, but they had nothing else to give me. Got to get it off by morning."

"I'm sorry."

"Not your fault."

"It is. If you hadn't helped me . . ."

"It would have been something else. My time was up. I'd lost faith."

"What will you do now? Go back to England?"

"Actually, not. I thought I might stay. It occurred to me when I was in prison. Nothing to go back for, and I have, well, some freedom here."

He looked around the room, as if searching beyond its narrow confines for the freedom that he had projected.

"Will they catch up with Archie?"

Mendoza paused before answering, and knocked ash off the end of his cigarette into a small green saucer that Esta had provided.

"I would think so, wouldn't you?"

"I have to find him."

"Yes."

They heard the sound of heavy footsteps on the stairs, then Weiss pushed open the door and came into the room. There were beads of sweat on his forehead and dark patches under the arms of his short-sleeved shirt. He set his bag of groceries down heavily on the kitchen table as if disburdening himself of an enormous weight.

"What took you so long?" He looked straight at Esta and ignored Mendoza's presence. "I had to go out and do the shopping myself. I shouldn't be climbing these stairs so often. You know what it does to my back? I hope at least you got a job out of this."

"No."

"But I heard Birnbaum on the telephone this morning. I was standing right next to him. He spoke to his son on your behalf.

What was it? Did you say something that you shouldn't have? Maybe it was the way you looked. You walk around dressing like I don't know what, a scarecrow in a field. Can I sit down here?"

Esta made to get up, but Mendoza had already risen from his chair. Weiss took his place at the table.

"Excuse me." He looked at Mendoza for the first time. "I didn't mean to make a rabbi get up. But my back."

"It's perfectly all right."

"You told her, Rabbi. I'm taking it you told her."

"Yes."

"You see that, Esta. The whole thing was a lot of nonsense. Now you got nothing to worry about. You know, Rabbi, we had a tragedy. Her mother. Perhaps you heard already. I've got a broken heart. But I have to go on. My daughter doesn't understand this. She doesn't understand how a man can cry and be dead in his heart and then sit in a café, see people, visit friends, enjoy refreshments. That's the nature of life."

"I'm sorry for your loss."

"That's right. What else can you say?"

Esta got up from the table and went to the toilet. She locked the door and sat on the seat. She felt mildly nauseous. She wondered how long she could conceal her condition from her father. She didn't want to tell anyone. She couldn't be exposed: what was inside her had to stay hidden; that was the only safe way. At the Prater, there had been a mother in a tree, holding her baby. She was a young woman with long straight hair. She crouched on a bough, cowering under the gray-green leaves of an ancient oak. The baby cried, and the mother tried to comfort her. The storm troopers made the mother flap her arms, knowing that she would have to let go of the baby if she did so. The mother flapped one arm and held the child with the other, as if under a crooked and broken wing. Esta didn't know what had become of them.

Her father banged on the door.

"Can I get in there?"

Esta rose from the seat. There was a spot of blood in the water. She opened the door, and Weiss pushed past her.

Mendoza stood in the kitchen, looking out the window toward the fading light beyond the shuttered garages. When Esta came in, he turned.

"I've been staring at the same view for weeks: back wall of a Russian church. It's nice to see something else."

"Can you help me?"

"Look for Rawlins? What would you like me to do?"

"Come with me."

Mendoza sighed, almost imperceptibly. "You're keen to get going, I imagine."

Esta nodded.

"I have to report back tomorrow. Return the uniform. I doubt they'll keep me long. We could leave after that, if you like. I'm afraid I have no transport. The bus, I suppose. Where . . . ? That is, are we traveling far?"

"I'm sorry. You're exhausted. I wasn't thinking."

"No, no, really. Just a little tired, that's all. A good night's sleep. I have a friend here in Tel Aviv."

Weiss appeared in the doorway. He had taken off his straw hat. The top of his head glistened with sweat.

"I'm going to lie down."

He removed his shoes and settled himself on the couch. Before closing his eyes, he conspicuously moved a framed photograph of Esta's mother, so that the face stared down on him like a benevolent icon.

Esta fell silent.

Mendoza continued to pour himself shots of whiskey. He had drunk almost half the bottle, and his eyes were bloodshot.

"I suppose I should be going."

He walked toward the door, swaying a little.

"First thing, then. Or perhaps that's a little ambitious. Shall we say nine? I'll meet you here."

Weiss lay snoring on the couch. Esta walked past him and out to the balcony. In the street, a mechanic in grease-stained overalls dropped the corrugated shutter of his bay and locked it up. He got on a bicycle and pedaled down the road, meandering to avoid the small pools of oil. There were dark clouds in the sky, and the moon, round and smoky as a burning tire, was hidden behind them.

She wanted to leave now, but her body was dead weight. She slumped down into one of her father's wicker chairs; the canes were splintered at the ends and dug into her uncomfortably. She tried to fight off sleep. In the past, she had managed to do so well beyond the point of complete exhaustion, but this time she had no resistance.

When she awoke, a figure loomed over her on the balcony. At first Esta didn't recognize him, but then she remembered the bow tie and the thick glasses.

"I'm sorry," Birnbaum said. "The front door was ajar. I didn't mean to wake you."

Esta looked at him, then out to the street. The moon had risen free of its black shroud and now scudded in brightness over the sky.

"I was worried about you. So I drove over. I hope you don't mind. I wanted to see if there was anything . . ."

"I'm all right now."

"Yes."

They sat in silence. It was Friday night, and Esta could see candles burning in the windows of the apartment house on the other side of the street. She was thinking about Archie: she saw him in his uniform, sitting at his desk in Cairo, tight and nervous, putting on airs for her. What if someone else had been sitting there? A different face, different eyes. It was stupid to think about it.

Birnbaum began to speak again.

"I've already made some inquiries—about a position. I should hear something on Monday. We get a long weekend because of our army connection; both Sabbaths, you see. Otherwise, I'd know a little earlier. Can you type, by the way? I forgot to ask you."

"Not very well."

"Well, that won't matter. There's plenty of other possibilities."

He continued describing the various jobs that were available in the lab, until Esta abruptly interrupted him.

"Did you say that you had a car?"

"I do, yes."

"Would you lend it to me?"

Birnbaum, taken aback by the request, stared at Esta as if her features had blurred and he was trying to get her in focus.

"Well, I suppose I could, yes, as long as it's at night, or on a weekend, of course. Even this weekend; short notice, but I could probably manage it. Where are you going?"

"Jerusalem."

"Perhaps I could drive you myself."

"A friend will drive me."

"Is it some kind of emergency?"

"I'm trying to find someone."

In the living room, Weiss turned his body on the narrow couch and twisted his face into the pillow; his snores were instantly muffled.

"Who are you looking for?"

"Someone I knew in Cairo."

Weiss stirred again on the couch and let out a small moan.

"His name is Archie Rawlins."

Birnbaum repeated the name, as if it might hold an explanation.

"You don't have to worry; my friend is a rabbi."

Birnbaum laughed. "Are rabbis good drivers?"

At first Esta didn't reply. She saw that Birnbaum was hoping for a kind word, or a smile, some acknowledgment that he was treating her well. Eventually she dredged up the appropriate phrases, but when she spoke, her words seemed to come out in a false, tinny voice, as if produced by a mechanical doll.

"Well," Birnbaum said, "if you want to get going in the morning, I might as well leave the keys with you tonight."

He reached in his pocket for his key ring, removed his car keys, and handed them to Esta. He moved over to the balcony rail and pointed out to her where his car was parked.

He sat down again. He seemed unwilling to leave, and Esta felt powerless to prevent him from staying. He began to tell her his family history. How his father, like her own father, had had the foresight to leave Europe—they were from Hungary—but how, luckily, they had all come out together. He had been in Palestine for eight years. As soon as the war broke out, he had volunteered for the British army, but they were reluctant to recruit Palestinian Jews, and in any case, as she could probably guess, with his flat feet and terrible eyesight, he wasn't exactly cut out for the infantry, but he did have a talent in science, and . . .

Esta half listened, but for the most part she gazed at the magnified shadows cut by the moon into the buildings on the street. She was waiting for Archie to emerge, for his tall, thin figure to step onto the roadside and be illuminated by the headlights of a passing car.

She heard Birnbaum suggest a cup of tea, and she got up to make it, stepping quietly past the couch where her father slept. When she returned, Birnbaum was sitting on the balcony, the tip of a lit cigarette burning between his fingers. His body seemed too big for the rickety chair that he had found to occupy, and the shape of his back—hunched, tilted forward—suddenly seemed to her to contain all the loneliness of the city's refugees and exiles. She saw them every day, wandering the streets of Tel Aviv in their inappropriate clothes: wool suits that hung on their skinny bodies like memories that were impossible to discard.

When he had drunk his tea, and after he had asked, stuttering and tentative, if he could see her again, and then immediately corrected himself because obviously he would see her again when she returned the car, Birnbaum left.

Esta returned to her chair on the balcony. For a long time she looked into the street. The candles in the windows had all burned down, and the occupants of the apartments had turned from prayer to sleep. The radio antennas on the rooftop looked to her like ships' masts. There was a brackish odor emanating from the unseen river behind the workshops, and the street itself, criss-crossed with floating shadows, suddenly seemed to Esta to be a dark canal carrying the debris—the broken furniture and cracked mirrors, smashed chinaware and soiled clothes—of its inhabitants' hastily abandoned former lives.

Eventually she slept, until, at first light, the harsh, raucous, throaty outcry of a stray crow awoke her.

Mendoza arrived while her father was still sleeping. He wore a shabby gray suit, and the collar of his white shirt, buttoned at the top, hung loose around his neck. Esta left a note on the kitchen table for her father and, after quickly explaining to Mendoza about the car, went out with him to the street. His eyes were still red, and Esta could smell the alcohol on his breath.

Birnbaum's car was a small white Ford, the back seat so over-loaded with books and laboratory equipment that the front seats were crushed up close to the windshield. Esta squeezed in and rolled her window down. Mendoza fumbled around with the keys. She felt that he was acting clumsily on purpose, slowing down his movements in order to give her a chance to change her mind.

A glaring sunlight filled the street, and almost as soon as they began to drive she heard the dull roar of the sea carry over the white houses and tree-lined streets. In the center of town, Mendoza lost his way and had to stop to ask directions. He pulled up outside the pillared entrance to a theater. Esta had time to scan the billboard: The Palestine Philharmonic Orchestra. Michael

Taube, First World Performance, Palestine Folk Symphony. Mahler-Kalkstein. A young couple stood arm in arm, reading the advertisement. When Mendoza called out to them they turned. The woman was pregnant, and while her husband spoke to Mendoza, pointing him toward Jerusalem with a vigorous combination of words and gestures, Esta stared at the woman's swollen stomach.

Mendoza started off again, peering nearsightedly at the road ahead. He seemed uncomfortable at the wheel, given to jerky movements and awkward gear shifts. His steering was erratic and generated a chorus of honks and yells from the other drivers.

As soon as they were out of the city, Esta made Mendoza stop. She walked away from the car, stood behind a bush, and vomited.

"I'm sorry," Mendoza said when she returned. "Been taking the curves too fast."

She knew that their journey was absurd. Mendoza had tried to indicate as much the previous night, and again today, but she wouldn't let him. She would never be able to locate the hut, and even if she did, Archie wouldn't be there. But she *had* to find him, especially now.

They reached Jerusalem at midday. Esta thought that she saw Archie among the group of soldiers standing by the bus station and then again in another crowd of Tommies, outside the Jewish market. In the space of half an hour, and in quite different parts of the city, she saw him entering a bank, crossing a street, and sitting in the back of a troop carrier. When Mendoza left the car to buy a bottle of brandy, she saw Archie playing backgammon in a pavement café. His hair had grown longer, but it was definitely him. Later, she caught a glimpse of him outside the Damascus Gate. An Arab man in a red tarboosh remonstrated with him over a business transaction, then Archie disappeared into the milling, jostling crowd. The long-winded cycle of an Arab love song spiraled through the air, surmounted the brown belches of exhaust fumes from the buses, and cut through the harsh calls of street vendors.

Mendoza drove, taking frequent swigs from the brandy bottle. Esta tried to remember the view from the hut, but all that came to mind was the swirl of dark rain clouds as Lewis Marks had carried her in his arms.

Late in the afternoon, they abandoned the city for the villages outside. In the most impoverished, mounds of rubbish and dirt had accumulated on the sides of unpaved roads. Dogs scavenged through rusty oil drums full of refuse, and animals stood among clouds of flies that sucked at their blood. A few barefoot children shuffled aimlessly in the streets, observed by groups of old men gathered in circles, smoking water pipes. In places, electric wires hung loosely from poles and the children played dangerously close, despite the shrill warnings emanating from their mothers.

Mendoza drove fast on the narrow roads, throwing up so much dust that the car windshield became smeared and increasingly opaque.

He began laughing to himself, talking, almost chanting.

"Money-grubbers, cheats, Christ-killers. They want their pound of flesh, they'll have their pound of flesh. Closer to God, that's the problem. Jealous. No priests in the way. No son to have to deal with before you get to the father. Stand in some dark unlit corner, all alone. Didn't have us, they'd have to invent us. Never talk about anything else. Put a man in prison after twenty years. Make him stand in that corner. Deprive him of everything. Make him smell his own shit."

Mendoza rammed his foot down on the accelerator. He sped down a narrow curving track flanked by a few dusty pines. Esta asked him to slow down, and he responded, but a big red-wheeled cart drawn by a donkey had appeared around the corner and was coming straight toward them. Esta shouted, and Mendoza swerved violently off the road. The car bounced, spun, skidded, and finally came to a halt on the edge of a cultivated terrace. The branch of an olive tree poked through Mendoza's half-open window; his cheeks were scratched, but a snapped-off, sharply pointed branch had narrowly missed penetrating his face. His hands were bleeding and covered with broken glass. Esta felt a wetness between her legs; she reached down and touched her fingers to the trickle of blood.

Mendoza's whole body shook.

"Are you all right?" he asked.

Esta stared at the red-brown stain on her fingertips.

"I don't know," she replied.

The driver of the cart, and his passengers, a sullen-looking Arab family, continued on around the corner, apparently oblivious to what had occurred.

PART
FOUR

JERUSALEM

1 9 9 1

1

I cleaned Mendoza's green Subaru last week and paid for an oil change. The mechanic who did the work, a new immigrant from Russia, threw me looks of intense hatred throughout the procedure. He even spat, incomprehensibly, into the drained oil. For the first time in weeks, I felt at home, back in England, and on familiar territory. My mother could never understand the English distaste for work, while I grew up to be an admirer of that particular trait. The English simply do not believe that everybody's got to serve somebody, which is why, despite the resilience of their religious prejudices, their churches are empty.

Mendoza and I have been driving around for days. We travel everywhere without restraint. Mendoza displays no anxiety over entering the Arab parts of town, or villages that might be hostile to our presence. Instead he is eerily nonchalant. As we drive, he likes to sing popular songs from the Second World War—"Roll

Out the Barrel," "We'll Meet Again." I must admit that his ren-
ditions get on my nerves, and from time to time I try to drown
him out by turning up the radio. The local rock and roll is abys-
mal, but occasionally a familiar chord strikes and a foreign import
hits the airwaves.

Mendoza more or less chain-smokes. The skin on his fingers is
leathery and yellow, and his teeth are brown. It is, of course, ridiculous to warn someone his age about the dangers of cancer.
When I return to my room at night, my clothes reek.

Often, especially on long stretches of road, Mendoza falls
asleep. He contorts his long body in the passenger seat, throws
his head back, and lets his mouth drop open. He says that the relentless summer heat deepens his stupor. He is almost ninety, after all, and we have no air-conditioning in the car. There is a
small white fan attached to the dashboard by a rubber suction
cup. I moved it to Mendoza's side, but it remains largely ineffec-
tual. As we drive, the whirred air ruffles and agitates his white
hair and throws it back from his high forehead or across his brow.

Sometimes he begins to doze in the middle of a sentence. I
wait an hour or more until he wakes, and then I need to jog his
memory. "You were in Cairo," I say, or "You were driving
through the desert." Occasionally, he loses the thread of his narrative altogether. When this happens he experiences a tremen-
dous frustration, in which I share, that he cannot put together the
pieces of the puzzle.

Last Sunday, as we left my mother's graveside and wandered
out of the cemetery, my head was throbbing. By the time we got
back to the car, I could hardly keep my eyes open. In the thin
shade thrown by a narrow cypress tree, Mendoza had given me
my father, in name if not fully in being. The dark, ragged figure
at the back of my mind had swung into the light, and I was
dazzled.

I drove, then, as now, without direction, and we arrived, quite
by chance, in a forest clearing beyond the newly developed sub-

urb of Gilo. The lot where I parked the car abutted an adventure playground. It was schooltime, and the wooden bridges and mock forts were abandoned. I wanted to walk, and although Mendoza was at first reluctant to get out of the car—he was worried that he might trip on the rocky path—I persuaded him to accompany me. I held his twig-thin arm, and we entered the forest, skirting the swings and the charred barbecue pits.

We made our way slowly down to a narrow bench that offered a view over a parched brown valley and beyond to the hills that surround Jerusalem. Mendoza collected some pine needles in his hands and rubbed them between his fingers. I could smell the pine resin, its scent rising into the dense blue air.

Of course, I was desperate to hear everything that Mendoza could tell me, but at the same time I was afraid of what I might learn. A part of me wanted to sit very quietly in the stillness of the forest and listen, not to Mendoza's voice, but to the beating of wings in the infinite blue space over our heads.

I was, it seemed, a Rawlins, half Christian, the son of a soldier. At the age of fifty, I had acquired a fresh description of myself, and as Mendoza spoke, I felt the contours of my life shift like a desert's windblown sands.

There is no pattern to our present journeys, because we have no firm idea where to look. Mendoza has only the vaguest of notions as to where my father was last seen. We have ventured as far east as Jericho, north to Ramallah and south toward Hebron. We drive through villages where the electric wires are strung with Palestinian flags and groups of masked youths hover by the roadside with rocks clenched in their fists. From time to time, the members of an Israeli army patrol stop us and ask what we think we're doing and don't we know what's going on? Mendoza describes our mission. The young soldiers respond with irritation or disbelief. We are simply adding to their security problems. On those occasions when, through perseverance on our part or indifference on theirs, we are let through the barriers, we have to run the gauntlet of the *shbab*, the teenage gangs that control access to the villages. Our presence, an old Jew and a middle-aged Englishman, is disturbing and makes them nervous. They are suspicious of us: What do we want? Are we journalists? If not, what are we doing there? The process of explaining is long and exhausting. Sometimes we are immediately turned away. Occasionally, our car has been stoned in a desultory way as we depart. When we succeed in securing passage, however, and our requests for interviews are granted, the old men of the village are courteous and helpful. Those who do not speak English are fluent in Hebrew and Mendoza translates their answers for me. It is absurd, of course, to expect that any of them will have knowledge of an obscure English soldier who may or may not have wandered through their village more than fifty years ago. But what choice do I have? We searched at the municipal registry in Jerusalem some time ago, but there is no record of my father's death.

I am aware that it seems almost an affront to those involved in the political battle to be pursuing my local and private quest in such turmoil. And yet the emotional prerogatives of personal life assert themselves with equal strength in times of war and struggle: lovers meet and break up, parents and children love and scuffle, wants and desires vie with needs and constraints. And I must, as the shrinks say, have some closure to this event, a cure for the long malaise of unbridled imagination that over the years has brought me too many faceless fathers. And perhaps, although this can only be whispered, he is alive.

Yesterday, as we drove past the burnished onion domes of the Russian Orthodox church on the Mount of Olives, I asked Mendoza if he believed in God. He laughed and said it was an impertinent question to put to a rabbi. I pressed him and found that it was no effort for him to reply in the negative. "But," he added, "I try to act as if there were one. And what is more, I accept the power of prayer." In the light of his words, I have taken to mumbling to myself odd little messages to the Lord: I ask for guidance, but I realize, to my distress, that in this holiest of places, I have come to think of God as nothing more than an accurate compass.

In the evenings, after I have dropped Mendoza off and helped him into his house, I return to Nahla'ot. Before going up to my room, I linger in the neighborhood. Generally, I sit for a while in Sami's, a brightly lit kebab house on the main thoroughfare. By eight in the evening, the streets are quiet, almost somnolent, and apart from the restaurants, the only establishment open is a small below-street-level hairdresser's, its door flung wide to reveal a line of women sitting passively under pastel-colored eggshell dryers.

What can we know of somebody else's life, especially, perhaps, if that somebody is a parent? My case, of course, as far as my father is concerned, is exaggerated, but even so, common sense suggests that at best you can only expect to arrive at a series of partial truths, and no matter how tight the bond, there will always be secrets that are never made available. It is only in novels, it seems, that you can learn everything about another person, and that person, of course, is a chimera.

Despite this truth, known to all, I have begun to reconstruct my father as carefully as I can from the stories that Mendoza tells me. Nightly, I log into my laptop all the information that he gives out during the day. I have learned, of course, that the first fantasies which engaged me in this city were misguided. The dreams I indulged in of my parents as Romeo and Juliet, wandering hand in hand through the atmospherically charged alleyways of Jerusalem, were naive and false: the creations of a sentimental son desperate to idealize his origins. On the other hand, the truth, as far as I have it, has failed to transform me in the manner that I expected. I had always believed that when I uncovered the deep mystery of my father's identity, I would be thrown into a state of shock: my character recast and transformed. It is almost embarrassing to admit, but aside from my initial dizziness, this has not been the case. When I ask myself why, it is clear that until I discover either my father or his gravestone, I will continue to treat the facts and details of his life in storybook fashion. As yet, I still cannot appropriately relate *him* to *me*, or *him* to *her*.

I type into the computer until I can no longer stay awake. By the time I stop, my only company is the stray cats that forage across the starlit rooftops and down to the bins on the street, piled high with fermented garbage. I sleep for three or four hours, and then I am ready to begin our search again.

In order to speed up my journey to his place, Mendoza has kindly lent me his car, but that means it is now my responsibility to find a parking place for it. Often, in the mornings, I forget where I left the car the previous night, and it is a good fifteen minutes or so before I discover its location. The narrow streets that surround my apartment are crowded with vehicles parked halfway up on the pavement, squeezed into corner spots, their trunks or hoods sticking out at odd angles. I search for the Subaru down lines of small, slightly battered cars covered in layers of dust, the interiors of their windshields readied for the rising heat by thick sheets of white cardboard, which lend them a blank Cyclopean stare.

At six in the morning there is usually a fair amount of street activity—lorries headed toward the market, boys pushing handcarts piled high with flat pita, soldiers on street corners waiting for a ride—except on Saturday, the Jewish Sabbath, when most of the city's inhabitants sleep late and it is only in East Jerusalem, and the surrounding Arab villages and towns, that the markets are active and crowded.

Usually, by the time that I arrive at his house, Mendoza is up and dressed. In his old age, he says, he finds that he needs very little sleep, and with the time he has left to him rapidly diminishing, he feels, in any case, that sleep is a waste of time.

This morning, however, there was no answer when I knocked. A ground-floor window was open, and after a suitable period of time had elapsed, I climbed through. I shouted his name but received no reply. I mounted the stairs, still calling, but fearing the worst. I must admit to a certain shame: imagining Mendoza dead, I was not sorry or sad, but angry that I would be unable to complete my quest.

Mendoza's bed was empty, but the counterpane was strewn with letters, documents, and photographs. A canister of pills and a glass of water stood on the night table next to his bed, along with a half-empty bottle of brandy. On his pillow there was a black-and-white snapshot of my mother. I had never seen one like it before: her hair was close-cropped, and her eyes held a vacant stare. In the background, a black goat with a bell hung on a string around its neck stood on a mound of rubble. I picked it up and put it in the back pocket of my jeans.

I followed a rough path round to the back of the house and found Mendoza sitting at a small table on a patio, sifting through more old papers. He was surrounded by a bare trellis. He heard me approach—his hearing is better than his vision—and lifted his head.

"You've been inside?" he asked.

"Yes."

"And you saw the picture?"

"Yes."

"I've been trying to remember. It's most annoying. That place, you see. I have a feeling, a recollection, it was the closest we came. Otherwise, why the photograph? We weren't exactly interested in holiday snaps, you know. Must have been trying to mark the spot."

"But you have no idea where you were?"

"Not much to go on, is it, really: a black goat, a pile of stones, and a few clouds?"

He got up from the table and took some tentative steps into the garden. The borders around his lawn were packed with fat, overblown roses, thick-stemmed and tangled. Mendoza bent his face to a fragrant bush and breathed deep. The hot wind picked up off the desert and heat exploded through the garden, as if someone had just opened the door to a blast furnace.

"Tried to make it English, you see." Mendoza waved his hand in the direction of the flower beds. "Hollyhocks over here, snapdragons, geraniums, the roses, of course. But I inherited a pomegranate tree from the previous owner—it's there, behind the lavender bush—and that put everything out of kilter. That's the point, I think. You can't hold on. Perhaps that's what happened to your father. The heat and light come first, then the scents and smells. The brain gets flooded. You start to stagger. Sounds like an old story, doesn't it? The colonialist abroad going under. But I'm not talking about 'pesky flies' and all that nonsense. I'm talking about an intensity of feeling that the place transmits. It reaches a level, you know, where it has the power to transform. There's a reason why religion has such a hold here."

He returned to his seat. The sun reflected off the rim of his glasses and sent thin laser beams of light across the table.

"Well, where shall it be today? Beit Jala? Sur Bahir? Silwan?"

His voice sounded tired, and I wondered if he had lost interest in our search.

"Perhaps we should take the day off," I suggested.

I removed the photograph from my pocket and began absentmindedly to finger the edges. Mendoza took it from me and stared for a long time.

"There were always rumors, you know. We heard things. But nothing ever came of the information. We drove around, on and off, for weeks. Toward the end we got a tip about a village that had harbored a British deserter. But no one knew where, or whether it was Christian or Muslim, whether on the outskirts of Jerusalem or miles away. Your mother became quite desperate. And she was ill, you know."

Here Mendoza paused, as the truth, dormant for so long,

dawned on him for the first time. He looked at me through the unpatched eyeglass and smiled.

"Two months. Then suddenly she gave up. I see now. I thought she'd left the country to continue looking for him. It wasn't uncommon, you know—abandoned war brides, or women who'd hoped to be brides. Some of them went after the men who'd got them pregnant. Most were stopped at the borders. Sad state of affairs, really. But your mother, well, obviously not quite the same. Her father . . . did you know him?"

"He died two years after I was born."

"Did he? Yes, perhaps your mother mentioned it in a letter. My memory, you know. Well, not an easy man. Not at all."

Mendoza insisted that we take our daily drive. We drove through the city and out toward the villages in the east. Mendoza seemed in oddly high spirits, singing a little to himself and look-ing out the window with a kind of half-smile and nodding his head. We passed a stone fountain where Arab children splashed in a wide brim guarded by lions and gorgons. We turned south-east and after a few miles reached the outskirts of a village where the walls were spray-painted in the colors of the Palestinian flag and covered with graffiti. A recently erected cinder-block wall bordered the street, topped by a wire-mesh fence.

We had the usual problems at the roadblock, but Mendoza seemed to have acquired a fresh energy on the drive and took an authoritative air with the young Israeli sergeant who stopped us. The soldier asked to see our weapons and was incredulous when we insisted that we were traveling unarmed. After a short argu-ment he let us go, banging on the boot as I started forward and shouting a final admonition after us.

"What did he say?" I asked Mendoza.

"He said, 'It's your funeral.' And I suppose in my case he's not far off."

We drove through a small gap in what had once been a barrier of tires. On both sides of the road, piles of rubble had been stacked into neat pyramids, ready for use as ammunition. It was close to midday, and the streets of the village were deserted, save for an old man who carried a sheaf of broomsticks on his back and wandered wearily in the direction of the roadblock.

The quiet was misleading, for as soon as we reached the center of the village, we were surrounded by a mob of boys, who seemed to emerge from nowhere. Most wore the black-and-white checkered masks of the Fatah and carried a ragamuffin weaponry of steel pipes and rocks. I kept the engine running while Mendoza conducted our negotiations. At one point he tried to get out, but the boys pushed him roughly back into his seat. I wanted to move forward, but the car was completely surrounded and acceleration could only have drawn me into the press of bodies. Someone reached in through my window and pressed the horn. I sat back, startled, and there was a peal of laughter. Suddenly the doors of the car were pulled open, and we were dragged out. Two young men stood guard over us while the car was searched. A lone fighter plane streaked low above our heads. No one, except myself, looked up.

Mendoza continued to speak in moderate tones, urging the young men to let us talk to someone in authority, although it was clear from their demeanor and self-confidence who was running the show.

Eventually they ordered us to abandon the car. We were directed toward a house at the end of the village. We walked slowly down a lane of small stone houses bordered by shrunken cacti.

Near the village cemetery, where the road fell away toward an olive terrace, we entered a pine grove that sheltered a large house. A small child played on the concrete porch, weaving a toy truck under the legs of a plastic chair and between tin cans that spilled over with pink and red geraniums. I rang the bell. An old woman answered, scooped the child up, and, without inquiring who we were or what we wanted, ushered us in.

We sat in the large, airy front room and waited. Mendoza, exhausted by his morning's exertions, sank back into the thick embroidered cushions that covered the sofa. After a few moments, a man entered. He wore a suit and tie, and his lank gray hair was combed over a bald spot. His dark eyes flickered behind thick pebble glasses. We stood and introduced ourselves. He asked us to please be seated and offered us coffee.

"We have so many journalists, you know. A visit from regular tourists is, well, a little out of the ordinary."

As the days had passed I had grown a little ashamed of my story. Each time I spoke, it seemed to me increasingly quixotic. In the village homes that we had previously visited, I had become used to a certain impatience creeping into the air before I had finished my tale. The men we spoke to were, after all, busy people, with the powerful diversions of both business and politics on their minds. In the current situation, a middle-aged Englishman searching for his missing father was hardly riveting material. I began to feel almost childish, and I got into the habit of peppering my narrative with apologies. On this occasion, however, our host listened with rapt attention.

When I had finished talking, instead of the usual polite shake of the head or halfhearted offer of more coffee, he simply leaned forward, unstrapped his wristwatch, and held it out to me.

"Take it," he said.

I reached forward, studied the watch face, then turned it over and read the inscription.

2

Mendoza and I stand in the shadow of tall cypresses by the unmarked grave in Ein Kerem where the El Asad family brought my father to rest. The nuns told us that this is the garden where Mary met her cousin Elizabeth and sang "Magnificat" to her. I have already made arrangements to purchase a stone from the same ecumenical mason who will provide my mother's.

I don't know exactly why, but I asked Mendoza to say Kaddish for my Christian father. He was silent for a while, and I sensed he was reluctant, but as I was about to apologize for my request, he turned toward me.

"By rights we should have a minyan here," he said. "But your father was a rabbi himself for a few hours, you know. So I suppose there's no harm."

He began, in a voice that trailed away and lost its strength as he proceeded, to recite the Jewish prayer of mourning, which never mentions death but praises God over and again and asks for peace.